THE RESCUERS
MISS BIANCA
THE TURRET

MARGERY SHARP'S "MISS BIANCA" SERIES

The Rescuers (1959)

Miss Bianca (1962)

The Turret (1963)

Miss Bianca in the Salt Mines (1966)

Miss Bianca in the Orient (1970)

Miss Bianca in the Antarctic (1971)

Miss Bianca and the Bridesmaid (1972)

Bernard the Brave: A Miss Bianca Story (1976)

Bernard into Battle: A Miss Bianca Story (1979)

THE RESCUERS

THE RESCUERS

Contents

1   The Meeting   3

2   Miss Bianca   15

3   In Norway   24

4   The Voyage   37

5   Marching Orders   51

6   The Happy Journey   58

7   The Black Castle   67

8   Waiting   80

9   Cat-and-Mouse   88

10   The Message   95

11   The Other Way Out   106

12   The Great Enterprise   117

13   The Raft   132

14   The End   139

The Rescuers

1

The Meeting

Ladies and gentlemen," cried Madam Chairwoman Mouse, "we now come to the most important item on our autumn program! Pray silence for the Secretary!"

It was a full meeting of the Prisoners' Aid Society. Everyone knows that the mice are the prisoner's friends — sharing his dry bread crumbs even when they are not hungry, allowing themselves to be taught all manner of foolish tricks, such as no self-respecting mouse would otherwise contemplate, in order to cheer his lonely hours; what is less well known is how splendidly they are organized. Not a prison in any land but has its own national branch of a wonderful, world-wide system. It is on record that long, long ago a Norman mouse took ship all the way to Turkey, to join a French sailor-boy locked up in Constantinople! The Jean Fromage Medal was struck in his honor.

The Secretary rose. Madam Chairwoman sat back in her seat, which was made from beautifully polished walnut shells, and fixed her clever eyes on his graying back. How she would have liked to put the matter to the meeting herself! An enterprise so difficult and dangerous!

Dear, faithful old comrade as the Secretary was, had he the necessary eloquence? But rules are rules.

She looked anxiously over the assembly, wondering which members would support her; there were at least a hundred mice present, seated in rows on neat match-box benches. The Moot-house itself was a particularly fine one, a great empty wine cask, entered by the bung, whose splendid curving walls soared cathedral-like to the roof. Behind the speakers' platform hung an oil painting, richly framed, depicting the mouse in Aesop's fable in his heroic act of freeing a captive lion.

"Well, it's like this," began the Secretary. "You all know the Black Castle . . ."

Every mouse in the hall shuddered. The country they lived in was still barely civilized, a country of great gloomy mountains, enormous deserts, rivers like strangled seas. Even in its few towns, even here in the Capital, its prisons were grim enough. But the Black Castle!

It reared up, the Black Castle, from a cliff above the angriest river of all. Its dungeons were cut in the cliff it-self — windowless. Even the bravest mouse, assigned to the Black Castle, trembled before its great, cruel, iron-fanged gate.

From a front seat up spoke a mouse almost as old and rheumatic as the Secretary himself. But he wore the Jean Fromage Medal.

"*I* know the Black Castle. Didn't I spend six weeks there?"

Around him rose cries of "Hear, hear!", "Splendid chap!", and other encouragements.

"And did no good there," continued the old hero gravely. "I say nothing of the personal danger — though what a cat that is of the Head Jailer's! — twice natural size, and four times as fierce! — I say only that a prisoner in the Black Castle, a prisoner down in the dungeons, not even a mouse can aid. Call me defeatist if you will — "

"No, no!" cried the mice behind.

" — but I speak from sad experience. I couldn't do anything for my prisoner at all. I couldn't even reach him. One can't *cheer* a prisoner in the Black Castle."

"But one can get him out," said Madam Chairwoman.

2

There was a stunned silence. In the first place, Madam Chairwoman shouldn't have interrupted; in the second, her proposal was so astounding, so revolutionary, no mouse could do more than gape.

"Mr. Secretary, forgive me," apologized Madam Chairwoman. "I was carried away by your eloquence."

"As rules seem to be going by the board, you may as well take over," said the Secretary grumpily.

Madam Chairwoman did so. There is nothing like breeding to give one confidence: she was descended in direct line from the senior of the Three Blind Mice. Calmly sleeking her whiskers —

"It's rather an unusual case," said Madam Chairwoman blandly. "The prisoner is a poet. You will all, I know, cast your minds back to the many poets who have written favorably of our race — *Her feet beneath her petticoat, like little mice stole in and out* — Suckling, the Englishman — what a charming compliment! Thus do not poets deserve specially well of us?"

"If he's a poet, why's he in jail?" demanded a suspicious voice.

Madam Chairwoman shrugged velvet shoulders.

"Perhaps he writes free verse," she suggested cunningly.

A stir of approval answered her. Mice are all for people being free, so that they too can be freed from their eternal task of cheering prisoners — so that they can stay snug at home, nibbling the family cheese, instead of sleeping out in damp straw on a diet of stale bread.

"I see you follow me," said Madam Chairwoman. "It *is* a special case. Therefore we will rescue him. I should tell you also that the prisoner is a Norwegian. — Don't ask me how he got here, really no one can answer for a poet! But obviously the first thing to do is to get in touch with a compatriot, and summon him here, so that he may communicate with the prisoner in their common tongue."

Two hundred ears pricked intelligently. All mice speak their own universal language, also that of the country they live in, but prisoners as a rule spoke only one.

"We therefore fetch a Norwegian mouse *here*," recapitulated Madam Chairwoman, "dispatch him to the Black Castle — "

"Stop a bit," said the Secretary.

Madam Chairwoman had to.

"No one more than I," said the Secretary, "admires Madam Chairwoman's spirit. But has she, in her feminine enthusiasm, considered the difficulties? Fetch a mouse from Norway — *in the first place!* — How long will *that* take, even if possible?"

"Remember Jean Fromage!" pleaded Madam Chairwoman.

"I do remember Jean Fromage. No mouse worthy of the name could ever forget him," agreed the Secretary. "But he had to be got in touch with first; and traveling isn't as easy as it used to be."

How quickly a public meeting is swayed! Now all Madam Chairwoman's eloquence was forgotten; there was a general murmur of assent.

"In the old days," continued the Secretary, "when every vehicle was horse-drawn, a mouse could cross half Europe really in luxury. How delightful it was, to get up into a well-appointed coach, make a snug little nest among the cushions, slip out at regular intervals to a nosebag! — Farm carts were even better; there one had room to stretch one's legs, and meals were simply continuous! Even railway carriages, of the old wooden sort, weren't too uncomfortable — "

"Now they make them of metal," put in a mouse at

the back. "Has any one here ever tried nibbling steel plate?"

"And at least trains were speedy," went on the Secretary. "Now, as our friend points out, they are practically impossible to get a seat in. As for motor cars, apart from the fact that they often carry dogs, in a motor car one always feels so conspicuous. A ship, you say? We are a hundred miles from the nearest port! Without a single mail coach or even private carriage on the roads, how long would it take, Madam Chairwoman, to cover a hundred miles in a succession of milk wagons?"

"As a matter of fact," said Madam Chairwoman blandly, "I was thinking of an airplane."

Every mouse in the hall gasped. An airplane! To travel by air was the dream of each one; but if trains were now difficult to board, an airplane was believed impossible!

"I was thinking," added Madam Chairwoman, "of Miss Bianca."

The mice gasped again.

3

Everyone knew who Miss Bianca was, but none had ever seen her.

What was *known* was that she was a white mouse belonging to the Ambassador's son, and lived in the schoolroom at the Embassy. Apart from that, there were the most fantastic rumors about her: for instance, that she lived in a Porcelain Pagoda; that she fed exclusively on cream cheese from a silver bonbon dish; that she wore a silver chain round her neck, and on Sundays a gold one. She was also said to be extremely beautiful, but affected to the last degree.

"It has come to my knowledge," proceeded Madam Chairwoman, rather enjoying the sensation she had caused, "that the Ambassador has been transferred, and that in two days' time he will *leave for Norway by air!* The Boy of course travels with him, and with the Boy travels Miss Bianca — to be precise, in the Diplomatic Bag. No one on the plane is going to examine *that;* she enjoys diplomatic immunity. She is thus the very person to undertake our mission."

By this time the mice had had time to think. Several of them spoke at once.

"Yes, *but* — " they began.

"But what?" asked Madam Chairwoman sharply.

"You say, 'the very person,' " pronounced the Secretary, speaking for all. "But is that true? From all one hears, Miss Bianca has been bred up to complete luxury and idleness. Will she have the necessary courage, the necessary *nerve?* This Norwegian, whoever he is, won't know to get in touch with *her,* she will have to get in touch with *him.* Has she even the necessary *wits?* Brilliant as your plan undoubtedly is, I for one have the gravest doubts of its practicalness."

"That remains to be seen," said Madam Chairwoman. She had indeed some doubts herself; but she also had great faith in her own sex. In any case, she wasn't going to be led into argument. "Is there anyone," she called briskly, "from the Embassy here with us now?"

For a moment all waited; then there was a slight scuffling at the back as though someone who didn't want to was being urged by his friends to step forward, and finally a short, sturdy young mouse tramped up towards the platform. He looked rough but decent; no one was surprised to learn (in answer to Madam Chairwoman's questioning) that he worked in the pantry.

"I suppose you, Bernard, have never seen Miss Bianca either?" said Madam Chairwoman kindly.

"Not me," mumbled Bernard.

"But could you reach her?"

"I dare say," admitted Bernard — shuffling his big feet.

"Then reach her you must, and without delay," said Madam Chairwoman. "Present the compliments of the meeting, explain the situation, and bid her instantly seek out the bravest mouse in Norway, and dispatch him back here to the Moot-house."

Bernard shuffled his feet again.

"Suppose she doesn't want, ma'am?"

"Then you must persuade her, my dear boy," said Madam Chairwoman. "If necessary, bully her! — What's that you have on your chest?"

Bernard squinted self-consciously down. His fur was so thick and rough, the medal scarcely showed.

"The Tybalt Star, ma'am . . ."

"For Gallantry in Face of Cats," nodded Madam Chairwoman. "I believe I remember the incident . . . A cat nipped on the tail, was it not, thus permitting a nursing mother of six to regain her hole?"

"She was my sister-in-law," muttered Bernard, flushing.

"Then I can't believe you're not a match for Miss Bianca!" cried Madam Chairwoman.

4

With that (after several votes of thanks), the meeting broke up; and Bernard, feeling important but uneasy, set off back to the Embassy.

At least his route to the Boy's schoolroom presented no difficulties: there was a small service lift running directly up from the pantry itself, used to carry such light refreshments as glasses of milk, chocolate biscuits, and tea for the Boy's tutor. Bernard waited till half-past eight, when the last glass of milk went up (hot), and went up with it by clinging to one of the lift ropes. As soon as the flap above opened he nipped out and slipped into the nearest shadow to wait again. He waited a long, long time; he heard the Boy put to bed in an adjoining room, and a wonderful rustle of satin as the Boy's mother came to kiss him good night. (Bernard was of course waiting with his eyes shut; nothing draws attention to a mouse like the gleam of his eyes.) Then at last all was still, and forth he crept for a good look round.

In one respect at least rumor had not lied: there in an angle of the great room, on a low stool nicely out of floor drafts, stood a Porcelain Pagoda.

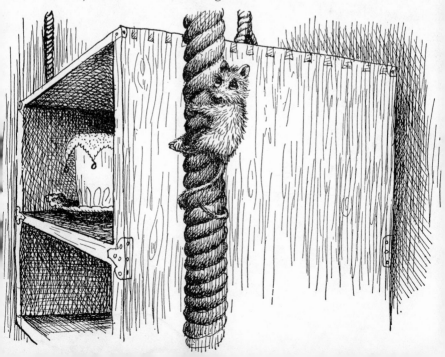

2

Miss Bianca

It was the most exquisite residence Bernard had ever seen, or indeed could ever have imagined. Its smooth, gleaming walls were beautifully painted with all sorts of small flowers — violets, primroses and lilies of the valley — and the roof rose in tier upon tier of curly gilded eaves, from each corner of which hung a golden bell. Round about was a pleasure ground, rather like a big bird-cage, fenced and roofed with golden wires, and fitted with swings, seesaws and other means of gentle relaxation. Bernard's eyes felt as big as his ears as he diffidently approached — and he himself felt a very rough, plain mouse indeed.

"Miss Bianca!" he called softly.

From inside the Pagoda came the faintest of rustling sounds, like silk sheets being pulled over someone's head; but nobody appeared.

"Don't be afraid, Miss Bianca!" called Bernard. "I'm not burglars, I am Bernard from the Pantry with a most important message."

He waited again. One of the golden bells, as though a

moth had flown past, tinkled faintly. Then again there was a rustling, and at last Miss Bianca came out.

Her loveliness took Bernard's breath away. She was very small, but with a perfect figure, and her sleek, silvery-white coat had all the rich softness of ermine. But her chief point of beauty was her eyes. The eyes of most white mice are pink; Miss Bianca's were deep brown. In conjunction with her snowy head, they gave her the appearance of a powdered beauty of the court of Louis the Fifteenth.

Round her neck she wore a very fine silver chain.

Bernard took two steps back, then one forward, and politely pulled his whiskers.

"Are you calling?" asked Miss Bianca, in a very low, sweet voice.

"Well, I *was* — " began Bernard.

"How very nice!" exclaimed Miss Bianca. "If you wouldn't mind swinging on that bellpull, the gate will open. Are there any ladies with you?"

Bernard muttered something about Madam Chairwoman, but too hoarsely to be understood. Not that it mattered; Miss Bianca's beautiful manners smoothed all social embarrassment. As soon as he was inside she began to show him round, naming every painted flower on the porcelain walls, and inviting him to try for himself each swing and seesaw. "Pretty, isn't it?" she said modestly. "Though nothing, I believe, compared with Versailles . . . Would you care to see the fountain?"

Bernard nodded dumbly. As yet he hadn't even noticed the fountain; it was in fact a staggering six inches high, made of pink and green Venetian glass. Miss Bianca sat down on a hidden spring, and at once a jet of water shot up out of the pink rosette on top. "There *is* a way of making it *stay*," she explained, "but I'm afraid I know nothing about machinery!" She rose, and the jet subsided. Bernard would have liked to have a go himself, but he was only too conscious that time was passing, and that as yet his message was undelivered.

Indeed it was hard to know where to begin. It was such a jump from Venetian glass fountains to the Prisoners' Aid Society. Moreover, though he no longer thought Miss Bianca affected, in fact he liked her very much, he couldn't for the life of him see her doing anything more strenuous than swinging on a gilt swing. And the turn the conversation next took fairly curled his whiskers!

"I see you've been decorated," said Miss Bianca politely. (She was naturally familiar with medals, and orders, and ribbons.) "May I ask what is it for?"

"Gallantry in Face of Cats," muttered Bernard. — First to his chagrin, then to his astonishment, she burst into musical laughter.

"In face of *cats?* How very droll! I dote on cats!" laughed Miss Bianca. "Or rather," she added sentimentally, "on one particular cat . . . a most beautiful Persian, white as I am myself, belonging to the Boy's mother.

I used to play in his fur; I'm told we made rather a pretty picture . . . Alas, he is no more," sighed Miss Bianca, "but for his sake *all* cats will ever be dear to me!"

Bernard was absolutely speechless. He didn't disbelieve Miss Bianca; he could, just, imagine some pampered lapcat fat enough and drowsy enough to have lost all natural instincts; but what an appalling thought — a mouse going out into the world, alone, on a mission of danger, *not afraid of cats!*

"My poor playfellow! Ah me!" sighed Miss Bianca tenderly.

"Look here, you've got to promise — " began Bernard; and gave up. There was a dreamy look in her eyes which warned him, though he didn't know much about women, that it was the wrong moment to run cats down. Instead, he attempted to console her.

"You've got all this," he pointed out, looking round at the swings and the seesaws and the fountain.

"And what trifling it seems!" sighed Miss Bianca. "What trifling it must seem, especially, to *you,* compared with the real and earnest life of a Pantry!"

Bernard drew a deep breath. Now or never, he thought!

"Would *you* like to do something real and earnest too, Miss Bianca?"

She hesitated. Her lovely eyes were for a moment veiled. Then one small pink hand crept up to finger the silver chain.

"No," said Miss Bianca decidedly. "I'm so fond, you see, of the Boy. And *he* is so attached to *me*. How many times have I not heard him call me his only friend! I feel so long as I do my duty to the Boy, my existence, however frivolous it may *appear,* is in fact quite earnest enough."

"That's one way of looking at it," said Bernard glumly. (They should have sent Madam Chairwoman, he thought, not him. Madam Chairwoman could talk about duty quite wonderfully.) "All the same," he persisted, "you're not with the Boy all the time. You're not with him now, for instance." (There was considerable point in this; it is at night that mice most want to be up and doing, and are most bored by inactivity.) "Actually, now that you've no longer your, h'm, playfellow, I really don't see how you occupy yourself."

"Well, as a matter of fact," said Miss Bianca modestly, "I write."

Bernard gaped. He had never met a writer before! — Though he was terribly afraid of wasting time, he couldn't help asking What.

"Poetry," confessed Miss Bianca.

How Bernard's heart leaped!

For so was the Norwegian prisoner a poet!

What a wonderful, fortunate coincidence! The very thing to make Miss Bianca change her mind! — Without giving himself time to think, and without any transition, Bernard blurted it all out — all about the Prisoners' Aid

Society, all about the great enterprise, all about Miss Bianca's part in it, all about everything.

The result was exactly what might have been expected. Miss Bianca fainted clean away.

2

Desperately Bernard slapped her hands, fanned her face, leaped to the hidden spring, turned on the fountain, with incredible agility leaped again and caught a drop of water before it subsided, sprinkled Miss Bianca's forehead. (Oh for Madam Chairwoman, he thought!) Seconds passed, a long minute, before the dark eyelashes fluttered and Miss Bianca came to.

"Where am I?" she murmured faintly.

"Here, in your own Porcelain Pagoda," reassured Bernard. "I am Bernard from the Pantry — "

"Go away!" shrieked Miss Bianca.

"If you'll only listen quietly — "

"I won't hear any more!" cried Miss Bianca. "I don't want anything to do with you! Go away, go away, go away!"

Greatly daring, Bernard caught both her hands and pressed them between his own. The action seemed to steady her. She stopped trembling.

"Dear, dearest Miss Bianca," said Bernard fervently, "if I could take your place, do you think I wouldn't? To spare you the least inconvenience, I'd walk into cat-baskets! But *I* can't travel by Diplomatic Bag, *I* can't get to Norway in twenty-four hours. Nor can anyone else. You, and you alone, can be this poor chap's savior."

At least she was listening, and at least she didn't push Bernard away. She even left her hands in his.

"And a poet!" went on Bernard. "Only consider, dear Miss Bianca — a poet like yourself! How can you bear to think of him, alone in a deep dark dungeon, when one word from you — "

"Is that really all?" whispered Miss Bianca. "Just one word?"

"Well, of course you've got to say it to the right mouse," admitted Bernard honestly. "And to find him I dare say you'll have to go into pretty rough quarters. I tell you my blood boils when I think of it — "

"Why?" whispered Miss Bianca. "Why does your blood boil?"

"Because you're so beautiful!" cried Bernard recklessly. "It's not fair to ask you to be brave as well! You should be protected and cherished and loved and honored, and I for my part ask nothing better than to lie down and let you walk on me!"

Miss Bianca rested her head lightly against his shoulder.

"You give me such a good opinion of myself," she said softly, "perhaps I could be brave as well . . ."

POEM BY MISS BIANCA, WRITTEN THAT NIGHT

Though timid beats the female heart,
   Tempered by only Cupid's fires,
The touch of an heroic hand
   With unaccustomed bravery inspires.

M. B.

3

In Norway

THREE days later, Miss Bianca was in Norway.

The journey, as usual, had given her not the least trouble. She traveled as always in the Diplomatic Bag, where she amused herself by reading secret documents while the great airplane flew smoothly and swiftly over mountain and forest, river, and, finally, sea. (To be accurate, there was a slight bumpiness over the mountain part, but Miss Bianca was too absorbed in a very Top Secret to notice.) Precisely twenty-four hours after departure she was reinstalled in her Porcelain Pagoda in the Boy's new schoolroom in Oslo, the capital of Norway.

It was then her mission really began; with, in Miss Bianca's opinion, far too much left to her own initiative. She was simply to seek out the bravest mouse in Norway! Without the slightest idea where he was to be found — or indeed where any mice were to be found! For Miss Bianca's life had been so remarkably sheltered, she really didn't know anything at all about how other mice lived. Except for Bernard, she had never even spoken to one.

Except for Bernard . . . Miss Bianca's thoughts flew to him so readily, she felt quite angry with herself. Now that the excitement of their midnight meeting was past, she couldn't help recognizing that good and brave as Bernard was, he was also completely undistinguished. — Yet how kind and resourceful, when she fainted! How understanding, when she came to, of all her doubts and fears! And how lost in admiration, how absolutely overcome, when she finally accepted her heroic task!

"I must be worthy," thought Miss Bianca. And mentally added — "Of the Prisoners' Aid Society."

So the very first night in her new quarters, she set out.

No one knew she was so slim that she could squeeze between the gilded palings of her pleasure ground. Certainly the Boy didn't know it. But she could.

The door of the new schoolroom didn't quite fit. In the morning no doubt someone would see to it; in the meantime, Miss Bianca slipped under. Outside immediately, she still felt pretty well at home — all Embassies being much of a muchness. There was first a broad corridor, then a broad landing, then a grand staircase leading down to a great grand entrance hall. (Miss Bianca, who had an eye for carpets, even recognized everywhere familiar patterns.) But she hadn't so far encountered any other mouse. "The Pantry!" thought Miss Bianca — remembering Bernard again. "But where on earth are pantries?"

However sheltered, all women have certain domestic instincts. Miss Bianca was pretty sure she ought to get lower down.

She also knew about service lifts. Passing from the entrance hall into the dining room, and observing a gap in its paneling (left open by a careless footman), up Miss Bianca ran to investigate. There inside, sure enough, were the proper ropes. "Obviously connected with the Pantry," thought Miss Bianca, climbing on. When after two or three minutes nothing happened, she boldly ran down — quite enjoying the easy exercise, and quite confident of finding herself in a pantry below.

Actually this particular service lift ran straight down to the Embassy cellars. Which was fortunate as it turned out, though Miss Bianca didn't immediately think so.

2

For what a sight, as she emerged, met her eyes!

Remember it was well after midnight, it must have been nearly two o'clock in the morning, the hour at which mice feel themselves most secure. In the Embassy cellar there was evidently some kind of bachelor party going on. At least fifty Norwegian mice were gathered there — singing and shouting and drinking beer. The most part wore sea boots and stocking caps; some had gold earrings in their ears, some a patch over one eye. A few had wooden legs. It was in fact the most piratical-looking party imaginable, and how any one of them ever got into an Embassy, Miss Bianca really couldn't imagine.

Never had she felt more uncomfortable. It is always trying to enter a room full of strangers — and *such* strangers! What a racket they made! The singing and shouting almost deafened her ears, there wasn't a moment of repose. (Miss Bianca had frequently assisted, from the Boy's pocket, at diplomatic soirees. *There,* always, was a moment of repose; in fact, sometimes the moments ran into each other and made *hours* of repose.) Even if she had shouted she couldn't have made herself heard, and Miss Bianca had never shouted in her life! She stood utterly at a loss, trembling with dismay; until at last a mouse nearby turned and saw her, and immediately uttered a long, low whistle. It was vulgar, but it did the trick. Head after head turned in Miss Bianca's direction; and so spectacular was her fair beauty, silence fell at last like refreshing dew.

"Forgive me for joining you uninvited," said Miss Bianca nervously, "but I am a delegate from the Prisoners' Aid Society, seeking the bravest mouse in Norway, on behalf of a Norwegian poet imprisoned in our parts."

Simply as she spoke, it was with a touching grace. Several mice at once cuffed one another for want of respect to the lady. Several tankards were kicked under benches. One of the soberest of the seafarers, who looked as though he might be a Petty Officer, stepped forward and touched his cap.

"Anyone from the Prisoners' Aid, ma'am," he said forthrightly, "finds all here ready and willing at the first tide. Just pick your chap, and he'll put himself under orders."

"How splendid!" said Miss Bianca, greatly encouraged. "Though how can *I* pick, stranger as I am? You must tell me who is the bravest."

"All of 'em," replied the Petty Officer. "All our lads are brave equally. Look about for yourself, ma'am, and count the Tybalt Stars!" (There was one on his own chest, with clasp.) "Some may look a bit rough to a lady — pipe down there, you by the bar! — but as to being brave, each and all rate A1 at Lloyd's."

Miss Bianca still felt any decision quite beyond her.

"Won't you choose for me?" she begged. "Of course it should really be a volunteer — but if you could give me any indication — "

The Petty Officer simply reached out a hand and clapped it on the nearest shoulder — only then looking around to see whom he'd got.

"You, Nils!" he snapped. "You a volunteer?"

"Aye, aye, sir," said Nils.

"Not a family man, or anything of that sort?"

"Not me," said Nils. (Several of his friends round the bar roared with laughter.)

"Willing to put yourself under this lady's orders?"

"Please, under the orders of the Prisoners' Aid Society!" cried Miss Bianca.

"All comes to the same thing," said the Petty Officer. "You just tell Nils what to do, ma'am, and Nils he will do it."

With that, as though no more had been settled than who was to run into the next room, all returned to singing and shouting and standing each other rounds of beer, and Nils and Miss Bianca were left alone.

She looked at him attentively. He was indeed rough to a degree. His sea boots smelled of tar, and his stocking cap had obviously never been washed since it was knitted. But he had good steady eyes, and he appeared quite unperturbed.

As simply as possible, Miss Bianca outlined the situation. She hoped he was taking it all in — he was so *very* unperturbed! — also he would keep humming softly under his breath.

"You're quite sure you understand?" she said anxiously. "How you travel in the first place I must leave to you — "

"Why, by ship — o' course," said Nils.

"I believe the Capital is some distance from the nearest port," warned Miss Bianca.

"Ship and dinghy, then," said Nils. "Wherever there's towns there's water — stands to reason — and wherever there's water, there us Norwegians can go."

"How resourceful you are!" exclaimed Miss Bianca admiringly. "As to reaching the Black Castle itself, for that Madam Chairwoman will have a plan. You must get in touch with her immediately, at the Moot-house."

For the first time, Nils looked uneasy.

"Could you let me have a chart, ma'am? On shore I'm a bit apt to loose my bearings."

"Certainly," said Miss Bianca. "If you will give me the materials, I'll do it now."

After a little searching, Nils produced from one of his boots a paper bag and a stump of red chalk. (He found several other things first, such as half a pair of socks, a box of Elastoplast, a double six of dominoes, a ball of twine and a folding corkscrew.) Miss Bianca sat down at a table and smoothed the bag flat.

At the end of ten minutes, all she had produced was a sort of very complicated spider web.

The Moot-house was in the middle — *that* was quite clear; but the rest was just a muddle of criss-cross lines. Miss Bianca felt so ashamed, she rapidly sketched a lady's hat — just to show she really *could* draw — and began again.

"Hadn't you best start with the points of the compass, ma'am?" suggested Nils.

Miss Bianca, alas, had never even heard of compass points!

"*You* put them in," she said, turning the paper over. Nils took the chalk and marked top and bottom, then each side, with an *N*, an *S*, an *E* and a *W*. Then he gave

the chalk back, and Miss Bianca again put a dot in the middle for the Moot-house — and again, out of sheer nervousness, drew a lady's hat round it. (The garden-party sort, with a wide brim and a wreath of roses.) Nils studied it respectfully.

" *That* I'd call clear as daylight," he said. "You should ha' set your compass first." He laid a finger on one of the roses. "Them, I take it, would be duckponds?"

"Oh, dear!" thought Miss Bianca. She knew perfectly well where the Moot-house stood — Bernard had explained everything so clearly — but she just couldn't, it seemed, put her knowledge on paper. And here was good brave Nils preparing to set forth with no more guide than a garden-party hat!

"Yes," said Miss Bianca recklessly. "Those are duck-ponds . . ."

An idea was forming in her mind, an idea so extraordinary and thrilling, her heart at once began to beat faster.

"All the same," added Miss Bianca, "I think it will be wiser to return with you myself, and conduct you to the Moot-house in person."

What on earth induced her to make such a mad, unnecessary offer? Her own personal mission was creditably accomplished; no one expected any more of her; upstairs in the Boy's new schoolroom a luxurious Porcelain Pagoda waited for her to come back to it. As the Boy waited for her — or would wait, how anxiously, should she quit his side! Miss Bianca's eyes filled with tears as she thought of him. But she thought also of someone else: of Bernard from the Pantry.

It has often been remarked that women of rank, once their affections are engaged, can be completely reckless of the consequences. Duchesses throw their caps over the windmill for grooms, countesses for footmen: Miss Bianca, more discerningly, remembered Bernard's modesty and kindness and courage. "Did I call him undistinguished?" she chided herself. "Isn't the Tybalt Star distinction enough for anyone?" To make no bones about it, Miss Bianca suddenly felt that if she was never to see Bernard again, life in any number of Porcelain Pagodas would be but a hollow sham.

Thus, since obviously Bernard couldn't come to *her,*

it was she who had to rejoin Bernard; and fortunately duty and inclination coincided.

"Which I take very kindly," Nils was saying. "Can you be ready, ma'am, by the dawn tide?"

"What!" exclaimed Miss Bianca. Her thoughts hadn't carried her quite as far as that!

"It so happens there's a cargo boat," explained Nils. "Nothing like cargo boats for picking up a passage upon! And not so many bound your way neither — we should take the chance! In fact, in my opinion, we should start for the docks straight off."

"Heavens!" thought Miss Bianca. — Yet in one way it made her decision easier. The thought of seeing the Boy again, possibly for the last time — of running up onto his pillow and breathing a last farewell in his ear — was already almost unnerving her. "Better not," she thought. "I might break down . . ." She rose, smiling.

"Pray lead the way," said Miss Bianca. "I'm quite ready!"

They left at once. (Nils just fetched his cutlass from the cloakroom, and he was ready too.) No one bothered to say good-by to them, in fact no one took any notice of them at all.

"Do you always set out on a voyage so — so casually?" asked Miss Bianca, as they passed through the wood cellar. She really felt quite nettled.

"Stands to reason," said Nils. "Us Norwegians be forever setting out on voyages."

"But one so fraught with peril!" exclaimed Miss Bianca.

"All voyages be fraught with peril," said Nils matter-of-factly. " 'Drowned in his seaboots' you might call the national epitaph." He paused, and looked down at Miss Bianca's tiny feet. "By which same token, ma'am," he added, "where's your galoshes?"

"I'm afraid I haven't any," said Miss Bianca.

Nils gave her an odd glance, a glance she couldn't quite read. She felt nettled again.

"Traveling by Bag, as one usually does," she explained icily, "one doesn't need them. In Bag, one's feet are always quite beautifully warm . . ."

"In Norway, you're better with galoshes," said Nils. "You stay here a minute."

He hurried off, leaving Miss Bianca to wait beside a chopping block. (How thankful she was that no one she knew was likely to come by!) But he wasn't gone long; within a very few minutes back he came hurrying with a pair of lady's galoshes under one arm. " I've borrowed a pair of Ma's for you," he panted. — Miss Bianca looked at them ungratefully; they were far too large, and dreadfully shabby. However, there was nothing to do but to put them on, and she did so. "That's more like!" said Nils. "Now we can be on our way!"

Up they went by the wood chute, into the broad Karl Johans Gate. Nils ran straight across, and almost immediately entered a tangle of byways leading down to the docks. Slipslop in her horrid galoshes, Miss Bianca followed. "I'm not seeing much of Norway!" she thought. There was light enough, too, if they hadn't been in such a hurry; a strange pearly grayness filled the streets, all the house fronts were clearly visible. "Are we passing anything of historic interest?" panted Miss Bianca. But Nils wouldn't stop. He never stopped once until they reached the docks. There, bidding Miss Bianca wait again, he ran swiftly up and down reading the names on the vessels until he found the right hawser. "Follow me!" he finally cried; and Miss Bianca, by now completely out of breath, followed up into a very old, very shabby cargo boat.

4

The Voyage

Of the first part of the full month's voyage that ensued, Miss Bianca afterwards, and fortunately, remembered almost nothing. Most of the time she was seasick. Nils with the greatest kindness and practicality found her a snug berth behind the galley lockers — warm, dry, and, as you might say, next door to a restaurant; but though thankful to be dry and warm, Miss Bianca turned in loathing from even the excellent local cheese. A few drops of water, a few crumbs of dry bread, were all she could face. She lay curled on a bed of potato peelings — how different from her pink silk sheets! — and merely suffered. If the North Sea was terrible, the English Channel was worse — while as for the Bay of Biscay, Miss Bianca could never subsequently endure even to hear it named.

The spirits of Nils, on the other hand, as soon as they were fairly out to sea, rose and rose. He sang sea chanteys almost continually, often breaking out as well into snatches of a long saga about someone called Harald Fairhair. He ran in and out of scuppers, up and down the

rigging; there wasn't a cat or dog on board, reported Nils joyfully — it might have been his own command! "Come up and see!" he urged Miss Bianca. "Come up and see the great billows, and how our vessel breasts them! Come up and see the lights of the ports, how they sparkle on the water! Come up and see the rays of the great lighthouses — each and all specially designed for the protection of us Norwegians!"

"I'm sorry, I have a headache," said Miss Bianca.

"A headache *at sea*? But the sea cures everything!" cried Nils incredulously.

"I'm writing poetry," said Miss Bianca.

So indeed she was. She hoped that in the event of shipwreck (which she fully expected), the following lines, sealed up in an iodine bottle, might be washed ashore and bring some comfort to the Boy.

POEM BY MISS BIANCA, WRITTEN AT SEA

Dear Boy! I would not have thee weep!
  Sooner forget thy Miss Bianca quite!
Yet know, 'twas only Duty's higher call
  Could e'er have torn her from thy loving side!

M. B.

The rhyme wasn't quite perfect, owing to seasickness, but it was the best she could do, and Nils kindly saw to heaving the bottle overboard.

He was as kind as possible — whenever he remembered her. It was a new experience to Miss Bianca not to be the center of attention, and led her to reflect a good deal on several points which she had hitherto taken for granted. Life in a Porcelain Pagoda had always seemed so natural to her! As cream cheese from a silver bonbon dish, and golden swings to swing on, and a silver chain to wear, seemed mere necessities! As she had told Bernard, Miss Bianca firmly believed that her devotion to the Boy made an ample return, and she believed so still; but it did not enter her mind that such an existence was unusual, and not the only possible one. Could one not find equal happiness, mused Miss Bianca, if not equal luxury, in devotion to another mouse? "Of course we should be very poor!" thought Miss Bianca. "I wonder how the poor live?"

She asked Nils. — She put it very delicately, in a roundabout way, so as not to hurt his feelings.

"What does your father do?" asked Miss Bianca.

Nils pulled his whiskers. — They were sitting together in the lee of a stanchion; it was a fine, calm night, very starry, and Miss Bianca had for once ventured up on deck.

"At a guess, he'll be voyaging — same as us," said Nils.

"But don't you *know?*" exclaimed Miss Bianca, astonished.

"Haven't seen the old buffer in years," said Nils casually.

"But who looks after your mother, and the family?" asked Miss Bianca. "How many brothers and sisters have you?"

Nils pulled his whiskers again. All mice have large families, and Nils was no better than any other man at keeping track of relations.

"A couple of dozen?" he suggested. "Soon as they're able, *they* go voyaging too — at least us boys do. The girls, until they marry, mostly stay home helping Ma. Ma takes in washing."

Miss Bianca shuddered. She had never imagined anything quite as dreadful as that! But she concealed her horror.

"No doubt it's because you're a race of seafarers," she said, "that your wives are left so much alone. Marrying a mouse in a good shore situation, such as a Pantry, for instance, would no doubt be very different. At least he would remain at one's side, in however modest a dwelling."

"As to that I couldn't say," replied Nils. "In Ma's opinion, the laundry runs a great deal better when she runs it herself."

"Poor soul!" thought Miss Bianca. Twenty-four children to support! — what deprivations *they* must have suffered! Perhaps not even new hats for Easter, and cream cheese only the rarest treat!

"How the poor live!" cried Miss Bianca uncontrollably. "It's quite dreadful to think of!"

"Is it? Myself, I don't know any poor," said Nils. He paused, and looked at her kindly. "Except, maybe," he added, "for one poor little female that hadn't any galoshes . . ."

Miss Bianca returned to her berth a thoughtful mouse indeed. She lay awake most of next day. To do her justice, Nils's silly misapprehension didn't occupy her long: Looked at in one way it was almost amusing — to own a Porcelain Pagoda, and yet be taken for poverty-stricken because one happened to borrow a pair of galoshes! (If only Nils *knew,* thought Miss Bianca, actually smiling.) No, what really engaged her attention was the fact that Nils didn't consider himself or his family poor. However small their income, he seemed to find it perfectly sufficient. Life outside a Porcelain

Pagoda was certainly *possible,* then, reflected Miss Bianca . . .

"But I could never, never take in washing!" she told herself.

With the best will in the world — and though she was rapidly shedding many of her prejudices — she couldn't believe Nils's mother to be *happy.* Alone all day at the mangle (except for say half a dozen daughters), and quite unsupported by a husband's company, how indeed could she be anything but wretched? — The picture would be very different, of course, with a loving husband in it as well . . .

"But I wonder if I could give drawing lessons?" mused Miss Bianca.

She was in a very distracted, uneasy state of mind; and to make matters worse, as the days passed and they began to near their destination, Nils started bothering her about the chart — a subject on which she was particularly sensitive.

Nils had taken charge of it at once, and kept it stowed in his left-leg sea boot, where it naturally rubbed against all the other things he kept there until it was quite smudged. Also the folding corkscrew must have come *un,* for there was a great round hole through one of the duckponds, or roses.

"*Really!*" exclaimed Miss Bianca, as he pulled it out. Secretly she was rather pleased; if *she* hadn't known how to draw a chart, Nils certainly didn't know how to take

care of one. "After all my trouble — !" exclaimed Miss
Bianca. Women can be dreadfully unfair, when prestige
is at stake.

"It looks all right to *me*," said Nils. "Why, Skipper's
chart up aloft you can't hardly read for cocoa! *I* can find
my way all right. All I was going to ask was, be they
duckponds linked by navigable streams?"

With growing horror, Miss Bianca realized that what
*she'*d intended for a map of the Capital, Nils took to be
a map of the route to the Capital from the port. In hon-
esty, she should have answered that she had simply no
idea — or have gone even further, and confessed that
the duckponds were in fact artificial roses. But what then
would become of Nils's confidence in her? It was dreadful to her to tell a lie; her only consolation was that she'd
practically told this one already, when she let Nils believe the roses to be duckponds in the first place, so it
wouldn't count twice.

"By navigable streams," said Miss Bianca.

"Simplifies things," said Nils happily.

"I'm sure I hope so," said Miss Bianca.

Nils took out the chart and studied it every day. He
liked studying charts. But poor Miss Bianca never
watched him without feelings of guilt and apprehension.

2

The days grew warmer and sunnier, the seas calmer.
They were in the Mediterranean. Miss Bianca, who had

done Greek and Latin with the Boy, spent more and more time on deck, gazing with a classical expression towards the fabled shores of Italy, Greece, and the Peloponnese. "Hector and the windy plains of Troy!" murmured Miss Bianca to herself. "The March of the Ten Thousand, the Spartans by the sea-wet strand, also foam-white Venus rising from the waves!" Never were the advantages of education better exemplified; she really forgot, for hours together, every distressing circumstance.

What she remembered was the Boy's schoolroom, in all its comfort and quietude; and the kindness of the Boy's tutor in allowing her to sit on the page; and the pleasure of shared intellectual achievement, as she and the Boy both got a verb right at the same moment, or memorized together some verse of splendid poetry. (Miss Bianca had had the best models.) In happy dreams, she saw Nils safe at the Moot-house while she herself ran back to the Embassy . . . She was quite confident that the new Ambassador would recognize her — if only by her silver chain — and take the promptest steps to return her to the Boy.

How she would enjoy traveling by Bag again!

It will be seen that Miss Bianca had once more changed her mind. Upon thinking it over she found she would prefer not to give drawing lessons. She was determined to bid Bernard but a last, fond farewell.

Two days later, they docked.

3

It is always agreeable to set foot on one's native shore again — and indeed Miss Bianca would have been glad to set foot on *any* shore; on the other hand, all seaports were equally foreign to her, and as she stood beside Nils on the quay (they had been among the first to disembark), she felt just as bewildered as upon the quayside in Norway. To make matters worse, it was now that her responsibility really began, and when Nils immediately suggested picking up a dinghy — obviously quite confident that she knew *where* one picked up dinghies — Miss Bianca could only pretend not to hear, for never was confidence more misplaced. She looked hopelessly about — up at the great hulls of the seafaring ships — up, even higher, at the great cranes unloading them — back towards the rows of customs sheds and warehouses — and really felt the situation quite beyond her. Then, fortunately, she looked down.

Bobbing against the foot of a flight of landing steps lay a model speedboat.

Miss Bianca could hardly believe her eyes. She recognized it at once. It was the Boy's, a gift to him from the American Naval Attaché — about fifteen inches long, and so wonderfully high-powered that the bathtub was scarred all round by its steely prow before some highhanded Someone indignantly fished it out. Then it had been lost. (Both the Boy and Miss Bianca suspected that

Someone of throwing it away.) And now there it lay, after what inconceivable journeyings by gutter, stream and canal, just as though dispatched by the Prisoners' Aid Society!

Miss Bianca instantly ran down, stepped on board and entered the cabin. What a relief it was to sit on proper cushions again! What a pleasure to see the elegant silver plating, the polished woodwork, the little bunch of artificial violets attached to a bulkhead! Even Nils, following, was impressed, as Miss Bianca welcomed him with the happy smile of the unexpectedly triumphant hostess.

"This is what I call organization," said Nils. "My word, she's a neat craft!"

"Custom-built," murmured Miss Bianca, "for a friend of mine. But do you know how to work it?" she added in some anxiety. "I believe it's what they call *atomic*."

"I was never yet aboard a craft I couldn't master," said Nils hardily. — Actually he pulled several wrong levers before he got the hang of things, and nearly swamped Miss Bianca in the process; but at last they were fairly under way.

What happened subsequently will be forever famous in naval annals. With a hundred miles to go, and navigating solely by Miss Bianca's sketch of a garden-party hat, Nils actually succeeded in reaching the Capital. If a duckpond, when he came to it, was bigger than he expected — actually a lake — Nils drove his vessel on regardless. There were navigable streams indeed, only they

happened to be rivers: Nils scorched up them like a motorist entered for the Grand Prix. Now and then he
yelled back to Miss Bianca, over his shoulder, such ex-
clamations as "Norway forever!", also his inevitable references to Harald Fairhair — but ever and always keeping an eye on the chart. (Miss Bianca, who naturally
didn't recognize their course, could only hope for the
best — but they were evidently getting *somewhere,* and
far, far more comfortably than she had anticipated.)
From time to time she fed Nils with coffee sugar out of
one of the lockers. — Coffee sugar! How well she remembered the Boy stocking it, that locker, with his mother's
specially imported coffee sugar! "How could I ever abandon him?" thought Miss Bianca, nibbling a pink bit herself. "Dear Boy, how could I ever think of abandoning
you — ingrate that I am? As soon as I have dispatched
Nils to the Moot-house, back, back to the Embassy will
I run!"

With a final swish and swoop Nils rammed a familiar
quay — one shallow marble step nudged by water lilies.
The little lagoon in which they rocked was actually the
Embassy's boating water. Almost overcome by relief and
thankfulness, Miss Bianca emerged from the cabin and
removed her galoshes.

"Correct landfall?" said Nils, switching off the headlights. (They had arrived about midnight, blazing like a
rocket.)

"Perfect!" Miss Bianca congratulated him.

"Thanks to the clearest chart I ever steered by," said Nils. "Where to now?"

Miss Bianca swiftly reminded herself of Bernard's directions. The tavern in whose cellar the Moot-house was situated backed onto the Embassy stables — no more than a mouse-run away, across shaven lawn; and once inside the stables, there were signposts (as there always are in the vicinity of any historic monument.) Nils could easily find the Moot-house by himself, while *she* ran straight back to dear familiar surroundings . . .

But for several reasons Miss Bianca rejected this sensible course. One reason, it must be admitted, was that she wanted to get full credit for her heroism and be publicly thanked. If it was conceited, it was also very natural!

"Now we must report at the Moot-house," said Miss Bianca, "to which I will conduct you myself."

She left the galoshes behind in the speedboat. She nearly popped them overboard, but remembered in time they belonged to Nils's mother, who might want them back.

5
Marching Orders

ONCE again the Moot-house saw a full meeting of the Prisoners' Aid Society.

For the last week, indeed, members had been gathering there every night, in case the bravest mouse in Norway suddenly turned up. There were also some skeptics among them who believed he never would turn up, and who came simply to bait Madam Chairwoman. (The most mean-minded thing on earth is to rejoice in seeing a high endeavor fail; but it is not, alas, unknown.) The great majority, however, were decent, honest, well-intentioned folk, just eager to be in on any excitement going — and getting a little bored with waiting for it.

It can therefore be imagined what cheers burst forth when Nils and Miss Bianca, escorted by Madam Chairwoman and the Secretary, suddenly appeared on the platform!

"Cheer yourselves hoarse, my dear friends!" cried Madam Chairwoman triumphantly. "You have every reason to! Not only has this heroine — " she bowed towards Miss Bianca — "successfully accomplished her mission

— as witness the presence of our gallant Norwegian comrade — but she has even returned herself to be his guide! Hip, hip — "

"Hooray!" cried all the mice. "Three cheers for Miss Bianca! Speech, speech!"

Miss Bianca shook her head modestly. She just advanced towards the edge of the platform and bowed. Even so, the graceful way she did it aroused a fresh burst of enthusiasm.

"As for you, sir," continued Madam Chairwoman, turning to Nils, "your gallantry and devotion — "

"Think nothing of it, ma'am," said Nils stolidly.

" — will ever be illumined in the annals of our race! The Jean Fromage Medal — "

"That's right!" cried the mice from the floor. "The Jean Fromage! Give him the Jean Fromage! Give 'em both the Jean Fromage!"

"I was *going* to say," said Madam Chairwoman, "that the Jean Fromage, if this enterprise is brought to a successful conclusion, may well be eclipsed by the 'Nils and Miss Bianca'! Hip, hip — "

"Hooray!" cried everyone again.

Where in all this joyful pandemonium was Bernard?

He was sitting in his usual humble place at the back. He wasn't even cheering. He was too much overcome by seeing Miss Bianca again. Moreover, there was a thought he couldn't keep from darting through his mind: Was it *only* to guide Nils that she'd returned? Could it be just possible that she had some other motive? As she advanced in all her loveliness to the edge of the platform, hadn't she appeared, however discreetly, to be *looking* for someone? Obviously she couldn't ask point-blank where that someone was — female delicacy forbade; but supposing, just supposing . . .

Bernard found himself tramping up on his big feet towards the platform. He didn't care what other mice his progress overturned — by now they were all out in the gangways — he just needed to get as close to Miss Bianca as possible.

"Thus you see how earnestly we thank you — " Madam Chairwoman was saying to Nils.

"Miss Bianca!" whispered Bernard.

She glanced quickly round and ran to the platform's edge. Across the row of potted plants, their whiskers touched.

"Bernard!" breathed Miss Bianca.

"But you shall not attempt the Black Castle alone!" cried Madam Chairwoman. (Bernard and Miss Bianca must have missed a bit.) "I now call for a volunteer to accompany and support our heroic Norwegian friend!"

Instantly, simply to prove himself in the slightest degree worthy of Miss Bianca's regard —

"I'll go!" shouted Bernard.

Miss Bianca drew a deep breath. Admittedly such a warmth of welcome — how different from the send-off in

Norway! — had gone a little to her head; but she was influenced even more by the look on Bernard's face.

"And I will too," said Miss Bianca — changing her
mind again.

2

They received all last instructions in the committee
room. (An old carriage lamp next door, tossed down into
the wine cellar by a long-ago postilion. Generations of
Prisoners' Aid Society members had made it extremely
neat; in fact it was much more comfortable than the main
hall, with walnut-shell chairs for everyone.)

"To pay compliments anew would be superfluous," said
Madam Chairwoman briskly. "Therefore to business! You
will travel by provision wagon. As you all know — or as
we must inform our Norwegian friend — the Black Castle is provisioned but once a year. Once in each year, and
only once, its gate opens to admit wagons from the country with flour, bacon, potatoes and so on. Thanks to Miss
Bianca, we are just in time to catch them. They will halt
at the Town Gate, to pick up cough-cure for the jailers,
and there you must be ready tomorrow morning at five
o'clock sharp. I believe the journey takes about two weeks;
within two weeks," said Madam Chairwoman impres-
sively, "you will all three *be inside!* The luck of the mice
go with you! Any questions?"

Miss Bianca shook her head. She relied entirely on her

male companions. Nils, as usual, for his part seemed perfectly content to take whatever was coming as and when it came. Only Bernard spoke up.

"What do we do, *exactly*," asked Bernard in his painstaking way, "once we're *in,* to get the prisoner *out?*"

"That I leave to you," said Madam Chairwoman blandly. "I can't be expected to think of everything!"

3

It was next morning. Outside the Town Gate, in the soft, misty autumn dawn, the great cases of cough-cure stood ready for loading. (The Black Castle was so damp, its jailers had coughs all the year round.) And Nils and Bernard and Miss Bianca stood ready too. If they huddled rather close together, and if Miss Bianca's teeth chattered a little, it was probably because the dawn, besides being soft, was also rather chilly.

Nils had on his sea boots. Though Bernard thoroughly pointed out their uselessness, and indeed inconvenience, he wouldn't be parted from them. "It's no use arguing," said Nils. "Without my sea boots I wouldn't feel myself. That's how us Norwegians are." Miss Bianca smiled at him understandingly: she felt the same way about her silver chain. Bernard had pointed out the unsuitability of this too, he feared it might attract robbers; but without it Miss Bianca wouldn't have felt *her*self . . .

She carried only a small hand valise containing toilet

articles and a fan. (There had been little time for shopping.) Bernard had a stout cudgel and an iron ration of sealing wax tied up in a large spotted handkerchief.

"Hark!" exclaimed Miss Bianca.

There was a jingle of bells, and suddenly, out of the dispersing mist, loomed an enormous wagon. Four great horses pulled it, their heads bobbing and bowing somewhere up in the sky; and from far above even them, a loud rough voice bellowed "Whoa!"

The wagon halted.

"All aboard!" cried Nils.

He ran swiftly up a trailing rope. Bernard seized Miss Bianca's valise and helped her to follow. Scarcely had they found shelter between two flour sacks when a series of shuddering thumps told them the cough-cure was aboard too; then came another loud shout, a whip cracked, and off the wagon rolled, on its way to the Black Castle.

6

The Happy Journey

THEIRS was the leading wagon. Behind rolled five others. All six were loaded with flour, bacon, potatoes and black treacle, but the first carried in addition cough-cure, chewing gum and cigars. These last luxuries were for the jailers — the cough-cure for the common sort, the chewing gum and cigars for the Head. So loaded, and bound for so terrible a destination, it might have been expected that the journey would be terrible indeed, and Miss Bianca was prepared to cry herself to sleep every night, in the little tent Bernard arranged for her among the flour sacks.

But not a bit of it.

It wasn't impossible to be happy, it was impossible *not* to be happy — as the great wagons rolled and swayed on their way, bells jingling, harness glinting, under a strong October sun, through a countryside scarlet with turning leaves and gold with stubble fields. How tuneful those jingling bells, how bright each star and crescent winking from martingale and brow-band! — and the ribbons, too, plaited into mane and tail! Red and yellow and orange, the colors proper to autumn, how they enhanced a chestnut or dappled beauty! But best of all was the rhythm of the six great wagons rolling together, keeping distance yet ever in touch, like six great ships at sea. "Us should have sails set!" shouted Nils, running up the tailboard. "Five capital craft in line astern — and us aboard the Admiral's!"

It was astonishing how quickly the mice felt at home. They had the whole place to themselves, for the wagoner sat on his high seat in front and only once a day cast an eye over the load to make sure all was shipshape. They soon knew the names of their four horses, which were King, Prince, Emperor and Albert. Albert was Miss Bianca's favorite. (He had a very noble, serene expression. Miss Bianca was convinced, she told Bernard, that Albert had not exactly come down in the world, but had renounced the world. — She imagined him winning prize after prize at horse shows, before recognizing their vanity and humbly devoting his great strength to better things.) As to food, of course, no mice could have been better off: the whole wagon was simply one great running buffet!

That was by day; each night, all six wagons drew up in company, and the six jolly wagoners, after they had built a fire and eaten a great meal, told stories and sang songs. Not even Miss Bianca found their voices rough, then, as in beautiful deep harmony they begged their loved ones, also their favorite inns, never to forget them. (As one touching melody followed another, Miss Bianca's eyes were frequently wet with tears — really just as she'd expected them to be, though for different reasons. These were *enjoyable* tears — as the saddest songs were enjoyable to the jolly wagoners.) Each night she and Bernard and Nils slipped out of the wagon and crept closer and closer to listen, and if any item had the slightest rhythm of a sea chantey, Nils would join in; and afterwards they would all stroll back from the concert together, under the glorious moon. It was just like being at Salzburg.

Nils and Bernard had become very good friends. They hadn't much in common, but each saw that in whatever peril lay ahead, he could rely on the other's stanchness. — They never discussed this peril, or made any sort of plan for their great task of prisoner-rescuing. As Nils sensibly pointed out, it was no use crossing bridges till they came to them, and besides, they were having such a happy time, it seemed a pity to cast a shade over it.

2

Sometimes fieldmice came to visit, and then indeed was the peace of the wagon shattered. Whole villages swarmed up at a time — mothers and fathers, aunts and uncles, and of course the children — all chattering and arguing and gossiping and passing remarks. They never stopped asking questions, and never waited for an answer.

"Where are you bound, and why?" chattered the fieldmice. "My goodness, what a quantity of sacks! Unbelievable! Where do they all come from? And what's in those boxes? I say, Amelia, look at this fellow's boots! What's he wearing boots for? And look at the lady's necklace! My word! Look at this other fellow's feet, why isn't *he* wearing boots too? Couldn't he get any big enough? Ha, ha, ha!"

"Pay no attention," said Miss Bianca to Bernard. "They are only simple country folk, with no opportunity to learn manners." She didn't mean to be overheard, she spoke behind her fan, but fieldmice have very sharp hearing, and at once they all took umbrage.

"No manners, indeed!" they chorused. "Hear that, Amelia? The lady says we never learnt no manners! Hands up who goes to dancing class! Hands up all who know strawfoot from hayfoot! My word, she should see one of our barn dances! Come on, let's give one now!"

And they actually began dancing Sir Roger de Coverly there on the floor of the wagon — hands across, back-to-back, down-the-middle and all the rest. They *began* — but in half a minute they were all doing something else again: jumping on and off the cigar boxes, nibbling at the sacks, sliding down the treacle tins, and never for one moment ceasing their chatter.

"How strange! One always thinks of country folk as being rather stolid," said Miss Bianca. "I think I shall lie down a little . . ."

Bernard had found her a delightful veranda between two of the upright slats that formed the wagon's sides,

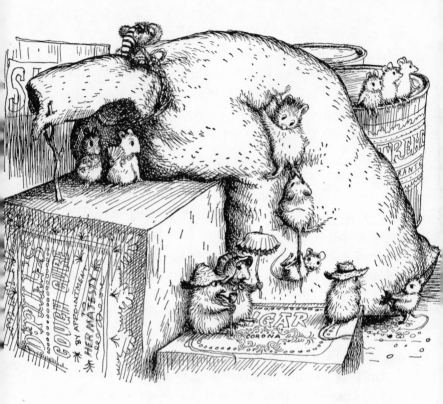

where she could rest in the afternoon and still look out at the changing landscape. It was considered Miss Bianca's private place, but she often invited the other two to share it, and Bernard at least never refused. (Nils preferred a spot higher up, on what he called the poop.) Miss Bianca and Bernard had many long conversations there, and told each other all about their past lives.

"What you must have seen," marveled Bernard, "of Courts, and Embassies! I'm afraid my society must seem very dull to you."

"Not at all," said Miss Bianca. "There is nothing more tedious than a constant round of gaiety. What *you* have to tell, of life in a Pantry, is far more interesting."

They talked in this way for hours, Miss Bianca describing things like musical evenings when the Embassy ballroom was decorated with six hundred pink roses, and Bernard describing things like Sports Day in the Pantry. (The biggest race twice round the top china shelf, five points penalty if you touched china.) They told each other their earliest recollections: Miss Bianca's of waking up on a pink silk pillow, and Bernard's of helping to roll home a walnut . . .

It was a happy time. By night songs and stories, by day agreeable conversation, and ever the beautiful landscape unfolding on either hand — it was a happy time indeed. If only it could have gone on forever! But the days passed, the wagons rolled, and presently the country began to change.

3

"The country's changing," said Bernard uneasily.

"Aye," said Nils. "We're out of the Mediterranean."

Miss Bianca at least knew what he meant. Bare heath and crooked firs, instead of fat farmland and scarlet maple — indeed they were approaching colder waters . . . She shivered a little, and put her fan away in her valise.

That was on the eighth day out; on the tenth, they entered The Barrens.

Here there were no trees at all, nor any sort of vegetation, only rocks and boulders strewing a great flat stony waste. The wagon trail still ran broad and plain, but the horses didn't like it; every mile or so they stopped and balked at something white under their hoofs, and the wagoners had to jump down and pull them past.

"What is it that alarms them so?" asked Miss Bianca curiously.

Bernard didn't want to tell her, but she persisted and he had to. "Bones," said Bernard grimly. "The bones of the prisoners who died on the march to the Black Castle."

Miss Bianca shuddered, and asked no more. Some of the bones had fetters still upon them, for as a prisoner fell so he was left to lie. Then the crows came down and picked him clean.

Albert was the bravest horse, but even he trembled all over. His bells trembled too, not jingling any more, but giving out a faint, mournful, funereal chime.

The fieldmice had vanished long since. In The Barrens, there was no life at all.

At night, the wagoners sounded like people singing to keep their spirits up. Nils and Bernard and Miss Bianca stayed in the wagon.

On the twelfth day, the trail began to climb. The boulders closed their ranks until it was like driving between rocky walls, and then between rocky bluffs, and then between great cliffs. High as the trail climbed, these cliffs rose ever higher, beetling overhead like storm clouds made solid; and here the bones lay thicker.

This lasted for two days more.

On the fourteenth day, quite suddenly, the summit was reached, and all dropped away before the one highest peak of all, which was the Black Castle itself.

They had arrived.

As though the very mountain split, an enormous iron gate swung slowly open, and the wagons rolled through.

7

The Black Castle

It was an appalling moment, and an appalling place.

Behind them was the huge buttressed gateway; on all other three sides of the courtyard great grim black walls, windowless, reared up quite out of sight. There wasn't a scrap of creeper or greenery upon them. Between the paving stones underfoot not so much as a toadstool sprouted. All was iron-hard, iron-chill, and black as old iron.

The air was like the air in a well. Not so very high up in it, a few carrion crows silently hovered.

In silence, as though the Black Castle awed even them, the wagoners began to unload their wagons; there was no need for orders or instructions, they had done the job before, and were only too anxious to get it over. The kind horses nickered and whinnied uneasily; but no human sound was to be heard save the coughing of the jailers waiting to get at the cases of cough-cure.

"What do we do now?" whispered Miss Bianca. The three mice had run down at once, and were now huddled together beside a wheel.

"Wait, then follow the best boots," muttered Nils.

There were boots stamping and shifting all round them — great cruel jailers' boots, black as everything else in the Black Castle. Even Bernard turned a trifle pale, but he nodded bravely.

"You be leader," he whispered.

They waited for what seemed like hours — Nils meanwhile scrutinizing attentively each pair of feet that passed. All seamen have an eye for a boot; and even though these weren't the sort he was used to, he had soon made up his mind. When at last the wagons filed out again, and the jailers began to disperse —

"Follow me!" cried Nils unhesitatingly.

Miss Bianca cast one longing farewell glance towards the tailboard of the last wagon. Even as it passed the gate, sunlight seemed once more to fall upon it; the wagoners were already calling and shouting to each other again, as they headed back into the jovial, sunlit countryside. How glad they were to be going! "And how glad *I* should be!" thought poor Miss Bianca.

She very nearly ran after them. The gates weren't yet quite closed. By running as fast as she could, she might have just caught up; and have run up on board again, and been carried back to safety and civilization . . .

"Miss Bianca," called Bernard urgently, "do please hurry!"

She sighed; and followed duty's higher call.

2

"See any hole?" muttered Nils.

"There, by the stove," whispered Bernard. (He was much cleverer than Nils *indoors.*) "Run in quick, Miss Bianca!"

A moment later they were all looking out, from at least temporary security, upon the Head Jailer's private sitting room.

For that was where the best boots had led, before stamping out again — and how luckily! What Bernard had spotted was actually *the only mousehole in the Black Castle.* The walls of no single other apartment were wainscoted. From the dungeons below to the battlements above, all was either natural rock or bare granite blocks. (Even the jailers' bedrooms weren't so much as white-washed.) As yet, of course, the mice didn't realize their good fortune; they barely glanced at the quarters they were in future to know so well, before examining the larger quarters outside.

"Oh, how *pretty!*" breathed Miss Bianca in surprise.

At first glance, the Head Jailer's sitting room was pretty indeed. The upper part of each wall, above the wainscot, appeared to be hung with the most charming varicolored paper — all reds and blues and browns and yellows. "Just like butterflies!" added Miss Bianca admiringly. — Then she shuddered. For when one looked closer, they *were* butterflies, each cruelly impaled by a lethal pin. Very many, as their poor broken wings showed, hadn't even died in a killing-bottle. And they covered half of every wall! The Head Jailer must have been collecting them, and tormenting them, for years and years . . .

He had evidently other horrid habits as well. Strewn all about the floor were cigar butts and the wrappers off packets of chewing gum: as though he couldn't live without something in his mouth, and hadn't been brought up to tidy as he went along.

"I'm so sorry, but really I feel quite faint," said Miss Bianca.

"Go and lie down a bit," said Bernard kindly. "It looks quite clean inside. — At least he's shortsighted, don't you think?" he added to Nils, as Miss Bianca thankfully withdrew. "He didn't notice us under his heels?"

"He's too fat to see past his own stomach," said Nils crudely. "So far as *he's* concerned, I'd say we could run where we liked. But it's to be hoped he doesn't keep a cat . . ."

The words woke in Bernard a most uncomfortable recollection . . . of an old, old member, at that meeting of the Prisoners' Aid Society when everything started. Hadn't he referred, quite positively, to the Head Jailer's cat? *"Twice natural size, and four times as fierce"* — Bernard recollected the very phrase.

"He keeps a cat all right," said Bernard gloomily.

At that very moment — for the Head Jailer liked to leave his own door open — Mamelouk lounged into the room.

With splendid presence of mind Bernard yanked a

cigar butt across the entrance to the hole, thus masking
all mouse scent, and above this malodorous barricade he
and Nils peered anxiously out.

The cat Mamelouk yawned, stretched, and finally
leaped up into the Head Jailer's armchair. He was an
enormous black half-Persian, with a coat like a thundercloud and eyes like dirty emeralds. When veiled, they
were menacing; when wide open, hypnotic. Even for a
cat, his self-assurance was staggering. With the Head
Jailer under his thumb, he was King of the Black Castle,
and well he knew it.

"Nasty customer, eh?" muttered Nils.

"We must keep Miss Bianca out of his way," said Bernard.

"No more than a couple of mouthfuls," agreed Nils, "*she*'d make for him . . ."

It crossed their minds that neither of *them* would make more than a couple of mouthfuls either. They watched Mamelouk in silence for a few minutes longer, and then thoughtfully rejoined Miss Bianca, and warned her that she was never, in any circumstances, to go out of the hole alone.

3

The hole was their home.

It had several disadvantages. Mamelouk was always liable to turn up in the sitting room outside, and the necessary smell of cigar butts at the entrance made Miss Bianca almost ill. But when Nils and Bernard, after several daring reconnaissances, discovered that there was absolutely no other accommodation available, they sensibly made the best of it, and at least it was a splendid listening post.

They made it really very nice.

The entrance passage, which ran directly at right angles from the wainscot, was quite two and a half inches long, and this was their lobby, where were kept Bernard's cudgel, Nils's sea boots and cutlass, and Miss Bianca's valise. (It was essential to be tidy; and they had the Head Jailer's awful example.) Beyond, between the wainscot and the original granite, and from the stove to the outer wall, stretched a quite commodious apartment. Bernard cleverly divided it with match-boarding — the sitting room floor was quite littered with empty matchboxes — to make Miss Bianca a bedroom by the stove, a slightly larger one for himself and Nils at the other end, and a parlor for general use in between. There Miss Bianca took charge. She had always had a taste for interior decoration, and the lack of professional assistance but sharpened her wits. Soon gay chewing-gum wrappers papered the walls, while upon the floor used postage stamps, nibbled off envelopes in the Head Jailer's wastebasket, formed a homely but not unsuitable patchwork carpet. Miss Bianca with her own hands fashioned several flower pieces — so essential to gracious living — from bread crumbs dyed pink or blue with red or blue-black ink.

At least they had no need to economize where food was concerned: the Head Jailer had all his meals sent up on trays, and was a very untidy eater. Miss Bianca even made one or two daffodils out of cheese.

All heavy work was of course done by Nils and Bernard — the carpentry and paperhanging and so on; Miss Bianca just had the ideas.

Naturally such an amount of work took time, but it was well they were kept busy, otherwise their spirits might have sunk unendurably low.

4

As it was, they sank low enough.

One of the mice's first acts had of course been to constitute themselves into a subsection of the Prisoners' Aid Society, Black Castle Branch. Nils and Bernard voted Miss Bianca Madam Chairwoman, Bernard was Secretary, and they held a General Meeting once a week. As meeting succeeded meeting, however, these grew shorter and shorter and gloomier and gloomier; for the more information the mice gathered, the more hopeless their mission appeared.

As witness the following digest of several earlier Minutes:

Each prisoner occupied a separate dungeon deep down in the rock, and these dungeons were never opened. Food (black bread and treacle) was let down, but once a day, each morning, through grids in the ceilings; and these grids were set in the floor of a long stone corridor itself cut off from the rest of the Castle by a locked iron door.

(SOURCE: Instructions from Head Jailer to new common sort of jailer, in H.J.'s sitting room: overheard by all Members.)

(QUERY: How were the prisoners got *into* their dungeons? The Members couldn't think.)

The door fitted too closely for even a mouse to run under.

(SOURCE: Nils.)

Once a day, of course, it was unlocked by the jailer
with the food pans, and then Nils was pretty certain he
could have got in too — if it hadn't been for Mamelouk
the cat, see below.

> Mamelouk regularly accompanied the jailer on his
> rounds. It was his horrible amusement to jump down
> into a dungeon, as soon as the grid was opened, and
> torment the prisoner by spitting at him while he ate,
> and then ride up again on the food pan.
> (SOURCE: Gossip of jailers: overheard by Nils and
> Bernard.)
> (MINORITY OPINION: Perhaps Mamelouk was try-
> ing to *cheer* the prisoners? — M. B.)

The jailer mightn't notice Nils, but Mamelouk certainly would.

"One of these days I'll risk it all the same!" cried Nils
desperately. "I'm no nearer getting in touch with the poor
chap than if I'd never left Norway!"

"Don't be an idiot," said Bernard, "you wouldn't stand
a chance. There can't be an inch of cover down there: it's
just one big trap."

As the whole Castle was an even bigger trap.

Except for the great gate, there was no way out at all.
The wagons had approached from the south: on the
northern side, it was as though the mountain range had
been sliced clean away; the Castle rose straight up from
the very verge of a tremendous cliff. Below flowed the
River, bridgeless as far as eye could see, and on the far-

ther bank stretched the same sort of country as The Barrens. No wonder *that* side was never guarded! But indeed there seemed as little reason for the jailers in the watchtower above the gate . . .

"Even suppose we could rescue him from his dungeon," said Bernard gloomily — "him" always meant the Norwegian prisoner — "how on earth would we get him *out?*"

This particular conversation took place not at a meeting but in the parlor, where they were all sitting round a fire of cedarwood. (Cigar boxes burn beautifully.) The leaping flames made it look very cozy, playing over the fresh wallpaper and the gay carpet and Miss Bianca's flower pieces. No amount of physical comfort, however, can lighten the burden of responsibility to a truly conscientious mind.

"Cross *that* bridge when we come to it," said Nils shortly.

"You mean you can't think of anything," said Bernard. "I'm not blaming you; *I* can't either."

"What troubles *me* — " began Miss Bianca. She hesitated. What was in her mind was something so dreadful, she felt she really ought to keep it to herself. Then she felt she really couldn't. "What troubles *me,*" whispered Miss Bianca, "is that we don't *know* . . . we have no means of knowing . . . whether he's even still *alive!*"

She looked anxiously at Nils and Bernard; they were looking at each other.

"We hoped you wouldn't think of it," said Bernard reluctantly.

"You mean you and Nils *have*?"

Nils nodded. "Stands to reason," he said gravely. "Put *me* in a dungeon, I wouldn't last a week!"

"But we won't give up hope," said Bernard quickly. "We don't *know* one way or the other. Remember the luck of the mice!" he added cheerfully. "Hasn't it brought us all the way here — found us this splendid hole — kept us all fighting-fit and ready for anything? Remember how beastly we thought the wagon ride was going to be, and how jolly it turned out! And you, Nils, remember that chap Harald Fairhair you're always singing about, remember 'Up the Norwegians!' "

Nils reached across and grasped him by the hand; Miss Bianca slipped hers into his other. Whate'er befell, at least they were three united, loyal companions. At the moment, it was their only consolation.

POEM BY MISS BIANCA, WRITTEN IN THE BLACK CASTLE

Black as the Castle press my mournful thoughts!
What ray of hope can e'er their gloom dispel?
Again, dear Boy, your Miss Bianca fond
Bids you a last, an ultimate farewell!

M. B.

Actually this was the most depressing poem she ever wrote, but even at the time, because it so exactly expressed her feelings, she was rather cheered up by it. Poets have uncommon advantages — as will be seen later on.

8
Waiting

THE pleasantest place in the Black Castle — or rather the least depressing — was a little stone ledge outside the Head Jailer's window. It wasn't a proper window sill, it couldn't have taken a flowerpot, but it was wide enough for a mouse to sit on, in the fresh air. Every afternoon, before setting out on his rounds, the Head Jailer used to raise the sash a couple of inches — his was the only window in the Castle without bars — and as soon as his back was turned Nils and Bernard and Miss Bianca used to run up and sit outside. It was really quite nice, though one of them had always to keep watch for the Head Jailer's return; he closed the window again immediately. Like most wicked people, he hated fresh air; this was the only airing his room ever got. So the three mice had to be careful to regain their hole in time, otherwise they would have had to make a long, dangerous journey round by a corridor window and back through the sitting room door. Nils and Bernard took turns watching — they took fair turns at everything — while the others looked at the view. In time it grew very, very familiar.

Far below ran the great River — sometimes angry, sometimes smooth: and when it was smooth huge rafts floated by, so stacked with logs they looked like floating woodpiles. In the stern of each was built a sort of hut or shelter made of reeds, for the raft-men to sleep in; and if there was a raft-woman — a raft-wife — aboard, there would be hens and hencoops as well, and most likely washing out. When it was rough, they evidently tied up somewhere along the banks, for then not a craft was to be seen, and when they reappeared it was in bunches of six or seven at a time.

"Where can they all be going?" marveled Miss Bianca.

"Why, to the towns, o' course," said Nils, "with winter firing. Don't you use firewood in these parts?"

"At the Embassy, we used central heating," said Miss Bianca.

Nils laughed loudly.

"And where d'you suppose the heat comes from?"

"You forget," said Bernard quickly, "that Miss Bianca has never had to occupy herself with housekeeping. In these parts, as you call them, ladies don't."

Miss Bianca threw him a grateful look. But she was very anxious there should be no bickering. Tempers fray so easily, when one is anxious and frustrated!

"Nils can never get used to my incompetence," said she gently. "But it didn't stop him being very kind to me, on shipboard!"

As a matter of fact, and to their great credit, their

bickerings were very rare, and never lasted more than a few moments. Just a touch of crossness, now and again, was inevitable, for they were frustrated and anxious indeed. The thought of the poor prisoner was never far from their minds, and yet their anxiety to be *doing* something for him was coupled with such a complete inability to think *what*. Bernard relieved himself a little by digs at Madam Chairwoman (not of course referring to Miss Bianca); whenever Nils made his remark about crossing bridges — "I'd like to see Madam Chairwoman cross *this* one!" Bernard would mutter bitterly; that absent figure became really quite a useful scapegoat. Very much, however, was due to Miss Bianca, whose perfect manners and unfailing *savoir-faire* would have soothed the tempers of tigers.

Which was all the more creditable to *her,* since she in one respect was having the worst of things. By day, the three mice could support each other's spirits; Bernard and Nils, sharing a room, could talk to each other at night too. Poor Miss Bianca was all alone.

Quite often she got up, and crept into the parlor, just to hear the sound of their voices. Although the things they talked about weren't particularly cheerful!

"*I* wouldn't last a week," she heard Nils mutter sleepily. "Not in a dungeon I wouldn't . . ."

"*I'd* last a month," mumbled Bernard. "I'd last two months . . ."

Nils evidently woke up.

"Bet you you wouldn't!"

Bernard woke up too.

"Bet you I would!"

"Bet you a double six of dominoes," said Nils, "you'd
be dead and gone, and carried out feet first, inside *ONE
WEEK.*"

"And *I* bet *you,*" countered Bernard, "two potatoes and
a walnut, that I'd still be there to shout 'Up the Norwegians!' as they shoveled you under — having still *ONE
MONTH AND THREE WEEKS TO GO.*"

"I take you," said Nils.

"And *I* take *you,*" said Bernard.

There was a slight pause.

"Who's to hold the stakes?"

"Miss Bianca."

Miss Bianca shuddered. — But in the morning, neither Nils nor Bernard said a word about it, and with a
mixture of relief and irritation she concluded that they
had just been playing a masculine game, like golf.

She still envied them. And how she envied them even
more, when the thunderstorms began!

Each year, it seemed, as winter approached, such un-
natural storms buffeted the Castle unceasingly. All too
soon the pattern became familiar: first an ominous still-
ness in the air, as though presaging snow — not a sound
in all the Castle save the coughing of the jailers — then
a little stir of wind, the storm's outrider, then the first
lightning flash, and then — crash! — instead of snow

the thunderbolts, banging like artillery fire against the Castle walls. From watchtower to dungeons the whole place shook; and Miss Bianca, in bed, put her head under her pillow. Or else she got up and sat in the parlor — and once at least met Bernard, coming to see if she was all right.

"Are you all right, Miss Bianca?" asked Bernard anxiously.

Miss Bianca pulled herself together.

"Thunderstorms always have played havoc with my nerves!" she apologized. "Even under the Boy's pillow, they used to set me quaking! — Actually I just came to see that the fire was out."

Bernard kicked at the hearth, and said yes it was, at least there was no danger from fire.

"Then I'll go back to bed," said Miss Bianca bravely. She paused a moment, however, and heaved a little sigh. "Oh, Bernard," she added wistfully, "how long ago it seems, that night we first met, in my beautiful, safe Porcelain Pagoda!"

2

Indeed it seemed long; and indeed it *was* long — from full summer until almost midwinter. First there had been Miss Bianca's air trip to Norway, then the long voyage back, then the wagon journey, and now nearly two months in the Black Castle. And without achieving any-

thing! That was the hardest to bear of all. "If only something would *happen!*" they began to think . . .

Something did.

They had been in the Black Castle exactly two months
and a day, when a most terrible event occurred.

Bernard was sitting on the Ledge alone. Miss Bianca
had one of her headaches, and since they never left her
by herself, Nils was staying indoors too. It was his turn.
Bernard would have been the one gladly, but in any situation of danger it is always best to keep strictly to rules.
— Imagine his amazement, therefore, to wake from a
light doze and see Nils coolly seated beside him!

"Don't worry," said Nils easily. "Miss Bianca didn't
want me, so I thought I'd join you for a breath of air. She
can, you know, be just a bit of a nuisance!"

Bernard was so horrified, he nearly fell off the Ledge.

"But suppose Mamelouk comes in?" he cried.

"Even if he does — " began Nils.

At that very moment, Mamelouk appeared inside.

Bernard dashed towards the window — too late! In
that very moment, an old sash cord irretrievably frayed,
and down the window slammed.

"Looks like we'll have to take the long passage round,"
said Nils, still unperturbed.

"And what about Miss Bianca?" shouted Bernard.
"Alone in there with Mamelouk?"

"She's only to keep safe in the hole," said Nils reason-
ably. "Stands to reason, she won't venture out — "

Bernard caught him by the scruff and shook him till his teeth rattled.

"You idiot!" he shouted. "You irresponsible idiot! Not venture out! Don't you know that Miss Bianca *isn't afraid of cats?*"

They stared at each other in horror.

"Come quick!" gasped Bernard. "We can do nothing here — and I couldn't bear," he sobbed, "to *watch!*"

9

Cat-and-Mouse

His fears were only too well founded. Scarcely had he and Nils rushed from the Ledge, when Miss Bianca innocently walked forth into the very jaws of death!

And not because she didn't see Mamelouk; because she *did* see him.

She was feeling bored. Her headache was better, and when she looked for Nils he had gone. Miss Bianca didn't particularly mind, she wasn't frightened, but all by herself she felt bored. If only she'd a book to read! — but she hadn't. The Head Jailer was practically illiterate, there was nothing to be borrowed from his shelves save one dog-eared pamphlet entitled *Cut Your Own Corns,* which Miss Bianca would have sooner died — O ominous phrase! — than look at.

She was bored, she had nothing to read: thus when a shadow fell across the entrance to the hole, she naturally put her head out.

About three feet away, big and black as a thundercloud, crouched Mamelouk.

This was the first time Miss Bianca had ever seen him

— Nils and Bernard being so careful to keep her out of his way — but she recognized him immediately from their description, and thought it a very unfair one. Indeed Mamelouk, except for color, was so like her old Persian friend, Miss Bianca was prejudiced in his favor at once. Nils and Bernard said he had a horrible leer; Miss Bianca thought it a rather nice smile. — It will be remembered, also, that though Mamelouk's tormenting of the prisoners, by leaping into their dungeons, was down in the Minutes in black and white, Miss Bianca had never been able to credit it, such was her misguided trust in feline chivalry. So she now looked out with no more than pleasurable excitement!

As for Mamelouk, his whiskers fairly twitched in anticipation. He'd suspected for weeks past that there was something of interest in that hole beside the stove; now he promised himself a proper mouse-tea — with a little game of cat-and-mouse first.

If only his prey could be lured from the safety of the hole!

"Little lady," purred Mamelouk suavely, "won't you come out and play with me?"

Miss Bianca advanced to the very threshold.

"Are you calling?" she asked hopefully.

"Certainly I'm calling!" purred Mamelouk.

"I'm sure it's very nice of you," said Miss Bianca; and to Mamelouk's surprise and joy tripped out into the room. "I should have been delighted to make your acquaintance sooner," she added, "but my friends are a little unsociable . . . How shall we play?"

"Like this!" grinned Mamelouk.

He flashed out a great black paw and touched her on the nape. Only a little more force, and he would have broken her back — as he intended to break her back; but only after reducing her to helpless terror. Such was his horrible nature.

"Now, run, little lady!" he ordered. "Run between my paws!"

"With pleasure," said Miss Bianca. She darted gracefully to and fro. "Touch, and touch again!" she cried. "What shall we do next?"

Mamelouk looked at her with renewed astonishment. She was the first mouse he had seen in years, for he had come to the Castle when only half grown — yet he couldn't believe his memory played him so false, that this was the usual way for a mouse to behave.

"A lady of spirit, I see!" he growled. "All the more sport, then, before the end! *This* is what we do next, my love!"

He flashed out his paw again and pinned Miss Bianca to the floor. She lay absolutely helpless, not an inch from his jaws, under a weight like a mattress stuffed with lead.

"What beautiful eyes you have!" observed Miss Bianca. "They remind me so much of a friend's . . . Were you ever in Persia?"

"No, I was not!" shouted Mamelouk. "And *this* is what

we do afterwards!" he shouted — with one movement scooping her up and flipping her through the air. From his point of view it was a mistake; Miss Bianca landed quite safe, if a little breathless, in the long hair of his back, where he couldn't immediately get at her. "Hide-and-seek!" cried Miss Bianca delightedly; and ran deeper in.

By this time Mamelouk was so baffled, and so angry, he would have made one mouthful of Miss Bianca there and then — if he could have got at her. But he couldn't. He rolled, and shook himself, then leaped and gallo-paded, but he couldn't shake Miss Bianca off. She nestled deep in his long thick coat, and clung on tighter and tighter, emitting little squeals of pleasure. ("I know it's a common taste," cried Miss Bianca, "but how I do enjoy a switchback!") It was Mamelouk who tired first, fling-ing himself down before the stove quite worn out.

Miss Bianca's voice next came from somewhere near the root of his tail.

"I'm sorry to tell you," she called kindly, "but your coat needs a *great deal* of attention. When were you last brushed?"

Mamelouk began to swear — using really the most dreadful language, but fortunately Miss Bianca couldn't quite hear. She just gathered that he was annoyed, and made haste to soothe him.

"Now don't get into a pet!" she begged. "I'm only speaking for your own good — "

"Cats aren't brushed!" shouted Mamelouk.

"Oh, indeed they are!" retorted Miss Bianca positively. "My friend often told me how uncomfortable it was, if his Page missed even one morning. — And what's this?" she cried, really distressed. "This dreadful matted patch?"

"Probably blood!" shouted Mamelouk. "Mouse blood!"

"No, it isn't," said Miss Bianca. "It's treacle. Really, what carelessness! — But at least I can get *that* out for you — if you'll only hold still."

Mamelouk held still. He was too exhausted to do anything else. Miss Bianca nibbled and nibbled, and at last nibbled the treacle patch clear. — But it wasn't *only* treacle: it was a tiny scrap of cloth, stuck with treacle to Mamelouk's fur! And with writing upon it!

"Do see about your brushing tomorrow," said Miss Bianca hastily. "Now forgive me if I run!"

Mamelouk had actually fallen asleep. Bernard and

Nils, rushing in at the sitting room door, could streak straight across to join Miss Bianca in their hole.

"Are you safe?" panted Bernard.

"Of course I'm safe," said Miss Bianca. "And just look at this!"

10
The Message

THEY had to scrape and scrape, and lick and lick till
their tongues felt like emery paper, being careful all the
time not to scrape or lick away any writing. (Mamelouk
was right in one respect; the message, for such it was,
was written in blood, from a pricked finger.) At last the
treacle was cleaned off, and there quite clear upon the
poor scrap of rag showed three or four words in an educated hand.

"And in Norwegian!" shouted Nils.

He pushed Bernard roughly aside, to see better. Bernard didn't mind.

"What does it say?" cried Miss Bianca.

They had never before seen Nils overcome by emotion. Now he actually used the precious rag to wipe his
eyes! "For goodness' sake don't wash anything off!" cried
Bernard — offering his own spotted handkerchief. "Just
tell us what it says!"

Nils gulped and controlled himself.

"It says . . . well, roughly, it just says, *Shall I ever
see Norway again* . . ."

For a moment, at these pathetic words, all fell silent. Then —

"But at least he's still alive!" exclaimed Miss Bianca.

It was wonderful what a difference the knowledge made. Each mouse felt a fresh surge of hope and energy. Discussing the matter among themselves — as they did for hours and hours — they decided that the prisoner must have prepared the message in advance, and seized an opportunity when Mamelouk jumped down into the dungeon to stick it to his fur. However despairing, then, the poor poet, besides being still alive, was still capable of resource! — and how much more should *they* be, at liberty at least within the Castle! "We've been idling!" cried Nils. "We haven't been using our heads!" This wasn't strictly fair, but both Bernard and Miss Bianca understood what he meant: while they didn't know the prisoner was *there* to be rescued, they had gradually let hopelessness get the better of them, and lived from day to day waiting on events . . .

"I shall explore the Castle more thoroughly," said Nils, wiping his eyes for the last time. "There must be *some* way out, besides the gate! I've just been sitting on the Ledge like a stuffed owl — "

"I shall make a timetable," said Bernard, "of exactly when the jailers go their rounds, and exactly when they unlock the dungeon corridor."

"And I," said Miss Bianca, "shall talk to Mamelouk."

The other two at once stopped making their own plans to argue with her. Even Nils now realized what risk she had just run, and as for Bernard, he could hardly trust himself to speak moderately.

"Don't think of it, Miss Bianca!" he begged. "Wonderfully as things have turned out, do please believe it's an even greater wonder you're not eaten up this minute! No mouse on earth could talk to Mamelouk *twice!* — and live to tell the tale! Why he *didn't* eat you — "

Miss Bianca looked down at her fan.

"I think I fascinate him," she said simply. "You may be perfectly right, perhaps he does mean to eat me — Oh, dear," sighed Miss Bianca in parenthesis, "how very different a nature, in that case, from my poor friend's! — but he *didn't,* you know. His expression, as I ran between his paws, was, really, quite fascinated. I'm sure he wants to meet me again — if only from dishonorable motives. Let me engage him in conversation, and guide it into the right channels, and what may I not learn, to our advantage? For if anyone knows everything that goes on in the Castle," said Miss Bianca, "it's Mamelouk."

Bernard and Nils couldn't deny it.

"But the danger — !" cried Bernard nonetheless.

"You and Nils make *your* plans," said Miss Bianca gently; "aren't they dangerous too? *You* have strength and agility; *I* — " she looked modestly down again — "have only charm. You must allow me to employ it. Now good night, dear friends, and in the morning to our tasks!"

She carried the prisoner's message to bed with her, and placed it tenderly under her pillow.

Before they all fell asleep, a short conversation took place in the room shared by Nils and Bernard.

"Nils," said Bernard.

"Um?" said Nils sleepily.

"Who called Miss Bianca a bit of a nuisance?"

There was a slight pause.

"I ought to be kicked," said Nils. "If you like you can come and kick me now."

"That's all right," said Bernard. "Good night!"

2

Now all was action and enthusiasm again. Nils and Bernard returned to exploring the Castle — Nils on the outside, Bernard within. (They left Miss Bianca alone as a matter of course.) Nils ran about the great walls, utilizing every nook and cranny, while Bernard even more daringly slipped to and fro at the jailers' heels, noting and memorizing their every movement. Miss Bianca deliberately threw herself in Mamelouk's way, and this was useful to the other two as well, since she kept him fixed in the sitting room for long periods at a time. Mamelouk couldn't tear himself away from her!

It is hard to speak too highly of Miss Bianca's courage — shot with vanity though it might be. Her gaiety and wit fascinated Mamelouk completely. At the same time, as she came to know him better, she recognized him to be just as cruel and wicked as Bernard said. He did indeed mean to eat her up! — He as good as told her so! "Can you really be as sweet as you look, little lady?" Mamelouk would purr, with horrible double meaning. "I wonder what's the way to find out?" Then it was always *just one more game,* or *one last game* — "To give me an appetite for my dinner!" purred Mamelouk. Miss Bianca's nerves were so taut, she had to go and lie down as soon as she regained the hole. — But she always did regain it: always, at the last moment, by some exquisite trick or clever piece of flattery, she held Mamelouk's paw suspended — and then skimmed like a hummingbird to safety.

Unluckily, when Mamelouk felt like conversation, it was mostly about himself, and Miss Bianca grew very tired of hearing what a handsome kitten he had been, and what an enormous sum the Head Jailer had paid for him, and how even dogs, in the days when he was out in the world, used to howl for mercy at the sight of him. (Besides all his other vices, he was a shocking liar.) One piece of information, however, she did gather, which she hoped might be highly important.

Every New Year's Eve, all the jailers in the Castle, including the Head, held a midnight feast. From midnight till dawn not a single one was on duty. "And not next morning neither," leered Mamelouk.

"Indeed? Why is that?" asked Miss Bianca.

"They've all got bilious attacks," leered Mamelouk, "they stuff themselves so! One's *supposed* to be on duty, the one who takes the prisoners their grub, but it's all he can do to stagger!"

Miss Bianca's heart beat with excitement, but she kept her wits.

"And do you have a bilious attack too?" she inquired solicitously.

"Not me!" swaggered Mamelouk. "I attend, of course, to prevent disappointment — and I eat everything going! — but the feast hasn't been spread yet that could upset my stomach! I am Mamelouk the Iron-tummed!"

But when Miss Bianca made her report to Nils and Bernard, she added that she was sure he was lying again!

"He protested too much," she explained. "I remember a child at one of the Boy's birthday parties who said the same sort of thing — until a footman carried him out! In *my* opinion, Mamelouk won't be on duty either."

"Which means," said Bernard eagerly, "that on *that* morning, the morning of New Year's Day — "

"We can get into the dungeon corridor!" shouted Nils. "All of us! *And* down through the grid — for a mouse can pass where a food pan can't! We may reach the prisoner at last!"

"But as to getting him *out*," said Bernard, more soberly, "we're much where we were. A man can't pass where a mouse can; and even if he could, he'd still be inside the Castle. The gate won't open till next autumn; and we could never hide the prisoner until then."

"At least Nils can speak to him in Norwegian," said Miss Bianca, "and keep his spirits up. Nils can call a few words of Norwegian through each grid (like Blondel and Richard the First), and as soon as he gets an answer — "

"Down I'll jump!" promised Nils. "But in the meantime," he added, "how long *is* it, to New Year's Eve?"

Bernard ran out and looked at the Head Jailer's calendar.

"Three days," he reported back.

"In the meantime," said Nils stoutly, "I shall go on exploring."

They then passed a vote of thanks to Miss Bianca, and retired for the night.

None of them slept much, however, partly through excitement and partly because there was another thunderstorm. The thunderstorms at this time were more furious than ever. So was the River more furious than ever — lashing and beating between its banks like a captive dragon. Even up in their hole the mice could hear its voice, ever present between the thunderclaps, and almost more alarming in its steady, thwarted rage.

Yet the River was to prove their best, if erratic, friend.

3

Two days passed in feverish yet unrewarded activity. Bernard gave up making timetables and explored with Nils. They discovered several fresh cracks and crannies — what a buffeting the Castle had taken! — but none of any use to a man-size prisoner. Then at last, very early after the worst night of all —

"Come quick!" cried Nils, pulling the pillow off Bernard's head.

To Bernard's surprise, Nils had evidently been out already; his fur was damp and staring from the morning air.

"What, before breakfast?" mumbled Bernard. He was still only half awake.

"Bother breakfast!" cried Nils. "Come on!"

He was away before you could say knife, and now Bernard leaped up and followed. Together they ran recklessly across the sitting room, out into the corridor, up through the bars of the corridor window, and then down,

down, down the Castle walls to a little boss of rock out-jutting from the cliff itself. The last of the gale almost whipped them off their feet; below snarled the still angry River, tossing and turning in its bed.

"See anything different?" asked Nils excitedly.

Bernard leaned so far over, Nils had to hold him by the tail. He gazed with all his eyes. There *was* something different, though at first he couldn't make out what. Then he discerned at the very foot of the cliff, where once rock rose sheer from water, a great jumbled heap of stones.

"The Castle's crumbling!" cried Bernard.

"Not the Castle," corrected Nils, hauling him back. "*It's* too solid. But there was just one weak spot — as the River's found out! Look at those stones — *cut* stone! Look at those *steps!* D'you know what *I* think's down there?"

"Go on, tell me!" implored Bernard.

"An old water gate," said Nils. "Some time, down there, there's been a water gate. Stands to reason! No one ever built this castle just for a prison," said Nils positively. "In its time it must have been an honest Castle, *with* — stands to reason! — a water gate. Then it was blocked up; and now the River's worried it free again, like worrying the stopping out of a tooth. So there *is* another way out!"

For a moment they gave themselves up to happy excitement — Bernard congratulating Nils and slapping

him on the back, Nils flourishing his whiskers in honest self-approval. Then Bernard looked over the edge again.

"I wonder what part of the Castle it leads to?" he said practically. "And if it's unblocked all the way?"

"That we must find out," said Nils. "Come on!"

11

The Other Way Out

Down the cliff they scrambled again, down and down towards the river brink. It was a perilous journey, but they achieved it. (On some particularly difficult ledges they had to use each other's tails as mountaineers use ropes: one of them held on tight while the other slid down, then the one below made a back for the one above, or even caught him as he jumped.) Down they went and down — fur scraped, tails aching — and at last stood gasping but triumphant upon the heap of jumbled stone.

"What did I tell you?" panted Nils.

There was a water gate all right. Up under a cavernous stone arch — cut stone! — rose a flight of granite steps that disappeared into the gloom above, and in the buttress to one side was even an old iron mooring ring!

But how well had the River done its work? Were those steps still blocked, higher up?

Exhausted as they were, the mice had to know.

At least it was easier going up than coming down: though the steps would normally have been too high even for tail-work, the River, retreating, had washed down ramps of sand and small stones against either wall. Nils and Bernard slipped a bit on wet mud and shreds of waterweed, but otherwise made good progress — and with each step passed felt their hearts lift. It looked as though the whole flight was clear! — As so indeed it proved, right up to the top, where a high rusted gate lolled half-fallen from its hinges . . .

Even a man could have squeezed by. Bernard and Nils of course simply ran between the bars.

Where were they now?

"We're still pretty deep down in the Castle," said Bernard.

"Aye; at dungeon level!" said Nils.

Before them stretched a long narrow passage cut from the rock itself. For a moment they thought it was the corridor where the jailer with the food pans came to let down the prisoners' food. But there were no grids in its floor, the floor was solid rock too. (Nils and Bernard ran up and down twice, to make sure.) So was one wall solid rock. But in the other was a row of iron doors.

Dungeon doors . . .

"And there's another door, don't you see, at the *end,*" cried Nils, "to bring the prisoners in by!"

At last it was clear, what the mice had never been able to discover, how the prisoners were got into their cells. (Small wonder, too, that the jailers weren't aware of the River's work. Until a new prisoner arrived, they had no reason to enter *this* corridor at all.) And as if to

confirm all speculation, at that very moment sounded a jailer's boots stamping overhead, accompanied by the clank of food pans. Nils and Bernard, by listening intently, could hear the grids creak up, one after the other, behind and above each iron door.

"All we need now," said Nils, *"is the key.* I see it all!" he exclaimed excitedly. "We get hold of the key — drop it through the grid — jump down ourselves — and all escape together by the water gate! All we need now is the right key!"

In Bernard's opinion this splendid plan had still a lot of loose ends. (How were they to *get* the key?) But he re-

frained from saying so. Indeed, it touched him to the
heart to see Nils now run from sill to sill, attempting, in
vain, to call beneath some Norwegian word of hope. The
doors were set in solid rock, no voice of mouse could possibly penetrate. "Come on back, old fellow!" urged Bernard — not unsympathetically, just practically. "Now is
the time, if there ever was one, for proper planning!
Come on back to Miss Bianca, and let's *think!*"

It was a desperate, perilous journey again: first down
the steps to the water gate, then up and up the cliff, and
up again over the castle walls. Again, the dauntless mice
achieved it. (Bernard was as dauntless as Sir John Hunt,
and Nils as Sir Edmund Hillary.) The thought of all
they had to tell Miss Bianca spurred them on, and though
they ached in every limb, they never paused once until they reached the little boss of rock from which they
had first peered down. There they allowed themselves a
brief rest, while they got their breath (and also discussed
whether to have a breakfast first and lunch immediately
afterwards, or lunch straight away). Then off they set
again. They had still a long way to go, but, as Bernard
said, the worst was over.

He was wrong.

Fatigue made them careless. When at last they regained the door of the Head Jailer's sitting room, they
hurried straight in without stopping to reconnoiter, and
at that crucial moment, for the first time, met Mamelouk
face to face. — Mamelouk was as surprised as they were,

but he wasn't tired. For just one instant they all three stood transfixed — Bernard and Nils foolishly huddled together — then out flashed a cruel black paw and pinned them both to the ground!

2

At the same moment, Miss Bianca peeped out of the hole. She had been worrying all morning, ever since Bernard and Nils weren't there for breakfast. As the hours passed, her anxiety grew; all morning she had been running to the door to look for their return. Now at the sight that met her eyes she almost fainted! But she had got out of the habit of fainting, and instead uttered but one piercing shriek of dismay.

Mamelouk looked around. He grinned with pleasure. From his point of view, the appearance of Miss Bianca was the one thing needed to make the fun complete.

"So *these* are your unsociable friends?" he purred. "Now I shall have sport indeed! Would you like to see me eat them up?"

The three mice exchanged agonized glances. "Whatever you do, lie still!" adjured the glance of Miss Bianca. What Nils and Bernard had to convey was far more complicated: each longed with all his might, before he died, to pass on to Miss Bianca all their discoveries about the River and the water gate and the dungeon doors. It was obviously impossible. She saw only that they had *some-thing* to convey, and of terrific importance!

"Ha, ha, ha!" laughed Mamelouk. "Come closer, little lady, and watch!"

He began to shake all over with cruel glee. (Nils and Bernard could feel it oozing from his very toes.) His grin stretched from ear to ear, revealing every one of his dreadfully sharp teeth, and even the wide red gullet behind; tears of mirth rolled down his whiskers and glistened in his fur like the spangles of a Demon King. Miss Bianca had never seen him so terrible as in this fiendish merriment — but she stepped bravely out towards him, summoning all her funds of wit, and resourcefulness, and feminine cunning.

"Which will you eat first?" inquired she. "You can't swallow both at once, you know!"

"Oh, can't I?" grinned Mamelouk. "You just watch me!"

"I meant, without spoiling your appetite for the midnight feast," explained Miss Bianca hastily. "It *is* tonight, isn't it?" she added. "The great feast when you eat more than anyone else, and everyone is so astonished at you? Dear me, they'll be astonished in a different way, if you're so full of Nils and Bernard you can't manage a bite!" said Miss Bianca, carelessly.

She was being very clever, both in disguising her true feelings and in thus playing on Mamelouk's vanity. It wouldn't be half so much fun for him to eat her friends before her eyes if she didn't seem to care about them, while his reputation as Mamelouk the Iron-tummed was his greatest pride. — He looked uneasily at the mice under his paw. After their months of good living, both Nils and Bernard had put on weight. Either one would have made a square cat-meal, and in point of fact Mamelouk was accustomed to eat nothing whatever all that day . . .

"Perhaps you're right," he admitted. "I'll just break their necks and have 'em tomorrow."

"Dear me!" said Miss Bianca again. "I thought you considered yourself quite a gourmet! My Persian friend, whom I may have mentioned to you, always told me mice shouldn't be hung even an *hour!* But I suppose you're forced to live coarsely."

Mamelouk was stung.

"I don't live coarsely!" he shouted. "I live on the fat of the land!"

"It's so nice to hear you take that view," said Miss Bianca blandly. "It shows a truly humble nature. My *Persian* friend, now — "

"Nor's my nature humble!" shouted Mamelouk.

" — my *Persian* friend," continued Miss Bianca, "had quite a little witticism on the subject. 'Fresh-killed mouse, caviar,' he used to say. 'One day old, ants' eggs!' Of course if you don't *mind* eating ants' eggs — which at the Embassy we fed to goldfish — I've really no advice to give," said Miss Bianca kindly. "You must do just as you think best."

Mamelouk was by now thoroughly confused. He didn't want to spoil his appetite for the feast, he didn't want to let Nils and Bernard go, and Miss Bianca had somehow

made it seem that if he killed and saved them up, he would be regarded as a goldfish! For a cat with two plump mice under his paw, the situation was really extraordinary.

The uncertainty in his mind began to transfer itself to his muscles. Very slightly, the grip of his paw slackened. Bernard and Nils looked at each other, hardly daring to hope.

"Or if I *might* make a suggestion," added Miss Bianca impulsively, "*do,* as you're dining out, pay a *little* attention to your coat. You might begin with your back."

"What's wrong with my back?" growled Mamelouk — confused afresh by this sudden change of subject.

"Just look!" said Miss Bianca.

Vain Mamelouk looked. Actually there was nothing wrong with his back coat at all, he'd groomed himself rather specially — but he couldn't help looking.

Over his shoulder.

Away from the mice.

"*Now!*" shrieked Miss Bianca.

With one instant's terrific effort Nils and Bernard wrenched themselves free and streaked like lightning for the hole. Miss Bianca skimmed in just ahead of them, and Mamelouk was left fuming outside . . .

3

Lunch was sausage and sauté potatoes, followed by treacle sponge, followed by cheese and biscuits. (Nils

and Bernard decided to cut breakfast after all and just have twice as much of everything.) With so much to tell Miss Bianca, they had to talk with their mouths full. She for her part was alternately so enthralled by their discoveries, and so alarmed at the dangers they had run, she could barely nibble a crumb.

"What heroism, and enterprise!" she murmured. "Dear Bernard, dear Nils, how warmly I congratulate you!"

"It is you who are the heroine," said Bernard soberly. "Without your wonderful coolness and resource, we should neither of us be here now."

"That's right," agreed Nils. "We'd be in Mamelouk's famous tum!"

Miss Bianca shuddered.

"Pray don't speak of it!" she begged. "Or I really *shall* faint! Indeed," she added gravely, "we must now have no more thoughts of ourselves, or of anything else, until the prisoner is free. It is positively New Year's Day tomorrow, and how much still remains to be decided! How many obstacles loom still in our way! — Oh, dear," suddenly, uncontrollably wept Miss Bianca (a prey to delayed nervous shock, and no wonder), "that dreadful, *dreadful* River!"

For a moment they all of them thought about the River.

"There we'll have to swim for it," said Nils hardily. "It's The Barrens on the other side," he added, "that bother *me* . . ."

For a moment they all thought about The Barrens.

"There we'll have to march for it," said Bernard.

Then they all thought about the prisoner, and their courage was renewed.

They began to plan in detail what had never been planned before — or, if planned, had never succeeded: the liberation of a prisoner from the Black Castle.

12

The Great Enterprise

It was determined in the first place to act on New Year's Day. (Tomorrow.)

This really went without saying. New Year's morning, with the jailer on duty, also Mamelouk, too bilious to be efficient, offered the mice their one and only chance of entering the corridor above the dungeons.

"Or may we not assume it a certainty?" proposed Miss Bianca.

"Seconded," said Bernard.

For such a momentous discussion they were having an extra, special meeting of the Prisoners' Aid Society, Black Castle Branch. They just cleared lunch away first.

"Call it a certainty," said Nils.

"Carried unanimously," said Miss Bianca, from the Chair. "We all three, then," she proceeded, "enter the corridor — "

"Question," said Bernard. "*I* suggest Madam Chair-woman join us below at the water gate, thus bypassing at least some of the peril."

"I certainly *won't!*" cried Miss Bianca. "To venture

alone down to a River," she added, more formally, "without other members to assist and guide, is something no Chairwoman should be asked even to contemplate. We all enter the corridor *together*. Nils then makes contact with the prisoner — "

"Trust me for that!" shouted Nils.

"I'm sure we do," said Miss Bianca. "Nils next, through the grid, throws down the right key — "

She paused.

"How do we *get* the right key?" asked Miss Bianca.

"The jailer will have it on his belt," said Nils, "along with all the rest. Bernard and I have seen 'em. I throw down the whole bunch, and the prisoner will sort out which is his."

"But how do we get the keys from the jailer?" persisted Miss Bianca.

"By force," said Nils.

Miss Bianca had an uneasy feeling that the point wasn't really settled. How exactly *did* one use force on a jailer, if one happened to be a mouse? But she didn't want to undermine the meeting's confidence; also she recalled a saying of the great Duke of Wellington's, to the effect that whereas his enemies made plans of wire, *he* made *his* of string — that is, he always left something to the inspiration of the moment. Frail and pliable as string, yet in the end strong as a rope ladder, Miss Bianca trusted *their* plans might prove! — and passed on to the next step.

"Thank you, Nils," she said, "for your excellent idea. "You then jump down yourself — Oh, dear!" added Miss Bianca, now losing a trifle of her own confidence. "How do *I* get down?"

Nils and Bernard went into committee for a moment.

"I will jump second," reported Bernard, when they came out, "and between us we will stretch my handkerchief like firemen. Then you jump into it. It won't be half so dangerous as saving us from Mamelouk."

"I suppose I *can*," murmured Miss Bianca — and returned to her role as Madam Chairwoman. "Next, we induce the prisoner to place his confidence in us — "

"Trust me for that too!" shouted Nils.

" — and conduct him, he having unlocked his cell with the key provided, to the River bank. There have been far too many interruptions from the floor," added Madam Chairwoman Miss Bianca severely, "and I don't want to hear anyone say, 'Then we'll have to swim for it.' The Meeting *knows* it will have to swim for it."

"And then march for it," muttered Bernard.

"And then march for it," agreed Miss Bianca. (She ought really to have called Bernard to order too, but somehow she didn't.) "It thus appears," she continued, "that until the jailer goes his round tomorrow morning, there is nothing we can usefully do. Our best course is to get as much sleep as possible, in order to recruit our strength; though I must say I should like to leave things tidy!"

In fact, after sleeping all the rest of the day (while Mamelouk watched fruitlessly outside), they spring-cleaned half the night. There was no real reason for it, probably no mouse would ever take that hole again, yet Miss Bianca's instinct was right too: there is nothing like housework for calming the nerves. Mamelouk went off to the party shortly before twelve, so they could put all the furniture outside, then for hours all was peaceful do-mestic activity. Faintly, as Nils and Bernard took the carpet up, they heard the songs and shouts of the jailers' midnight feast; faintly, as Bernard and Nils cleaned the wallpaper with dry bread crumbs, they heard a last burst of merriment die away. As dawn broke, Miss Bianca, sweeping out a last pan of rubbish through the lobby, saw Mamelouk the Iron-tummed totter back and collapse before the hearth; by which time the nerves of all three mice were as calm as could be.

It was pleasant, too, as after a sustaining breakfast they took a last look round, to see everything so neat and clean.

"It wasn't such a bad hole after all," admitted Nils, as he got into his sea boots and buckled on his cutlass.

Cudgel in hand, Bernard nodded silently. He couldn't trust himself to speak. In spite of all the terrible circumstances, the hours he spent hanging wallpaper for Miss Bianca had been among the happiest of his life.

He was glad to hear *her* give the hole a kind word too.

"Adieu, dear hole!" murmured Miss Bianca softly. "Dear hole, adieu!"

Bernard picked up her valise. Nils looked out first, to see if the coast was clear. It was. Beside the stove, Mamelouk still snored and tossed in queasy dreams. For the last time, they picked their way among the cigar butts and the matchboxes and the chewing-gum wrappers. Miss Bianca cast a last compassionate glance towards the poor butterflies on the walls. But they were none of them sorry to see the last of the Head Jailer's sitting room.

2

Along the corridor they hurried, down some stairs, along a corridor and down more stairs again. It was all strange territory to Miss Bianca, but Nils and Bernard, after their explorations, ran on unhesitatingly. Not a soul besides themselves was about. Empty stretched the corridors, unguarded the stairs: all jailers save one, as Mamelouk had foretold, lay still abed, quite unable to lift head from pillow . . .

But where was that *one*?

As the mice approached the corridor above the dungeons, they began to take more care. At the last flight of steps Nils crept on in advance, while Bernard and Miss Bianca waited halfway down. "I hope he won't be long!" whispered Miss Bianca — for now that even their own footsteps were stilled the silence was frightening; the whole weight of the Castle seemed to press down on them like an enormous, million-times-magnified paw . . .

Then back Nils called in triumph, they hurried after, and beheld inert against an iron door — *holding it open,* like a doorstop — the jailer with the food pans!

He had got just so far before collapsing. The pans and their contents lay scattered all about. To Miss Bianca's extreme relief there was obviously no need to use force on him, for he was sound asleep.

What a moment that should have been! — What a *half*-moment, indeed, it was! But scarcely had the mice savored their triumph when they perceived something they hadn't bargained for.

There was no bunch of keys at the fat jailer's belt. The key ring dangled far out of reach overhead, where he had left it in the lock of the smooth, iron door.

No mouse can run up smooth iron.

"Now what do we do?" muttered Nils desperately.

"*Think!*" said Bernard. "We can't be beaten now!"

Enormous above them, like a mountain, loomed the bulk of the big fat jailer. — Like a mountain! Bernard had been mountaineering with Nils half the previous day; and the top of the jailer's head lolled only an inch below the lock . . .

"Stand ready to catch!" cried Bernard recklessly.

The Duke of Wellington would have been proud of him, as Bernard now acted on the inspiration of the moment. So was Miss Bianca proud of him, as Bernard with-

out the slightest hesitation leaped up onto the jailer's outstretched foot, and ran up his leg, and then across his big
heaving stomach — it heaved like an earthquake — and
then up onto his shoulder. "Oh, pray take care!" called
Miss Bianca — almost too far below to be heard! Bernard
waved back, and mountaineered on. Across the jailer's
face was a traverse to dismay the most expert; where
beard stubble gave place to bare flesh it was like travers-
ing polished rock. Bernard only just managed it — and
only just in time. The mountain turned volcano, as the
jailer sneezed; but Bernard, his foot at the roots of bushy
hair, had plenty to hang on to.

The jailer sneezed but in his sleep. Courageous Bernard plunged ever on, now as through a greasy jungle.
He attained the jailer's very scalp, and thence with a
supreme effort launched himself at the dangling keys
above. Twice and thrice he swung his full weight from
them; then out they came from the lock, and he and key
ring together cascaded jangling down!

"Over to you, Nils!" gasped Bernard.

Nils instantly ran on. (There was no time, now, for
praise or congratulations.) Bernard and Miss Bianca followed, dragging the keys between them. Beyond the
comatose jailer stretched the dungeon corridor itself;
with, set in its floor, at intervals of two or three yards,
the gratings over the dungeons. Nils ran swiftly from
one to the next, calling through each a word of Norwegian. The suspense was almost unbearable, for suppose

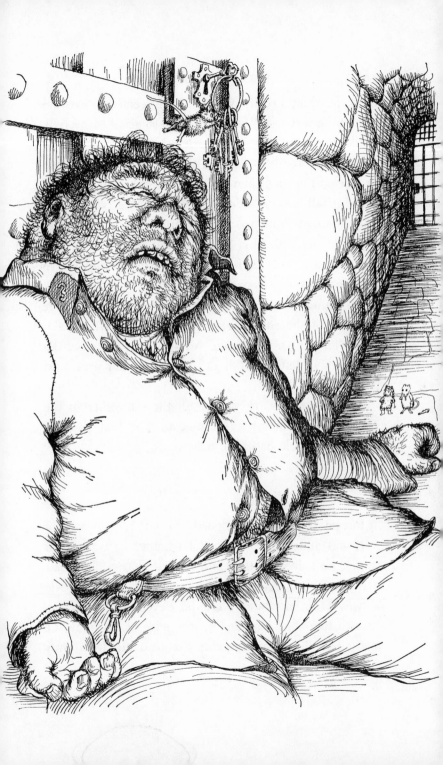

the jailer should really wake? An age seemed to pass before at the very last Nils halted. Had someone answered? Evidently yes! "The keys!" cried Nils. Between them they pushed the keys through the bars, easing them side by side on the ring, then eased the ring through too, and heard it fall below. "Norway forever!" cried Nils — and unhesitatingly launched himself after.

So did Bernard. Miss Bianca, peering down, in a matter of seconds saw his handkerchief stretched to receive her. Fortunately it was a very large handkerchief, more like a young tablecloth, but even so she had to shut her eyes before she could nerve herself to follow. Indeed, only a joint cry of "Be brave, Miss Bianca!" gave her the necessary impetus. But it did. She shut her eyes, and jumped.

A moment later, they were all three together in the Norwegian prisoner-poet's dungeon. The first stage of the unachievable had been achieved.

3

But poor prisoner, poor poet!

It was difficult at first to tell whether he was old or young, he looked so thin and ill and shaggy. The hair that streamed in elflocks over the rags of a prison-uniform — was it fair, or white? Were those eyelids red with age, or with weeping? Huddled on the edge of his bunk, he might have been twenty years old, or a hundred. Only something in the *way* he huddled — elbows on knees, chin on fists — reminded Miss Bianca of the way the Boy used to huddle, if ever the Boy was terribly, terribly unhappy . . .

"Oh, he's *young!*" she whispered. "Poor, poor prisoner!"

What spoke most eloquently of his despair was that the bunch of keys lay still where it fell, on the ground beside his bed; he hadn't even stretched out a hand to see what it was. Or perhaps things had been thrown down at him before, in jailerish sport, just as Mamelouk sportively jumped down to spit at him . . .

For a moment the mice could only gaze in pity, while the eyes of Miss Bianca at least filled with tears. Then Nils again said something in Norwegian.

"Be still, my poor brain!" muttered the prisoner. "Is not one such delusion enough?"

In fact Nils had to repeat himself, shouting, about four times, before the prisoner looked wonderingly up. — First up, then around. Nils was almost hoarse before the prisoner looked *down.* As soon as they had his attention the three mice lined up, and Nils and Bernard took two steps back, then one forward, and politely pulled their whiskers. (There is nothing like sticking to manners, in any unusual situation.) Miss Bianca, in the middle, bowed.

After only the slightest pause, to get his legs properly under him, the prisoner rose and bowed back.

It must be remembered that he was a poet. It is the gift of all poets to find the commonplace astonishing, and the astonishing quite natural. The sight of Bernard and Nils and Miss Bianca — Nils in his sea boots, Bernard carrying a valise, and Miss Bianca wearing a silver chain — therefore didn't disconcert him in the least, and when Nils again addressed him in Norwegian, he was far more delighted than surprised.

— Yet how feeble his own poor voice, after the long silence of solitary confinement, as he courteously bade them welcome! Miss Bianca again felt her eyes prick with tears.

"Tell him we are come to save him!" she prompted.

"That's what I'm *trying* to," said Nils, rather impatiently. "But here goes again!"

He launched into quite a long speech, interrupted from time to time by questions from the prisoner.

"He just wants to ask after his relations!" translated Nils, more impatiently than ever.

"Tell him there'll be opportunities for that later," urged Bernard. "Tell him that just now we've got to hurry!"

By this time the prisoner, partly through weakness, partly to see his visitors better, had sunk down to his knees. Nils jumped onto his hand, and ran up his arm, and began to shout directly in his ear. ("I'm having to tell him all about the Prisoners' Aid Society!" Nils called down irritably.) Again an age seemed to pass before the

prisoner's expression turned from dreamy pleasure to as much as ordinary attention. But at last he began to understand, and his eyes grew brighter and brighter. He picked up the keys, and cradled them lovingly in his palm — bending on Bernard such a look of admiration that modest Bernard blushed; and at last, with a few brief words, rose shakily to his feet.

"What does he say now?" asked Bernard. "Will he come with us?"

"He says," translated Nils soberly, "that he puts his life in our hands."

The three mice looked at each other. They looked at

the prisoner's gaunt, feeble frame, and Nils and Bernard thought of the slippery steps down to the water gate, and of the angry River beyond. What a responsibility! But their courage was high, and so, it seemed, was the prisoner's. (He was a poet. He didn't think he was dreaming, as a prisoner who wasn't a poet might have done — and so missed his chance of escape.) Shakily but resolutely — his fingers trembling but his spirit firm — he tried one key after the other in the lock of his door . . .

At the third, it opened.

There is no more wonderful moment in life than when a prison door opens. It was not through weakness that the prisoner, for a moment, again sank to his knees. Then up he rose; only once shuddered, as the cold damp air whistled through his rags; followed the mice along the passage, and with a smile set his foot on the topmost of the water gate steps.

4

The River had lapped back; yet even as they descended, the roar of water sounded louder and louder in their ears. The River was angry still! But there was no help for it, they had to go on. Each step seemed a separate precipice, slippery with washed-up mud; the mice skidded and slipped, the prisoner had to brace himself for support against the wet, rough, rocky wall. In fear and trembling, yet all resolute, they descended. In fear and trembling they reached the bottom —

And there, wonder of wonders, beheld a raft hugging the bank for shelter, tied to the old iron ring in the old, newly revealed water gate wall!

"The luck of the mice!" cried Bernard. "The luck of the mice at last! — Nils, tell the prisoner to get on board! You, Miss Bianca, run along the rope, and Nils and I will follow!"

Nils said something in Norwegian. The prisoner nodded. He was at the very last step; only a yard separated him from the raft. Then that foot slipped, in he fell, a powerful undertow sucked him down, and the faithless River carried him away!

13
The Raft

Without an instant's hesitation, Nils and Bernard jumped in after. "Keep his chin up!" spluttered Bernard. "We must keep his chin up!"

"But where's he got to?" spluttered Nils.

At that moment, the poet rose to the surface; they struck out desperately towards him.

"Kick off your sea boots, you idiot!" choked Bernard to Nils; Nils kicked them off, and made better progress. But they couldn't help. The dead weight of the prisoner's head was too much for them.

"Swim! Swim for dear life!" shouted Nils in Norwegian. It was no use. The poet was too weak from his long imprisonment to manage more than half a stroke, and indeed by this time Nils and Bernard needed all their strength to keep going themselves. With a faint smile of gratitude — even in his extremity! — down the prisoner went for the second time . . .

Where was Miss Bianca, during these dreadful happenings?

She had done what everyone should do in an emergency; she had obeyed orders. She ran straight along the mooring rope and onto the raft. A woman came out of the reed house, but Miss Bianca didn't even notice her. She ran up onto an empty hencoop where she could see what was going on — and seeing, shrieked in dismay!

So did the woman shriek. The raft-woman took one look at Miss Bianca, and instantly kicked the hencoop overboard, right into the Norwegian poet's arms as he rose for the last time.

After that, for some moments, all was noise and confusion. The raft-wife shrieked again; out from the reed house rolled a couple of men, and between them they hauled the prisoner aboard — Nils and Bernard clinging to his clothes, and Miss Bianca clinging to the hencoop. All four were so full of water, the prisoner had to be life-saved by the raft-men, while the mice lifesaved each other; but everyone was safe aboard!

2

All who use waterways, be it by sea, river or canal, speak essentially the same language. If each separate word isn't understood, at least the general drift is. The raft-people soon learned all they needed to — and besides were the very reverse of inquisitive. For instance, no one said anything about the Black Castle, though it loomed so directly above them; in the same discreet, almost off-hand way they supplied their guest with dry and anony-mous clothing, and when he had changed made his old prison rags into a bundle, and weighted it with a flatiron, and sank it in the River. (The raft-wife also cut his hair for him.) And the moment the River had a little calmed, they unloosed the mooring rope and cast off.

"What splendid, kind people!" exclaimed Miss Bianca.

"Aye; proper seafarers," said Nils.

The mice made this last journey in the poet's pockets. He somehow explained to the raft-wife, when she wanted to chase them off, that they were friends of his. "Mind they don't run about loose, then!" warned the raft-wife grudgingly. (She had sacrificed her flatiron, but she couldn't abide mice.) So the poet put them one in each pocket — Bernard in the left, Miss Bianca in the right, and Nils over his heart.

From this snugness and security, each day, again, as on the wagon ride, they looked out upon a changing landscape. But now it was the *reverse* of the wagon ride: first they floated between cliffs on one side and The Barrens on the other, then through a country of bare heath and crooked firs, then through fat farmland, all tucked up for the winter but still very friendly and comfortable-looking. Here they sometimes passed wagons quite close to the bank, and then the three mice all leaned out and waved. (Miss Bianca once thought she saw Albert, but it may have been just a likeness.) The River, as though sorry for having nearly drowned them, behaved beautifully: it flowed with a strong, even current, just powerful enough to keep the raft floating steadily, but without sending so much as a ripple on deck. The raft-people told each other they had never known such fair weather! — and it made them all the kinder to the poet (though they would have been kind to him anyway), because they believed he was bringing them luck.

The poet grew stronger every day. Each day he ate three enormous meals of pork, fried potatoes, and apple jam. Some might have found this diet monotonous, but not the poet, after years of nothing but bread and treacle. — He always kept back three little portions for the mice, which they ate behind the hencoop, under his strict supervision on account of the raft-wife's prejudices. Then they had a short scamper and got back into his pockets.

Sometimes at night, because the moon was so beautiful, he let them run out again, just for a few minutes; and Miss Bianca was so inspired she wrote two new poems.

POEM BY MISS BIANCA, WRITTEN ON A RAFT

How beautiful the night!
　　What silver ripples swim behind our wake!
All nature hushed, winds stilled, the waters calm,
　　'Tis as we sailed upon an argent lake!

How beautiful the dawn!
　　Aurora's fingers part the fading mist,
Sweet birds strike up their morning roundelays —
　　'Tis as we sailed on seas of amethyst!

　　　　　　　　　　　　M. B.

The other was perhaps not quite so poetic, but even more heartfelt.

RAFT-SONG, BY MISS BIANCA

Day and night, between faraway banks,
　　Smoothly glided a beautiful raft.
Sun and moon and the stars of the sky
　　Look in blessing on cargo and craft!

Three brave Rafters with hearts of gold —
　　Four poor Mariners saved from the foam —
Look down in blessing, sun, moon and stars,
　　Carry them safely, swiftly home!

　　　　　　　　　　　　M. B.

This one had a rather appropriate, watery rhythm; the three mice used to sing it each night, from pocket to pocket, while the poet slept.

Safely indeed, if not very swiftly, the raft bore them on. How glorious it was, to be headed for freedom at last! For their cargo was due at the Capital, and once there, said Nils confidently, the prisoner-poet, his strength now quite recruited, would be able to make his own way home.

"And I shall go with him," said Nils yearningly. "Ah, it'll be good to see Norway again, and take a glass of beer with the lads!"

Bernard looked at Miss Bianca. *He* was going home too; but where, oh where, was Miss Bianca's home? Would she disappear again into the world of high society — into her Porcelain Pagoda?

Miss Bianca was asking herself the same question.

14
The End

THE return of Bernard and Nils and Miss Bianca, their mission successfully accomplished, has been so often described in mouse history that only a brief account of it is now required.

Their welcome at the Moot-house was naturally tumultuous. The ceiling rang to shouts of "Three cheers for Miss Bianca!", "Three cheers for Bernard!", also "Up the Norwegians!" (led by Nils). Madam Chairwoman was actually observed to kiss the Secretary. The Secretary kissed Miss Bianca. All Bernard's relations kissed Bernard. Nils was presented with both the Jean Fromage Medal and the Tybalt Star — he'd in fact had one of these already, but swapped it for a mouth organ — and also, what he appreciated far more, with a replacement for every single possession lost with his sea boots.

Bernard and Miss Bianca made the list together, and they remembered everything: half a pair of socks, a box of Elastoplast, a double six of dominoes, a ball of twine and a folding corkscrew. When Nils saw them all neatly laid out on a silver tray, he showed emotion for the second time. As to the sea boots themselves, cobblers were working night and day on a new pair to his special measure.

It was more difficult to know how to reward the raft-people — until Miss Bianca recalled how the raft-wife had shrieked at the sight of her, and had made the poet carry them all in his pockets. Then a solemn declaration was drawn up, and signed and witnessed by Madam Chairwoman and the Secretary on behalf of all members,

to the effect that no mouse should ever in any circumstances set foot on the raft in question; and Bernard
undertook to point it out, where it lay alongside the
woodyard, to parties of not more than twenty at a time.

Miss Bianca's famous chart was richly framed and
hung up beside the Aesop's fable picture over the speakers' platform. Below, a glass case enshrined her fan, Bernard's spotted handkerchief, and Nils's autograph, for
the inspiration of future generations.

The Nils and Miss Bianca Medal, struck in pure silver,
was awarded to Nils, Miss Bianca and Bernard. (Bernard himself quite agreed that "and Bernard" would have
made it sound awkward. He had the most generous nature possible.) On one side was depicted the Black
Castle, on the reverse a broken fetter. Particulars of this
new award were at once distributed to every regional
branch of the Prisoners' Aid Society, also to Societies
overseas, with the request that it should rank above both
the Jean Fromage Medal and the Tybalt Star.

"And we mustn't forget your mother's galoshes!" said
Miss Bianca to Nils.

"You're right there," said Nils. "Ma promised she'd
fair skin me, if I didn't bring 'em back!"

"Or would she prefer a new pair?" suggested Miss
Bianca.

"Not Ma," said Nils positively. "Ma gets so attached to
her old galoshes, you wouldn't believe."

So they went together to find them in the speedboat.

There it still lay, just as they had left it, gently a-rock on the Embassy boating water; and there were the galoshes too. Leaving Nils to look round, Miss Bianca took them into the cabin and filled each quite full of coffee sugar, and also wrote a grateful note of thanks on ship's writing paper.

When she came out again, Nils was still looking round. He was looking and looking, as though he couldn't bear to tear himself away.

"It *is* nice, isn't it?" said Miss Bianca.

Nils sighed.

"The neatest craft I ever saw!"

"So I think too," said Miss Bianca.

"A1 at Lloyd's!" sighed Nils. "I dare say the Owner," he added casually, "would have no use for a Nils and Miss Bianca Medal?"

"Now, really — !" began Miss Bianca. She was about to scold him quite severely, for she'd suspected all along that he took that splendid honor far too lightly. The wistfulness in his eyes, however, made her pause.

"As a swap," suggested Nils.

"In the first place," began Miss Bianca again, "decorations are never to be 'swapped' — " and again she broke off. If ever anyone wanted anything, badly, Nils wanted that speedboat. His hand, caressing a lever, quite shook with yearning! "And why not?" Miss Bianca asked herself. "I'm sure the Boy, if he knew all Nils's care of me on the voyage from Norway, would give it to him gladly!"

Aloud, she said impulsively, "Would you like the speedboat for your own, Nils?"

Nils was speechless with joy. He just pulled every lever in sight — turned on the headlights, rammed the quay, nearly swamped Miss Bianca, and reversed.

"But how will you get it home?" asked Miss Bianca, on second thought. "We know you mean to travel with the poet — "

"Far sooner under my own steam!" cried Nils.

"What, through all those dreadful oceans?" exclaimed Miss Bianca, aghast — and almost regretting her offer. "Please don't think of it, dear Nils!"

"Why, I can think of nothing else!" cried Nils. "Just hand me over the ship's papers, send a wire to Lloyd's telling them of the change of owners, and I shall be the happiest mouse alive!"

So Miss Bianca let him have his way. She felt he deserved it. — Also she felt she would never really understand Norwegians!

2

The farewell between the poet and his three rescuers was very touching. (As Nils had foretold, the poet made his own arrangements for getting home. He fell in with a Norwegian captain, with whom he was going to travel back to the port, and there sign on as supercargo, no questions asked.) The night before he left he met Bernard and Nils and Miss Bianca, by appointment, outside the Moot-house door.

"Little Miss Bianca," said he, stooping tenderly down, "as soon as I get back to Norway, I shall write a poem about you."

(Of course Nils had to translate.)

"Can I really deserve such honor?" exclaimed Miss Bianca modestly. "When all I did was but any mouse's duty? Yet I thank you from all my heart, and from all my heart wish you well."

With extreme delicacy, the poet but laid a finger, caressingly, on her head. Miss Bianca allowed her whiskers but to brush it. They still understood one another!

"As for you," continued the poet, to Bernard, "no stouter soul e'er breathed! I shall never forget your heroism, which it is quite beyond me to thank. And as for you," he added, to Nils, "all I can say is, look me up in Oslo, and we'll make a proper night of it!"

Then he tried to hug them all, which was manifestly impossible, and overcome by emotion turned hastily away.

"Farewell, dear poet!" called Miss Bianca.

"Farewell!" he called back over his shoulder. "Farewell, and God bless you all!"

Bernard and Miss Bianca then accompanied Nils to the Embassy boating water to see him off too. He couldn't take Miss Bianca's famous chart with him because it was already hanging in the Moot-house, but he assured them

he remembered the route backwards. ("Finest chart I ever set eyes on!" declared Nils.) Wearing his new sea boots, he stepped joyfully on board the speedboat; shook hands with Miss Bianca, slapped Bernard on the back, and with his usual cry (which we will not here repeat), blazed away, headlights flaring, towards the Mediterranean, the Bay of Biscay, and the North Sea.

Afterwards it all seemed very dark and quiet.

There was a long pause.

"And where shall *you* go, Miss Bianca?" asked Bernard in a low voice.

Miss Bianca hesitated. She was actually staying for the moment with Madam Chairwoman — who brought her breakfast in bed each morning, who couldn't spoil her enough! — but she obviously couldn't stay with Madam Chairwoman forever.

"Really I don't know," murmured Miss Bianca. "For the last six months, everything has been so extraordinary . . ."

"If the most devoted affection," began Bernard, "even though limited within a Pantry — "

At which moment he was interrupted by a loud voice from overhead.

"Why, if it isn't Miss Bianca!" cried the voice. "The Boy's Miss Bianca, that he's so a-fretting for! So she *was* left behind!"

A big hand reached down and scooped her up. Holding her carefully in his palm, one of the Embassy footmen was now displaying her to an Embassy housemaid. (They had met for a tender interview by the boating water.)

"Let alone the reward offered," added the footman, "I've always had a kindness for the Boy! — I'd be glad to send her back to him anyways! As it is, five golden guineas for us, and off by Bag she'll go — the little beauty!"

From that callous yet altruistic palm Miss Bianca looked down at Bernard.

"Did you hear?" she called softly.

"I heard," said Bernard.

"*Fretting for me!* Ah, it's not for my Porcelain Pagoda," called Miss Bianca, "that I quit you, dear Bernard! Pray believe me! It is but Fate, that casts our lots so far apart! I must return to the Boy!"

"I always thought you would," said Bernard bravely. "I always knew it, in my bones. Farewell, dear Miss Bianca!"

"Farewell, dearest Bernard!" called she.

The footman carried her into the Embassy. What a welcome there awaited her! Amid universal rejoicing cream cheese was at once set out in a silver bonbon dish; the new Ambassador offered one of his own silk handkerchiefs to furnish her with temporary sheets; and a place was immediately booked for her in the next Bag to Norway.

So ends the heroic tale of Bernard and Nils and Miss Bianca.

Nils, after innumerable adventures, reached Norway in safety; and met the poet again in Oslo, where they went out to dinner and the theater and supper afterwards. The poet kept his word and wrote a beautiful poem about Miss Bianca, which was printed in several anthologies.

Bernard became Secretary of the Prisoners' Aid Society, and had a useful, respected and happy career.

Miss Bianca, reunited with the Boy, and once again domiciled in her Porcelain Pagoda, was happy too. It was really the life that suited her best.

But they none of them ever forgot each other, or their famous adventures in the Black Castle.

THE END

MISS BIANCA

Contents

1	The General Meeting	3
2	The Happy Valley	18
3	The Ladies' Guild to the Rescue!	29
4	The Diamond Palace	40
5	The Awful Truth	50
6	Back at the Moot-hall	66
7	The Grand Duchess	72
8	The Captives	83
9	False Hopes	94
10	A Coach Ride	101
11	The Hunting Lodge	108
12	Bloodhounds in the Forest	124
13	The Last Stand	134
14	The End	145

Miss Bianca

1

The General Meeting

HOWEVER PERILOUS and astonishing the exploits of the Mouse Prisoners' Aid Society, each separate adventure always starts off at a formal General Meeting. (Corporate rules and regulations, order and decorum, provide a solid foundation for individual heroism.) On this particular occasion the chair was taken by none other than the celebrated Miss Bianca, whose part in rescuing a prisoner from the Black Castle earned her the first Nils and Miss Bianca Medal ever struck.

What a picture she made, as she stood modestly waiting on the platform for the applause to subside! — her coat ermine-white, her long dark lashes fluttering over her huge brown eyes — round her neck a very fine silver chain — her whole tiny, exquisite figure thrown into graceful relief against a background of potted palms! But beneath that composed exterior her heart was in fact beating like a very small

3

sledge hammer, for Miss Bianca had been drawn into public life against her will; the elegant retreat of a Porcelain Pagoda, in the schoolroom of an Ambassador's son, was far more agreeable to her than the agitation of a Moot-hall. Fortunately the handsome building, converted from an empty wine cask, still retained the aroma of a notable claret; it acted on Miss Bianca's nostrils like a sort of sal volatile. Even so, her famous silvery voice, when she was at last able to speak, slightly trembled.

"And now," said Miss Bianca, consulting her notes, "we come to the main item on the Agenda. It is really the Secretary's place to put it to you —"

"No, no!" cried all the mice at once. (At least a hundred; the Ladies' Guild was out in force, every matchbox bench was filled, there was standing at the back.) "No, no! Miss Bianca!"

Miss Bianca glanced apologetically over her shoulder; the Secretary smiled, and shook his head. He was a rather commonplace-looking mouse named Bernard: though he too had adventured to the Black Castle no one ever seemed to remember it, and he would probably have been made Secretary anyway, just because he was so reliable about mailing notices.

"Very well, then," said Miss Bianca. "Can everyone hear me at the back?"

"Aye, aye!" "Clear as a bell!" "Even Granddad!" called several of the standees.

"Then I will proceed," said Miss Bianca. "What I am about to say will no doubt surprise you, but I rely as always upon your open minds and generous hearts." (Miss Bianca might be a nervous speaker, but she was by this time also a practiced one, and knew there was nothing like flattery to win an audience to one's side. Moreover, people *told* they are generous and open-minded often discover that they really *are,* so that flattery of the right kind — and Miss Bianca would have scorned to employ any other — does nothing but good.) "In the past," continued Miss Bianca, "as you are well aware, our Society has directed its efforts along the traditional lines of cheering, consoling, and generally befriending the prisoner in his cell —"

"One of 'em us even got out!" cried an excited young mouse. "And from the Black Castle! If it's a rescue operation again, ma'am, count on me!"

"And me!" "And me!" shouted two more, jumping to their feet and flexing their biceps. For a moment there was quite a turmoil as their mothers tried to make them sit down and their friends slapped them on the back; it was such a scene of excitement and disorder as the Moot-hall rarely witnessed. — Miss

6

Bianca, however, again glanced anxiously at the Secretary, and he knew exactly what she was thinking: that their common adventure had given mice an unfortunate taste for *flamboyance* in welfare work. Not one, now, thought anything of sitting up to beg a prisoner's crumb! — in the long run one of the most useful acts a mouse can perform. Crumb-begging, like waltzing in circles (even with a jailer outside the door), was regarded as mere National Service stuff, barely worth reporting on one's return from the regulation three weeks' duty . . .

"Only tell us, ma'am, what chap it is we're to rescue *this* time!" one of the would-be heroes was shouting. "A soldier taken in the cruel wars?"

"Or a brave mariner taken by pirates?" shouted his friend. "Oh what joy to nibble at the halyard, till the Jolly Roger hits the deck!"

Miss Bianca cut them both short.

"*This* time, it isn't a 'chap' at all," she said severely. "*This* time, it's a little girl."

2

As she had only too rightly anticipated, the excitement dwindled and dissipated like the air from a pricked balloon. Quite apart from the general feeling

7

of let-down, mice have small use for little girls. Little girls are too fond of kittens. There was a sudden rumble in the Hall as the audience shifted in its seats — of matchbox jarring against matchbox, of voices lowered to be sure, but definitely grumbling-ish. Miss Bianca saw that she must employ all her eloquence. She did. Dropping all note of severity, and just as sweetly and blandly as if the grumbling had been applause —

"The child's name," she proceeded, "is Patience. A pretty one, is it not? — reminding us also of that virtue which I'm sure every mother present, especially those with bold sons, needs to employ twenty times a day! *Patience* has no mother, however, nor father, nor indeed any relative in the world; and she is only eight years old."

This touching exordium was not without effect. All mice have such large families themselves, and are so used to counting aunts and uncles by the score, and first cousins by the hundred, they can imagine nothing worse than having no relations at all. A motherly-looking member of the Ladies' Guild began to sniff at once.

"Poor little thing!" she sniffed. "Are her eyes open yet?"

"Only just wide enough," said Miss Bianca gravely,

"to appreciate the full horror of her situation. For horrible it is, as I am sure you will agree, when I tell you that this unfortunate innocent has been kidnapped into the service of the Grand Duchess!"

3

What a change, again, came over the Moot-hall! — instead of rumbling, utter quiet; instead of grumbling, the tense silence of bated breath! For even the stern rulers of the State feared the Grand Duchess — so old, and rich, and tyrannical, so withdrawn from all eyes within her Diamond Palace!

Humbler folk believed her to be a witch.

The three would-be heroes' mothers absolutely pulled them down by the tail. Not that they needed much pulling.

"So she's in the Diamond Palace, eh?" said a sour voice.

"Indeed she is," said Miss Bianca, more brightly than she felt. "Within the very center of our city! At least there will be no perilous journey to undertake first, as there was to the Black Castle! I don't suppose there's one of you here couldn't find your way to the Palace blindfolded."

"Aye, but not with our eyes open," objected the

9

voice. It belonged to a peculiarly disagreeable old Professor of Mathematics, who made a point of objecting to everything, from barn dances to lending libraries; in this case, however, he obviously had the Meeting with him. Miss Bianca looked urgently towards Bernard — it was just at such junctures as these that the Secretary's stolid, matter-of-fact manner was most valuable. He at once rose and stumped to the platform's edge.

"Erected in 1775, and thus one of the country's most historic monuments," began Bernard, just like a guidebook, "of course the Diamond Palace isn't actually *built* of diamonds. It's built of rock crystal. That is, there's nothing magic about it. It's just an ordinary, rock-crystal palace."

"As I suppose the Duchess is just an ordinary Duchess?" sneered the Professor.

"Born in 1883," agreed Bernard, "only d. and sole issue of the late Grand Duke Tiberius, therefore inheriting all his titles and properties — the Diamond Palace among 'em, also a certain hunting lodge — "

"Never mind the hunting lodge," interrupted the Professor. "Does she ever open *bazaars?*"

"Not that I know of," admitted Bernard.

"Or flower shows?"

"Not that I've heard of," admitted Bernard.

"Then of course she isn't an ordinary Duchess," snapped the Professor. "In my opinion, she's a witch."

Undoubtedly he had the Meeting with him. Low mutterings of "Hear, hear!" rose from every side. This was particularly chagrining to Bernard, who had really done his best. — However, Miss Bianca, as she swiftly advanced again, threw him a very kind look. (Bernard noted it in his diary that night.)

"Such I know to be the common view," said Miss Bianca smoothly, "among the uneducated." (This was of course a dreadfully shrewd hit at a Professor of

Mathematics.) "To the educated view, the Grand Duchess is simply a cruel, cold-hearted, tyrannous old woman, which Heaven knows is bad enough! — Has anyone here read *Jane Eyre*?"

The question, however unexpected, was almost superfluous. Mice are great readers — as every librarian knows. A forest of hands shot up; quite a shudder ran through the Hall as half the assembly recalled poor Jane's various, unmerited hardships — such as being made to stand on a high stool, also nothing but burnt porridge for breakfast. Several members of the Ladies' Guild, in telepathic communication with each other and Miss Bianca, squeaked that it didn't ought to be allowed.

"I agree with you," said Miss Bianca gravely. "Yet what was the worst hardship of all? The deprivation of all affection. Not to be kissed good-night (at the tender age of eight) is a deprivation indeed."

At this point many of the mothers present kissed their offspring so to speak on principle, and just in case of accidents. It was amid a general wiping of whiskers that Miss Bianca launched her boldest stroke.

"To the imagination of the *male* members of our Society," she continued, with rising intensity, "it is perhaps impossible for me to appeal. How carelessly indeed each son takes for granted a mother's love! But surely the female breast, though so much more tender, is no less heroic? — I don't appeal to the *men*," cried Miss Bianca, "I appeal to the Ladies' Guild!"

4

Here was something new indeed!

Hitherto, the Ladies' Guild had never done anything more exciting than provide supper. Its members listened all the more eagerly. Many of them stood up

13

on the benches — pushing their husbands off in the process!

"If the adventure be too doubtful for our menfolk," went on Miss Bianca, more sweetly and persuasively than ever, "may not we ladies undertake it? Of course I wouldn't ask you to attack pirates, or armed sentries — that would be *quite* beyond us: but the child Patience is under the surveillance only of ladies-in-waiting. Should you wish to hear my plan —"

"Yes, yes!" "Tell it quick!" cried all the Ladies' Guild.

"First, then, we infiltrate into the Diamond Palace. — As you have just heard the Secretary explain, it's a perfectly ordinary Palace," added Miss Bianca reassuringly, "and no more difficult to infiltrate than any other. — Next, being assembled, under my leadership — if you will accept of it —"

"Yes, yes!" cried the Ladies' Guild again.

"— at a given signal all rush squeaking forth. What will the ladies-in-waiting do *then*?"

Instantly the full beauty of the plan was apparent.

"Jump on chairs!" cried an excited voice.

"*Some* may," conceded Miss Bianca, "but for the most part they will *run*. Anywhere, in all directions — flinging open every door before them! Certainly

14

not one will have a thought for the child! — who may thus, in the general confusion and panic, easily make her escape. It will not be a case of 'see how *we* run,' " cried Miss Bianca — referring to one of the oldest mouse legends of all, that of the Three Blind Mice — "but 'see how *they* run'!"

She sat down amid a positive hurricane of shrill cheers. One section of the Ladies' Guild tried to storm the platform, while other members gathered in excited groups discussing ways and means of infiltration. A tough games-mistress mouse offered to arrange training courses up chair rungs. They were all filled with pride and enthusiasm at the thought of doing something so daring and important, and such a wonderful change from just providing suppers.

It was not to be expected, however, that their husbands were going to take all this lying down. As the wives gathered in chattering knots, so did they (except that they rather muttered). Nor was it long before they found a spokesman. Miss Bianca had scarcely recovered from her exertions when up rose the Professor again.

"Just a minute," said he.

Miss Bianca sighed. But with her usual beautiful manners she with a graceful gesture of one hand silenced the Ladies' Guild (who were quite ready to shout him down), and with an equally graceful gesture of the other invited him to proceed.

"No one less than I," proceeded the Professor, "denigrates the heroic potentialities of the Ladies' Guild — particularly under the leadership of our esteemed Chairwoman. In fact, I consider the child Patience as rescued already. All I ask — and am maybe not alone in so asking —"

("Hear, hear!" muttered all the husbands.)

"— is what do we *do* with her when we've *got* her? Other prisoners — *proper* prisoners — have homes to go to. This child, on Madam Chairwoman's own admission, has no home at all."

"If she's not very big, I dare say she could come in with my lot behind the stove," suggested the motherly mouse. "One more in a dozen won't make much differ!"

"Don't forget she's going to *grow*," warned the Professor. "My word, what a size she'll be, in a month or two's time! Eating enough for a couple of hundred! — Is she to be on our hands for *generations?*"

Undoubtedly he scored a point. Mice have enough work to feed their own enormous families. Even the whiskers of the Ladies' Guild members began to droop, as they recalled what a struggle Sunday dinner sometimes was . . .

Loyal and devoted to Miss Bianca, and the Prisoners' Aid Society, as they wanted to be, their whiskers undeniably drooped.

Not for long!

"But of course all *that's* been arranged for," said Miss Bianca. "She will go to the Happy Valley . . ."

2

The Happy Valley

IN THE BIG comfortable kitchen of a farmhouse in the Happy Valley a farmer and his wife were sitting after supper. It was a lovely room. All the furniture was beautifully polished, and the floor strewn with fresh-cut sweet-smelling rushes: in the window sill a row of geraniums splashed big scarlet blossoms against the warm woollen curtain-stuff, colored pale green with brown stripes. Two big lamps — one for the wife's mending basket, the other for her husband's newspaper — cast each a pool of soft amber light, while up on the ceiling little lesser gleams, reflected from the log fire, made ever-changing patterns as they chased the shadows. Nothing could have been more cosy and secure, or more pleasant and peaceful. — But the woman sighed.

"What ails you, wife?" asked her husband kindly.

She tried her best to smile.

18

"Only foolishness, husband. 'Tis only that when the flames play so over the ceiling I remember our little lost one most. She called them — don't you remember? — the elves going to market."

"You've two great boys still," said the farmer.

"Which don't I well know and am thankful for," said his wife. "There's their supper waiting hot in the oven till they get home from their dancing — my big bad boys, handsome as their Dad, out breaking hearts right and left! But I still miss our little daughter."

"I no less," said the farmer, "bringing me my slippers . . ."

"So do the boys miss their merry little sister," said his wife. "What games they had together in the hay — and snowballing in winter, and cowslip-gathering in the spring!"

"Aye, and going after nuts in autumn," said the farmer.

"What care they took of her, too! I could trust her with them even paddling in the brook . . . Now there's the cowslips and the hazelnuts still, and two kind brothers still, but no little maid to find happiness in 'em."

"She was happiest of all on my knee," said the farmer sadly, "or in your lap, wife."

The little flames chased in and out among the

rafters as though they were looking for someone. As though at a breath of wind, or a sigh, one of the geraniums in the window gently let fall a scattering of scarlet petals.

"D'you know what I dreamed last night, husband?" said the woman softly. "Of a little girl-child coming to our door, to be taken in and cherished . . ."

"Such dreams are only dreams," said the farmer, "it's best not to think of them. — I've seen a mouse in the larder," he added, in a clumsy though well-meant effort to change the melancholy subject. "Give me a bit of bacon and I'll set a trap."

"Not in *my* larder you won't!" said his wife. " *'Let nibble who needs,' "* she quoted, "I'm sure we've enough and to spare!"

2

Actually the mouse in the larder was Miss Bianca! Here it is necessary to go back a bit.

As soon as she heard of Patience's dreadful fate, Miss Bianca, who was as sensible as she was kind, not only determined upon a rescue but also looked ahead to the child's future, and at once circularized all the Country Members of the Prisoners' Aid Society for news of a suitable foster home. When a reply came in from the Happy Valley, she was delighted. It was the most beautiful part of the whole country — farmland so rich, gleaners left a whole winter supply (for a mouse) in each furrow; the cheeses and sausages and sides of bacon stored in the larders of its farmhouses, only the pen of a poet could describe. Nor were the fortunate inhabitants less generous than their soil; they were simply the kindest, best-hearted folk imaginable, and probably not a farmwife in the Valley would have refused to take Patience in — only this particular one, as has been seen, was particularly suitable.

Nonetheless, Miss Bianca investigated. Reliable as her correspondent had sounded, when it came to an enterprise of such moment she felt she must see things for herself; and unknown to Bernard took the occasion of a Diplomatic picnic to do so. The Ambassador's car, slowing down at an awkward turning by the farmhouse gates (where a great oak tree took up half the road), more or less put her down at her destination; the Ambassador's son (who knew he shouldn't have had Miss Bianca in his pocket at all) raised no alarm; and off Miss Bianca ran to investigate.

She always did things thoroughly. Before entering the house at all, first she looked into the cow byre —

all sweet and wholesome, warm with the breath of clean contented cows. ("Pray pardon the intrusion," said Miss Bianca. "None needed, none needed," mooed the clean, contented cows.) Then she ran across the neat vegetable patch, noting a lavender-bush at each corner — sure sign of a nice farmwife — and peeped into the dovecote. No dovecote is ever really quite tidy, owing to the habits of its occupants; Miss Bianca but paused on the threshold, and certainly didn't attempt the ladder leading to the first broad ledge behind the nesting-boxes; but the plump rows of sleeping doves looked in their way just as contented as the cows . . .

"This is evidently a very well-run farm indeed!" thought Miss Bianca.

In the house itself, she took the upstairs first, and within a matter of moments found the prettiest little bedroom imaginable.

Its windows were hung with buttercup-patterned chintz. A quilt in the same gay design covered a child-size bed. Upon the child-size dresser sat a whole row of dolls, just as though waiting for a little girl to come and play with them . . .

"Really quite ideal!" thought Miss Bianca.

The conversation overheard between the farmer and his wife amply confirmed this opinion; with a light heart Miss Bianca rejoined the Ambassador's party (again at the awkward turning by the oak tree), and thoroughly enjoyed the moonlight drive back.

Thus she had no difficulty at all — here we return to the General Meeting — in convincing even the male members present that the rescue of the child Patience could be safely undertaken without risk of having to lodge her behind the stove or go without Sunday dinner. As for the Ladies' Guild, they were even more determined to keep such a nice, rewarding adventure in their own hands.

"How I do pity that poor farmer and his wife," sighed the motherly mouse, "and what joy, girls, to think 'twill be we who restore their content!"

But as Bernard handed Miss Bianca from the platform, he gave her a very severe look.

3

"You might have been eaten by ferrets," said Bernard.

"I didn't go anywhere *near* ferrets," said Miss Bianca. "I didn't go into any woodland at all: just round the farm."

25

"Watchdogs, then," said Bernard gloomily. He was always more nervous for Miss Bianca than she was for herself.

"They don't keep a watchdog, I'm happy to say," retorted Miss Bianca. "Poor souls, hurling themselves against their collars all day long! It's quite pitiful to think of."

"I suppose if there *had* been a watchdog you'd have wanted the Prisoners' Aid Society to rescue *him*," said Bernard grimly. "I know you're not afraid of cats —" (this was a reference to their adventures in the Black Castle) — "but when it comes to pitying watchdogs, all reasonable limits are passed."

He spoke so crossly only because he was so devoted to her. Miss Bianca knew this, and gave him her sweetest smile before tripping off to head the supper table.

What a hubbub of animated conversation rose on every side! It was a peculiar source of pleasurable interest that the child Patience was bound for the Happy Valley, for though all present were city mice, nearly every family had country cousins: some merely exchanged Christmas cards, others were on picnicking terms, but there was no one unacquainted, if only by hearsay, with the Valley's delights. — A winter's supply left for the gleaning in each furrow! — And what a motto that was, *Let nibble who needs!* More than one mouse was heard to regret that his parents had put him into a bank instead of on a farm — but they were just the ones who enjoyed talking about the Valley most, while rare is the masculine intelligence, however satisfied by retail trade, unresponsive to the charms of a combine-harvester. The Ladies' Guild dwelt chiefly upon home-cured bacon and fresh cheese and sausages not the shop sort; also upon buttercup-patterned curtains . . .

The menfolk's voices were louder, but just before coffee that of the games mistress topped them all.

Surveying the rows of empty dishes — so recently heaped with sardine tails in aspic and puffed wheat *au fromage,* let alone plain toast-crumbs —

"On a point of order, Madam Chairwoman!" cried the games mistress. *"I* suggest that upon the triumphal return of the Ladies' Guild from their heroic feat of rescue, it should be the *male* members of our Society who provide supper!"

Of course it wasn't a proper point of order, because the General Meeting was already ended. Miss Bianca, bowing to the spirit of the occasion, nonetheless took a show of hands.

27

By a narrow majority, the Ladies' Guild — as though in advance — proved triumphant!

POEM BY MISS BIANCA, WRITTEN THAT SAME NIGHT

How sad and lone sit farmer and his wife,
How fond their thoughts of her who is no more!
Yet oh what happiness awaits them both,
Greeting a new-found daughter at their door!

M. B.

3

The Ladies' Guild to the Rescue!

THE NEXT FEW days were the most exciting the Ladies' Guild of the Prisoners' Aid Society had ever known. The games mistress set up an assault course in a disused attic, and classes rapidly formed for training — up two chair rungs and down again, *up* again and *down* again — "Don't weaken, girls!" cried the games mistress — also with special emphasis on skirt-climbing, the skirts represented by a pair of velvet curtains left hanging over a clothes horse. It was far more exciting than doing housework; many a husband came home to find the table unlaid — his wife was romping up chair rungs! No less pleasant was the general burgeoning of community spirit: neighbors who hadn't spoken to each other for weeks broke silence to exchange their experiences — "Catches you in the back, dear? With me it's behind the knees" — or useful hints, such as put a pinch of table salt in the bath, or always get a good grip on the hem.

Members too elderly for such violent exercise found almost equal satisfaction in preparing after-class snacks of competitive deliciousness, also in sewing neat arm-bands with P.A.S.L.G. on them. It was actually the mouse who'd offered Patience a home behind the stove who had the brilliant idea of fabricating scent-masks from strips of balloons.

"For what powerful perfumes, as is well known, don't ladies-in-waiting and such adorn their persons with?" she pointed out. "One whiff, very like, and no telling up from down!"

The little rubber masks were of all colors, pink and blue and yellow, just as the balloons burst and discarded by children are of all colors. Some mice looked so coquettish in them they had their photographs taken.

Naturally each class had a group photograph taken as well, with their armlets on and the games mistress in the middle.

Yet beneath all this surface frivolity purpose continued strong, and no class ever broke up without the singing of a brief anthem composed by Miss Bianca to a well-known air.

> *Shall little Patience be forgot*
> *And never brought to mind?*

31

We'll rout the Diamond Duchess yet
And show we're nae so blind!

But there was one thing about the Diamond
Duchess's household that even Miss Bianca, perhaps
fortunately, didn't know.

2

At last the great day dawned. — It was a Thursday,
because Miss Bianca, though recognizing every member of the Ladies' Guild prepared to infiltrate the
Diamond Palace on foot, felt they would stand a far
better chance of all getting there together by public
transport, and Thursday was when the municipal
dust-cart went around.

Devoted Miss Bianca! Customarily she traveled by
Diplomatic Bag in a Diplomatic airplane. At a pinch,
she went first class (by train), in a reserved coupé,
or by road in a Rolls-Royce. *She* could have gained
the Palace simply by popping out of the Ambassadorial
car as it drove by on its daily visit to the Chancellery.
But like those other great leaders Napoleon and the
Duke of Wellington, she scorned not to share the
hardships of her troops.

"And we can put on our scent-masks straight
away," said Miss Bianca to the games mistress.

The games mistress was second in command. Unlike Miss Bianca, she was very fond of giving orders. At her cry of "Scent-masks up!" all the members of the Ladies' Guild gathered waiting for the dust-cart hastily obeyed. Some had difficulty with the strings, but these Miss Bianca quietly helped, and then the games mistress counted them all up. — "Dear me, this is very curious!" said the games mistress. "There ought to be twenty-four — don't run about so, girls! — but I keep counting twenty-five. Who can the twenty-fifth be?"

In point of fact, it was Bernard.

So anxious was he for Miss Bianca, and so determined not to let her out of his sight again, he had actually attempted to disguise himself as a Lady. About his brawny right arm a circlet of sticky tape bore the letters P.A.S.L.G., his masculine features were shadowed by a bonnet out of the Boy Scouts' dressing-up box: it still wasn't a heavy enough disguise, once she got a good look at him, to deceive Miss Bianca! — Her nerves were naturally a little on edge; swiftly drawing him aside —

"My dear Bernard," said Miss Bianca, "how ridiculous you look!"

"I didn't mean to look ridiculous," said Bernard humbly. "I just meant to look like a member of the

33

Ladies' Guild. So that I could come with you."
Miss Bianca's nerves really *were* on edge.

"My dear Bernard," she repeated, more sharply,
"pray remember the dignity of a Secretary. Though
your solicitude is very touching, pray remember also
that this is not an expedition to any Black Castle!
The Diamond Palace, by your own account, is merely
an historic monument built in 1775. Now for goodness' sake take off that absurd bonnet and go home!"

At this moment the dust-cart loomed into view and
halted. Under the leadership of the games mistress,
up by wheel and trailing bucket every member of the
Ladies' Guild ran. To cries of "Where is Miss Bianca?"

34

up ran Miss Bianca too; and poor snubbed Bernard was left behind.

He hadn't even deceived the games mistress.

"Silly mistake, that of mine," said the games mistress. "And I must say I think it was jolly decent of the Secretary, to come and see us off . . ."

3

On the dust-cart rolled with its devoted cargo — twenty-four members of the Ladies' Guild, each wearing armlet and scent-mask. Pink and blue and yellow, a positive nosegay of bright colors displayed each group, as it sat (holding hands) between the horrid garbage bags. Only Miss Bianca's mask was black, fabricated from oiled silk, so that all might recognize and follow her. — Actually her ermine coat alone would have sufficed, but she was not beyond coquetry, and knew how wonderfully becoming was black silk against silvery fur. In fact it was a rather coquettish-looking party altogether. But not on that account did the spirit of heroism burn less bright in any breast. On the contrary: to be looking one's best, as every female knows, helps one to *be* one's best . . .

The dust-cart rumbled on, picking up the early-morning detritus of the city. None of it was very nice:

discarded fish-and-chip papers made the scent-masks a sheer necessity: even despite them the aroma from an empty beer bottle nearly asphyxiated the games mistress, and only the devoted efforts of her prize class saved her, by holding her head out over the tailboard until she recovered. It was a very exciting incident — as were no less the incidents of the bent fork, the broken jam jar and the dead kitten. This last — all feuds forgotten under the shadow of the Grim Reaper — the Ladies' Guild interred as neatly as possible under potato peelings, while Miss Bianca said a few appropriate words.

Actually the journey took all day, because the city had only one dust-cart, so it had to go all round. (The City Fathers were so conceited, they spent all the city money putting up showy monuments to themselves.) But a late arrival at the Diamond Palace was part of Miss Bianca's plan, and the Ladies' Guild had brought picnic lunches. These made a really nice funeral-feast for the dead kitten, after which all took naps, and then Miss Bianca employed the rest of the time in a final briefing.

"The Duchess having held her Evening Circle in her State Saloon," explained Miss Bianca, "all her ladies will naturally attend her to her bedchamber . . ."

37

Miss Bianca's familiarity with the domestic habits of the aristocracy, and Court etiquette in general, always quite fascinated the Ladies' Guild. They listened with rapt attention.

". . . the child Patience of course being with them," continued Miss Bianca, "in her quality of Tirewoman; and there they will remain until their mistress is asleep. *We* shall not meet the Duchess at all."

Several members actually objected that they'd *like* to! — such was the mounting spirit of heroism!

"Personally I prefer not to make the acquaintance," said Miss Bianca coolly (and thus impressing her followers afresh). "What is equally to the point, no more shall we encounter the Duchess's Major-domo — naturally excluded from the bedchamber by his sex. The only members of the Household *we* shall encounter are the Duchess's ladies-in-waiting, as they re-emerge, Patience among them, through the State Saloon."

"And that's when we up and at 'em?" cried the games mistress eagerly.

"Precisely so!" said Miss Bianca.

"And carry away the poor child," cried the motherly mouse, "and all subscribe for her coach fare to the Happy Valley?"

"Precisely so!" agreed Miss Bianca.

38

"Mightn't she just come and sup with us first — just to show the menfolk?" cried another mouse.

"I'm sure she'll be delighted to!" smiled Miss Bianca.

In such happy plans the last stages of the journey seemed to pass quite quickly, and it was with one enthusiastic voice, as the Diamond Palace at last loomed into view, that all the Ladies' Guild shouted out:

"There it is!"

There it was indeed.

4

The Diamond Palace

IT GLITTERED LIKE an iceberg — as huge, and bright, and beautiful, and cold.

It was strange. The Diamond Palace was so beautiful, tourists came from all parts of the world in coach-loads to admire just the sparkling balustrades and balconies, turrets and minarets, that could be seen towering above the outer wall. To make out the more elaborate traceries on the upper pinnacles they had to use field glasses — sun glasses too, in fine weather, when each rock-crystal facet caught and flung back the sun rays like the facet of a prism. All the tourists saw of the Diamond Palace was its top part, yet they compared it favorably with Blenheim, Versailles and the Taj Mahal. The strange thing was that however pleased they felt to have beheld such a sight, and however hot the day, as their coaches bore them on again they felt, also, cold.

Inside, it was cold indeed.

Icy-cold.

Diamond-cold.

A child's hands were ice-cold always, polishing the diamond figurines in the great glass cases, and the big diamond drops of the lustres, and the innumerable lesser diamonds with which every single piece of furniture was studded.

But if you didn't polish properly, you were whipped . . .

Perhaps something of this penetrated even to the tourists in their coaches.

2

Descending from the dust-cart, however, and as they crept in file under the sill of the back door, the members of the Ladies' Guild were still too hot with excitement to be affected. One or two of the more sensitive attributed a slight shiver to nerves, while Miss Bianca herself shivered simply — or so she thought — with repugnance at being set down at a tradesmen's entrance. "But such is a dust-cart's nature!" she recognized sensibly. As for the other mice, gazing up at the arches of a mere pantry, and at the even greater arches (as they crept into the kitchen) above the enormous ovens, they imagined themselves in the State Saloon already!

To be sure, there wasn't any smell of cooking; nor any clatter — indeed more probable, considering the lateness of the hour — of washing-up.

"Strange!" thought Miss Bianca to herself. "With such an establishment — for each lady-in-waiting, of whom I have heard there are a dozen, will surely have a maid, and that makes twenty-four persons dining at least — one wouldn't expect everything in order quite so soon? Yet here is not even a scullion still at work!"

She kept her own counsel, however, and merely observed that State Saloons were usually upstairs.

"Through that baize door, don't you think?" suggested Miss Bianca. "Through that baize door and then probably up a Grand Staircase . . ."

Of course she was used to palaces, and it was fortunate the mice had her for leader, otherwise they might have lost themselves irretrievably just in the rock-crystal basement. But under Miss Bianca's guidance every right corridor was safely followed, and every wrong door safely passed —

"But I think I'll just look into the Steward's Room!" said Miss Bianca.

She slipped under the sill. There at his desk snored

the Duchess's Major-domo, his head pillowed on his arms beside a bottle of port. Much as she reprobated excessive drinking, Miss Bianca nodded with satisfaction! — then on she led the Ladies' Guild again, now up the right service-stair, until at last all emerged in good order on the ground floor.

Here there was a brief pause to get their breaths back — not only from their exertions, but before the splendors of the Grand Staircase!

It rose in an enormous double sweep, like a horse-shoe, from the main entrance hall below to an arcaded gallery above. Every inch of balustrading (Greek-key pattern) was thick with diamonds. So were the stair rods holding down the cloth-of-gold carpet. — Miss Bianca set foot upon it as negligently, and ran up it as lightly, as if it had been mere drugget.

Yet even the splendors of the Grand Staircase paled before the splendors of the State Saloon.

Here the floor was so vast, the mice could scarcely see the farther end. From the ceiling hung six great diamond chandeliers of unexampled brilliance. In cabinets ranged round the walls diamond-studded *objets d'art* glittered through the glass like frost under a December sun; while from a central dais blazed the most dazzling object of all — the Grand Duchess's throne!

44

This was carved in the shape of two dragons supporting between them a seat of stretched sharkskin. The four diamonds set as their eyes were the size of walnuts. In front of the throne stood a sharkskin footstool coiled about by a diamond snake . . .

Personally Miss Bianca thought it all extremely vulgar. But as she glanced back over the awestruck ranks behind her she recognized this was no moment to give a talk on good taste in interior decoration. Far more immediately useful (and in any case there was no danger of mice buying themselves diamond chandeliers, even on hire-purchase) was to pretend to be equally impressed.

"Stupendous!" exclaimed Miss Bianca. "Really quite stupendous! I don't remember ever seeing anything quite like it."

Several members of the Ladies' Guild murmured that no more did they.

"Which makes it all the more extraordinary," mused Miss Bianca, as though to herself but still loud enough to be overheard, "to think that within an hour at most these splendid halls will be the scene of our humble Society's triumph! — The disarray of the Duchess's ladies," exclaimed Miss Bianca, more loudly, "the leading forth to freedom of the child Patience — such scenes as *those* I'm sure these halls have *never* witnessed! What a blessing indeed that the eyes of the Ladies' Guild are neither dazzled by diamonds nor dismayed by dragons, but see only the clear light of Duty!"

Her words acted on her followers just as tonically as she had intended. They burst into such prolonged cheering, the games mistress had to shush them. Then, with renewed confidence, at Miss Bianca's directions, all scattered behind and beneath the cabinets round the walls, ready at her signal to rush forth as soon as the ladies-in-waiting, and the child Patience, appeared.

Miss Bianca herself took up station under the Duchess's very footstool. — If she shivered again, she thought it was just because it was a footstool in such horribly bad taste.

Indeed, Miss Bianca was feeling every moment more and more confident. All was evidently just as she had foreseen: the Duchess's ladies and the child Patience still within the Duchess's bedchamber waiting for the Duchess to fall asleep, the Duchess's Major-domo most obviously off duty; all things considered, when Miss Bianca pictured the rout of those mouse-harried ladies, her only slight anxiety was a rather snobbish one . . .

"Games mistress!" called Miss Bianca softly.

"Ma'am!" replied the games mistress — leaping out from behind a cabinet and springing to unnecessary attention.

"If the more active *rôle* appeals to you," murmured Miss Bianca, "and if while *I* but take charge of the child, *you* will lead forth our members to harry the ladies-in-waiting —"

"You bet it appeals to me!" cried the games mistress.

"Then perhaps you would be so good as to harry them down the Grand Staircase towards the front door."

It wasn't entirely snobbishness. Miss Bianca had willingly *infiltrated* the Diamond Palace by the tradesmen's entrance. Quite apart from her personal repugnance to dust-bins, she felt that the child Patience's first steps to freedom deserved to cross a more worthy sill, and so wanted to make sure *which* door the ladies-in-waiting flung open first.

"Leave it to me, ma'am!" cried the games mistress. "The front door it shall be!"

But there was still something even Miss Bianca, let alone the Ladies' Guild, didn't know, about the Duchess's household.

They were soon to find out.

3

Suddenly a door opposite the dais opened. Through it, in two lines of six each, the Duchess's ladies-in-waiting filed. Their tall erect figures, from sweeping velvet skirt to nodding ostrich plume, were so accurately reflected in the rock-crystal floor, there seemed indeed not twelve but twenty-four of them. But did the brave Ladies' Guild on that account quail? No!

"Up, girls, and at 'em!" shrieked the games mistress.

Forth rushed all the Ladies' Guild squeaking like little railway engines. Recklessly they advanced upon the velvet hems . . .

Which swept on as smoothly and mechanically as before.

Even the one the games mistress had her teeth into.

Within a matter of seconds it was all too dreadfully apparent that the Duchess's ladies-in-waiting, far from jumping on chairs, had no fear of mice whatever!

In fact — as this alone would have sufficed to demonstrate — they weren't real ladies-in-waiting at all, but some sort of dreadful, inhuman, clockwork monsters . . .

5

The Awful Truth

NOT BECAUSE SHE was a witch did the Grand
Duchess choose to be so served: but because she was
worse than a witch. The rumors of witchcraft that
hung about her name were at once ill-merited and
above her deserts. Most witches are such humble folk,
a little magic (black or white) gives them their only
importance. The Duchess, rich and powerful from
birth, simply gave rein to a completely odious nature.

Once there had been proper ladies-in-waiting in the
Diamond Palace; but so autocratic was her temper,
not even the meekest could avoid displeasing her. If
this one smiled, the Grand Duchess took it for mock-
ery; another who looked grave would be accused of
sulking. A third who tried to make light conversation
would be called a chattering parrot; a fourth who
prudently held her tongue, a dumb beast. Nor did the
Duchess's selfish tyranny stop at mere abuse; herself
seated on a cushioned throne, she kept the ladies

standing all day long — not the slightest movement allowed save for a deep curtsey every quarter of an hour; on the hour itself, they had to curtsey as many times as the clock struck, for this was the way the Duchess liked to tell the time. Poor ladies — afraid to speak, afraid to be silent; afraid to smile, afraid to frown; afraid even to *sit down!* Yet because each had been chosen for her extreme docility and high sense of duty, they bore it; until one midnight, when no fewer than six fell in faints, the Duchess screamed that they did it on purpose and dismissed them all.

"Find me ladies who won't faint after even *forty-eight* hours!" screamed the Duchess to her Major-domo. "And who'll neither keep silent nor say anything I don't want to hear!"

The Major-domo, who was a very clever man, thought for three days (while the Duchess stayed in bed), and then went to a friend of his who was a very clever clockwork-maker. When another three days later the Duchess got up, there in her antechamber stood the most perfect lady-in-waiting ever seen. Upon the Duchess's approach she sank into a deep curtsey; then rose to stand as perfectly motionless as before. Not a finger-tip stirred, nor a hair!

"Humph," said the Duchess.

"As your Grace pleases," said the lady-in-waiting.

"Can you stand like that four times round the clock?" asked the Duchess suspiciously.

"As your Grace pleases," said the lady-in-waiting.

"Humph," said the Duchess again. "You're a bit monotonous, but those happen to be the only words I like to hear. — Engage her," she added, to the Major-domo.

"Of course your Grace has observed," said the Major-

domo rather nervously, "naturally your Grace's exquisite powers of observation have not failed to remark,
that the lady is in fact a mechanical figure . . ."

"She is, is she? No, I hadn't," said the Duchess.
"All the better! — order eleven more like her."

So the Major-domo ordered eleven more.

There were still some things, however, the mechanical ladies-in-waiting couldn't do. They couldn't for
instance, put the Duchess's shoes on for her in the
morning, or put her wig away at night. (She was far
too proud ever to do anything for herself.) They
couldn't polish all the diamond ornaments in the
State Saloon. Worst of all, they couldn't flinch when
reprimanded, or burst into tears when told how stupid
they were. There was something to be said for human
beings after all, decided the Duchess! — and determined upon engaging just one more, a very small and
weak specimen, whom she could make cry whenever
she pleased, besides having her shoes and wig and
ornaments attended to.

Thus it was that whenever the news of an orphaned
girl-child reached his ears, the Major-domo at once
sent out his spies to kidnap her. Patience was but the
last of a series, all the others having died young.

What a life poor Patience led! — polishing all day
long, with ice-cold fingers, when she wasn't running

at the cruel Duchess's beck and call! Putting on the
Duchess's shoes each morning was bad enough —
stuffing the Duchess's big gouty toes under the big
diamond buckles, and being rapped on the wrist
whenever the Duchess felt a twinge! — but even
worse was putting the Duchess's wig away each night.
It was a horrible wig, never combed from year's end
to year's end: the pomaded curls just grew greasier
and greasier, and the big diamond stars in it dirtier
and dirtier, until handling it was like handling a
greasy hedgehog. Patience never once managed to set
it on its stand without getting her fingers pricked, as
the blood spots on her one-and-only handkerchief bore
witness . . .

Worst of all, just as Miss Bianca told the General
Meeting, was the deprivation of all affection.

The child instinctively sought even a simulacrum
of it. Very late one night (after putting the Duchess's
wig away), she found one of the Duchess's ladies
standing alone in the Duchess's closet. — There was
nothing particular in that: she was the lady on night
duty. Nor could Patience normally have distinguished
her from any of the other ladies, save by her gown of
carnation velvet. But away from the diamond chandeliers of the State Saloon some trick of gentler light,
through the closet window, made the enameled face

look for once almost human — and almost kind. Patience ran up close and caught a fold of the carnation skirt between her hands.

"Oh, please won't you talk to me a little?" she begged. "I'm so lonely! I don't ask anything more — I know it would be as much as your place is worth — but if you'd only just talk to me a little, couldn't we almost be friends?" pleaded Patience. "I need a friend so badly!"

She paused; for it seemed the lady was really about to answer.

So she did — though first, as the clock struck one, sinking into a deep curtsey.

"As your Grace pleases!" replied the lady-in-waiting.

"Oh, don't say that to *me*," begged Patience. "I'm not the Duchess! Just say something you'd say to a little girl!"

"As your Grace pleases," said the lady-in-waiting.

For once something must have gone wrong with her mechanism. As Patience still knelt half incredulous, still pressing a fold of carnation velvet to her cheek, the high inhuman voice whirred into repetition.

"*As your Grace pleases, as your Grace pleases, as your Grace pleases . . .*"

55

2

What could the simple though devoted Ladies' Guild do against such monsters as these? Alas, it was the *Ladies' Guild* that ran!

As the sweeping skirts mechanically advanced, half the members were in retreat already — even before a pair of steely shoes began to stamp and click beneath that same carnation velvet hem. The sound, so precisely like that made by the spring of a mousetrap, completed the disarray of all — and helter-skelter higgledy-piggledy tripping and squeaking and slipping and squealing away all the Ladies' Guild ran just as fast as ever they could!

All save Miss Bianca.

When the ladies-in-waiting at last halted, drawn up in a semicircle round the Duchess's throne, there were left confronting each other just Miss Bianca and a little girl.

She was a very little girl. Although to Miss Bianca's certain knowledge eight years old, she looked no more than five or six, she was so pitifully undernourished. Her little thin arms, her little thin neck, were blue with cold. Elf-locks of pale gold hair, that should have been brushed to prettiness, hung in wisps about her

56

pale, hollow cheeks. She looked like a neglected little scarecrow. But that she had once been nicely brought up was apparent from her very first words.

"Poor little things!" said the child Patience. "Poor little mice! I do hope they all get safe home!"

"Do not doubt of it," said Miss Bianca rather bitterly, "under the leadership of the games mistress!" — She checked herself. Why shouldn't the Ladies' Guild run for home? Indeed, wasn't it their *duty* to run for home — their valiant, well-intentioned efforts having so obviously failed? They had their families to think of . . . "They have their families to think of," explained Miss Bianca.

"How lovely!" sighed the child Patience. "But are *you* going to *stay?*" she added eagerly.

Miss Bianca hesitated. She glanced swiftly towards the ranks of ladies-in-waiting. They were now standing quite still. It didn't make them much less frightening, but at least they were standing still. — Could it be possible, thought Miss Bianca, that her plan was still viable after all? — and that some means of exit could be flung open, if not by the ladies, then by the child Patience herself?

"Can you open the front door, my dear child?" asked Miss Bianca.

"Oh, no," said Patience. "Why, *that's* never opened at all!"

"Then the back door?" suggested Miss Bianca bravely.

"That's kept locked too," said Patience, "and I don't know where the key is. — Oh, do *please* say you'll stay with me, and be my friend!"

She pressed her little thin hands together beseechingly. Down each thin cheek, in her earnestness and anxiety, the tears began to trickle. It was an appeal impossible (at least to Miss Bianca) to resist.

"Until we both leave together!" promised Miss Bianca.

3

She spoke more stoutly than she felt. As the child carried her up to a little attic bedroom — up winding rock-crystal stairs innumerable, along a last winding rock-crystal corridor — Miss Bianca felt a chill to her marrow. "Can those things outside the window be *icicles?*" inquired Miss Bianca. "No," said Patience, "just horrid rock-crystal carvings." "But all these lumps of ice on your bedstead?" asked Miss Bianca. "Oh, *they're* just diamonds," said Patience, "and you

can't think how uncomfortable! But won't you please get in beside me all the same?"

Into bed she crept, just taking off her frock first. (The poor child, Miss Bianca noted, hadn't even a nightgown. What was even worse, she hadn't even a toothbrush. For all toilet she just dipped a torn old rag into a jar of cold water.) Miss Bianca, herself accustomed to nightly massaging with eau de Cologne, still curled up on the thin pillow with her usual grace. — It wasn't she but the child Patience who tossed and turned, and who from each first brief dream woke so pitifully sobbing. "No doubt it is in her dreams she remembers most," thought Miss Bianca compassionately, "of all the affection she once enjoyed . . ."

"Try and lie still," said Miss Bianca gently. "Would you like me to sing you to sleep?"

"Oh, yes please," said Patience. "Long ago, when I was just a little girl, I remember being sung to sleep every night . . ."

So in her sweetest, most silvery tones Miss Bianca began to sing a lullaby:

Long, long ago and lemon trees and lilacs,
*   Long, long ago and lily bud and leaf,*
Two turtle doves lived in an old, old elm tree
*   Far away from sorrow, far away from grief.*
Oh lemon trees and lullaby, oh lavender and lilac,
Oh long ago and lullaby and lily bud and leaf!

She had to sing it three times over, the first two because Patience liked it so much, and the third while the child's tear-wet lashes shut quite tight, and with her cheek still nestled against Miss Bianca's soft cool fur, she fell fast asleep.

4

Miss Bianca stayed awake much longer.

It wasn't only from cramp (if she moved, she was afraid of disturbing Patience), nor because a diamond-studded bed is so uncomfortable. (Miss Bianca's delicate frame felt every knobble through the pillow as accurately as a certain Princess once felt a pea through seven mattresses.) Mental distress alone would have destroyed Miss Bianca's repose even in her own Porcelain Pagoda.

For the more she contemplated the situation, the more uncomfortable *it* appeared too — the Ladies' Guild utterly routed, herself left but a fellow captive in the Diamond Palace with the very prisoner they should have rescued — and surrounded by mechanical ladies-in-waiting!

To be truthful, the mechanical ladies-in-waiting, though *she* hadn't run away from them, really frightened her. Miss Bianca hadn't been afraid of the jailers in the Black Castle — they, however cruel and odious, had at least been *natural,* as cats are natural, or ferrets, or any other traditional enemy of mice. But when she recalled the cold, inhuman bearing of the Duchess's ladies-in-waiting, Miss Bianca shuddered as before witchcraft indeed . . .

63

"If only the Ladies' Guild puts in a proper report!" thought Miss Bianca. "If only *Bernard* knows!"

But alas, the memory of Bernard didn't make her feel better, it made her feel worse.

"Oh that I had not spoken so harshly to him!" Miss Bianca now reproached herself — recalling Bernard's honest features beneath the borrowed bonnet, and the hurt expression on them as she chid him and turned away. "How unkind I was," sighed Miss Bianca, "and even worse, how impolite!"

She who so rarely failed in courtesy and understanding now paid almost too hardly for a single lapse. It was really quite pardonable — her nerves so naturally on edge, at that moment of waiting for the dust-cart — but now, in the small hours after midnight, when everything always looks blackest, she felt Bernard would be thoroughly justified in abandoning her forever and perhaps even helping to vote the games mistress into her place as Madam Chairwoman . . .

A second, deeper sigh agitated Miss Bianca's breast. — The sound, slight as it was, penetrated her companion's uneasy slumber.

"Are *you* unhappy too?" asked Patience drowsily.

At least Miss Bianca wouldn't fail in courtesy again!

"Not at all, my dear child," she said cheerfully,

"with such a nice little friend as yourself to bear me company!"

She composed herself afresh, taking care that her smooth cool fur still brushed Patience's cheek like a good-night kiss. Both slept at last — as around them the whole cruel, cold Diamond Palace slept. The child Patience and Miss Bianca made but a very small kernel of warmth and affection at its cold, cruel heart.

6

Back at the Moot-hall

MEANWHILE THE DEFEATED Ladies' Guild had naturally made the best of things. Who could blame them — their menfolk awaiting their return only too ready to make the *worst?*

The games mistress took charge. It was she who got them all out again from the Diamond Palace. She had in her time organized so many paper-chases and treasure-hunts and such for the Boy Scouts, she remembered every step of the way back from the Grand Staircase to the tradesmen's entrance; whence (having checked each member in turn under the sill) she marshaled them all onto a late-night bus for newspaper staffs, which passed actually by the cellars in which the Moot-hall stood.

Here, before entering, she again called a hasty roll to make sure no one was missing — as, with the unfortunate exception of Miss Bianca, no one was — and made them tidy themselves up. "Right turn and

66

brush the back in front!" cried the games mistress. "Comb whiskers and adjust arm-bands!" When this had been done at least the members of the Ladies' Guild didn't *look* defeated. In fact, as they marched into the Hall with the games mistress at their head — "Ears up, girls!" — they looked so smart and apparently victorious that every husband, son and brother rose spontaneously to his feet.

"Reporting to the Prisoners' Aid Society and Committee," called the games mistress loudly, "the Prisoners' Aid Society Ladies' Guild is happy to announce jolly nearly complete success!"

There was an immediate, and generous, burst of cheering, led by Bernard on the platform. Cries of "Good old Mum!" "Hip hip for Auntie!" and "Well done the missus!" shook the rafters.

"Indeed I think we *have* done well," said the games mistress modestly. "The confusion created no one who wasn't there could believe! As for the child herself —"

Here she paused, because this was where things were getting tricky, also there was a general rush for the door — bench after bench rapidly emptying as their occupants hurried out to take a look at Patience for themselves: whom they naturally expected, after the games mistress's words, to find just outside. (She wouldn't be able to get *in,* on account of her size.)

Among the first was the old Professor of Mathematics. He returned wearing an expression the games mistress didn't like at all.

"Hum," said he. "Not there. Where exactly *is* the child?"

There was a dead silence. Bernard on the platform stood up and scanned the ranks of the Ladies' Guild with growing anxiety. Up till then, when he didn't see Miss Bianca among them, he had assumed her modestly allowing the Guild its moment of glory — or possibly staying outside with Patience to lend the child moral support, and possibly coach her in a little speech of thanks . . .

"Is she perhaps already in the Happy Valley?" inquired the Professor.

"Well, not exactly," said the games mistress.

"Or on her way to it?"

"Not exactly either," admitted the games mistress.
"In fact, she's still in the Diamond Palace . . ."

"*AND WHERE IS MISS BIANCA?*" shouted Bernard.

"Well, she's in the Diamond Palace too," admitted
the games mistress.

A couple of pot plants went for six as Bernard
rushed to the platform's edge.

69

"You mean you *left* her?"

How often had the games mistress pulled a hockey match out of the fire in the last moments of play! She was famous for it.

"Not at all; she *stayed*," corrected the games mistress. "Personally I thought it a jolly good show. — And now I'm sure we all deserve a jolly good supper," she added briskly, "which I only hope the men haven't forgotten to provide!"

2

Actually the men had neither forgotten *nor* provided it — that is, in the sense of preparing anything themselves; they had just hired a catering firm, with the happy result that it really *was* a good supper. Cold bacon-rinds *à la souris* neighbored sardine-bones deviled and whole whitebaits in aspic. The centerpiece was a marshmallow studded with grape pips, while to drink there was elderberry wine, or sink water for the teetotalers, both ad lib.

Again (so swiftly can appetite obliterate the higher instincts) the very same cries resounded, of "Hip hip for Auntie!" and "Good old Mum!" as the mice set to. Even the Professor of Mathematics didn't disdain such a feast: he tucked into whitebait with the youngest.

His quaffing of elderberry wine even set them a bad example!

Only one seat remained vacant: Miss Bianca's; and halfway through, Bernard's.

3

Small heart had Bernard for festivity; he slipped away as soon as he decently could. He knew there was no hope, just then, of getting any sense out of the Ladies' Guild — and indeed when he saw how soon their whiskers began to droop again, and their coats to stare, he lacked the harshness even to attempt it.

After all, they'd *tried:* had performed (for *them,* so unused to adventures) genuine feats of heroism; and if they were now making the best of things — who could blame them?

But alone in his bachelor quarters Bernard paced the floor far into the night.

7

The Grand Duchess

SADLY ENOUGH HAD Miss Bianca and the child Patience fallen asleep: to what perils did they not awake!

But when Patience saw Miss Bianca on her pillow, she smiled for the first time in months.

"Oh, how lovely!" she exclaimed. "I thought you were a dream!"

"Certainly not," said Miss Bianca — feeling it high time to introduce herself. "I am Miss Bianca."

If this didn't make quite the usual impression, it was because Patience had led such a secluded life; Miss Bianca readily forgave the childish ignorance.

"How pretty!" cried Patience. "I shall love to have a friend with such a pretty name! — And are we *really* going to leave this horrid place together, just as you told me last night?"

Miss Bianca was feeling so much better (as people usually do in the morning), and in fact so sure that

Bernard *wouldn't* abandon her (a belief, as has been seen, fully justified), she nodded quite cheerfully.

"At the earliest opportunity," she promised. "Until when, you must do nothing to arouse suspicion, but go about your duties in the usual way. What are your first duties?"

Patience, wriggling into her dress, sighed.

"First I polish in the State Saloon, then I go and put the Duchess's shoes on for her, and her dreadful, horrible wig, and then there's the Morning Levée —"

"Ah!" said Miss Bianca. "I believe I shall attend it."

To be truthful again, and this time it does Miss Bianca nothing but credit, she made the decision purely as a test of courage. She was entirely *blasée* about Levées and Duchesses, and certainly had no wish even to appear to be paying respects to such an evidently odious and vulgar Duchess as this one was. Miss Bianca would truly have preferred to remain secluded in the attic and not set eyes on the Grand Duchess at all. But she *had*, during the night, admitted herself frightened — of the mechanical ladies-in-waiting. Fear was an emotion Miss Bianca despised; and now that she was herself again, felt it would be impossible to quit the Diamond Palace with such a stain on her honor. So she resolved to wipe it out by confronting the monsters once more.

73

She made her usual careful toilet — indeed taking so long over it, Patience was forced to run off. For Courts are Courts, however *outré,* and simply to show her own good breeding Miss Bianca took rather special pains with the gloss of her coat and the set of her whiskers. She spent an hour rubbing up her silver chain, until it shone — not like diamonds! Dear me, no! — but like a very fine thread of moonshine. Then she made her way to the State Saloon.

2

Patience was already gone to attend the Duchess's toilet. But the ladies were there.

Still drawn up in a semicircle before the hideous throne. They hadn't stirred all night!

Miss Bianca advanced towards them. — Not a finger now moved, nor the toe of a shoe!

"Evidently 'twas but a faulty mechanism," thought Miss Bianca, pausing by the figure in carnation velvet, "that made her stamp so!"

She walked all the way round. Carnation, orange, purple — peacock and green and yellow and scarlet — glowed the velvet skirts; heavy too with gold embroideries, and stiffened by buckram petticoats. "Certainly they make a fine show!" thought Miss Bianca.

But not a hem lifted, not a heel clicked. "What simpletons we were," thought Miss Bianca, "myself no less than the Ladies' Guild, to feel fear of such mere, if expensive, effigies!"

Just at that moment the air grew perceptibly colder.

"This is really the draftiest palace I ever entered!" thought Miss Bianca, still in a spirit of criticism. — Or rather, *began* to think; because just the next moment the door opposite the dais opened to admit first the Duchess's Majo-domo, then the child Patience, then the Grand Duchess herself.

Courageous as she was, and sophisticated as she was — and no longer afraid of the ladies-in-waiting as she was — at her first glimpse of that tall dreadful figure, Miss Bianca felt suddenly too cold to think properly at all.

3

Very tall indeed was the Grand Duchess: taller even than her ladies, and gaunt as a gallows. The dirty stars in her wig seemed at least six feet from the ground. They were not the only diamonds she carried; big necklaces and chatelaines of diamonds clanked from bosom and waist down to the big diamond buckles on her shoes. The brilliant set in the

crook of her cane was bigger even than those set for
eyes in the heads of the dragons supporting her
throne.

If Miss Bianca noticed all these details first, it was
because even she flinched a moment, before looking at
the Duchess's face.

One glance, and she looked away again; from a
countenance that might have been carved by some
gargoyle-maker, as grotesque as evil, inhuman in its
stoniness, yet marked too by the (worst) human
traits of arrogance, selfishness and cruelty. Deep fur-
rows of anger barred the forehead; out from each
nostril flared the lines of pride; cruelty itself, about
the mouth, grimaced triumphant. "No wonder,"
thought Miss Bianca incoherently, "the air is so cold!"
— and she shivered uncontrollably.

Slowly, between the ranks of her ladies, stalked the
Duchess — kicking contemptuously at them as she
passed.

"And what d'you say to *that,* my ladies?" inquired
the Grand Duchess sardonically.

With one whirring mechanical voice —

"As your Grace pleases!" answered all the mechanical ladies-in-waiting.

"Very proper," grinned the Duchess, seating herself on her throne, "if a trifle monotonous! And now

what does the *child* say — who hasn't placed my footstool?"

"Please, your Grace, I — I was only waiting for your Grace to sit," stammered Patience.

As she pulled the footstool into place, down whipped the Duchess's cane across her wrist; she couldn't help but cry out.

"Even better!" grinned the Duchess. "The human note! — Don't you agree, you old fool?"

"Certainly, your Grace!" fawned the Major-domo. "A very human note indeed! I selected the child specially on account of it."

"Then we'll hear it again!" snarled the Grand Duchess.

Never before had Miss Bianca suffered the indignity of being struck — even vicariously. For the second time she flinched, as the child Patience flinched. She was all this time sheltered beneath one of the velvet skirts, and evidently unobserved; she was in no immediate personal danger. But every nerve in her body quivered nonetheless; and as she again forced herself to look into that cruel, lowering, diamond-starred-about visage, she felt quite numbed before such a force of wickedness as even the Black Castle had not prepared her for.

"Oh that we were in the power of but a simple

78

witch!" thought Miss Bianca. "Oh Bernard," she added mentally, "pray come quickly! — If I have ever underestimated your humble, beautiful nature, pray forgive me and *come at once!*"

4

But that day passed, and the next, and the next: no Bernard.

No fresh rescue party from the Prisoners' Aid Society — not even a postcard from the Ladies' Guild: nothing.

The reasons for this were rather complicated. Let it not be supposed that the Society regarded the loss of its Chairwoman as a bagatelle. Encomiums of Miss Bianca's kindness in remaining at the side of the child Patience took priority on every next agenda at every next General Meeting, also several resolutions were passed affirming complete faith in her. In a way, the Society had only too *much* faith in Miss Bianca — and while planning in detail the gala supper to celebrate her return, gave no thought as to when, and still less as to *whether,* that return might be expected.

All save Bernard; and Bernard's difficulty was that he still couldn't find out exactly what had *happened* in the Diamond Palace. The Ladies' Guild indeed now talked freely enough about their adventures there — but only up to a point. They quite reveled in descriptions of diamond chandeliers, and Grand Staircases, and State Saloons, but when it came to the crucial point of why Patience (and so Miss Bianca) had been left behind, no one seemed to remember anything at all. Secretly, of course, they were a little ashamed of themselves, and to cover this guilty feeling a theory somehow grew up that Miss Bianca had rather encouraged Patience to stay on, just for a few days, so that she could stay too as Patience's guest.

"After all, old man," said the games mistress, "Miss Bianca, let's face it, does rather *like* Palaces. It's only natural, moving in Embassy circles as she does: personally I've always thought it jolly decent of her to act as our Chairwoman at all."

Bernard listened uneasily. To a mouse of his particularly humble (and beautiful) nature it all sounded quite possible: devoted as he was to Miss Bianca, he had never thoroughly understood a character so much more sophisticated, and the idea that a Diamond Palace could be positive anathema to her never occurred to him. He just thought that as Miss Bianca was so much the most beautiful of mice, such a beautifulest palace was but a fit setting for her, and one she would naturally enjoy.

81

"So if *I* were you, old man," said the games mistress bracingly, "I'd just wait until she decides her leave's up from the Embassy, and comes tripping back with the child of her own accord!"

It all sounded quite reasonable to Bernard. He still paced the floor each night (wearing quite a track in his stamp-paper carpet), but he didn't do anything. He was too confused.

"Oh Miss Bianca," thought Bernard confusedly, "if you aren't in deadly peril, I do hope you're enjoying yourself!"

8

The Captives

ENJOYING HERSELF! Poor Miss Bianca, who never in all her life had been so miserable as amid the cold, cruel splendors of the Diamond Palace!

The Major-domo's name was Mandrake. He had once committed a very wicked crime, of which only the Duchess now had evidence. Thus he was as much her slave as the mechanical ladies-in-waiting — and had to work much harder! There was only he to pre-pare, in the deserted kitchens, out of an enormous Deepfreeze, the Duchess's daily food of pheasant, or partridge, or jugged hare — her tastes ran strictly to game — as there was only Patience to attend the Duchess's toilet. Mandrake even had to put out the garbage, since he dared not trust Patience to unlock the back door; and all this so embittered a tempera-ment already harsh and morose, his only relaxation when off duty was to sit alone in the steward's room (as Miss Bianca had observed him), drinking bad port.

In the stables, a couple of wall-eyed old coach-horses were carelessly fed, and still more carelessly groomed, by a couple of dissolute ostlers — both, like Mandrake, with criminal records. (Even the two horses had criminal records: each having once kicked a man to death.) But the stables were quite separate from the rest of the Palace, and no rumor of human jollity (however dissolute) ever penetrated therefrom to challenge, even momentarily, the mechanical voices of the mechanical ladies-in-waiting.

"As your Grace pleases, as your Grace pleases, as your Grace pleases . . ."

It made no difference whether it was the Duchess who addressed them, or Mandrake who in passing uttered a bitter oath, or the child Patience a piteous sigh. *"As your Grace pleases!"* answered the mechanical ladies; just as whether the Duchess observed them or not they curtseyed once at every quarter, and then again to the strokes of the hour. Thus the Grand Duchess's dreadful, cold-dispensing presence could never be forgotten, even when out of reach of her cane.

Miss Bianca helped Patience with the polishing.

Her tiny fingers could explore where even a child's hands couldn't: never had the ornaments in the State Saloon gleamed brighter! But Patience was rapped across the wrist no less often for that.

They made their scanty meals from the Duchess's leavings. Patience almost starved from lack of nourishment — and Miss Bianca from pride. There was plenty left for a mouse, on each pheasant or partridge bone! — but Miss Bianca, discovering that the Duchess never touched her roll, preferred a farinaceous diet; and even so nibbled just enough each day to sustain the vital spark.

A dreadful, cold, cruel life it was indeed, day by day in the Diamond Palace; and at night no better. Still in the State Saloon curtseyed the mechanical ladies; in the stables the ostlers snored. — Why should they ever rouse? The great carriage-gates in the rock-crystal wall were overgrown by bindweed, and the padlocks rusted to the bars. In the Steward's Room Mandrake the Major-domo snored too. Miss Bianca, singing Patience to sleep each night with the lullaby about the doves, sometimes fancied she could hear the horrid sound even in the remoteness of the attic . . .

2

What troubled her most of all, however, as the days passed, was that the child Patience, now that she had herself, Miss Bianca, for company, seemed almost prepared to accept her dreadful lot.

"Mr. Mandrake's often told me," said Patience, "how grateful I should be . . ."

"For what?" asked Miss Bianca.

"Mr. Mandrake says, for a roof over my head," explained Patience.

"If we none of us ask more than a roof over our heads," said Miss Bianca, sharply, "lodgment in *any* prison at all must obviously be acceptable! Even in one so vulgarly diamond-studded as this!"

Patience (they were at work in the State Saloon) looked at the glittering dragon-throne, then up at the blazing chandeliers.

"Are they really vulgar?" she asked uncertainly.

"Quite odiously so," said Miss Bianca.

The child sighed.

"Do you know," she said, "sometimes I think I can remember *candles*. At least, I think they were called candles . . ."

"Did they shed a kindly light?" asked Miss Bianca.

"Oh, *yes!*" said Patience. "Especially the one by my

86

bed. And there was a bigger one as well — much bigger — that someone sat sewing by . . ."

"That would be a lamp," said Miss Bianca. "Lamps are kindly too."

Though she knew it was her mother Patience was trying to remember, Miss Bianca for the moment said no more, lest any further recollection should prove too distressing. But she herself recalled the kind face of the farmer's wife in the Happy Valley, and determined to lose no more time, but act at once — while Patience still remembered candles.

With or without assistance!

3

"For which I have waited too long already!" Miss Bianca chided herself. "Quite possibly by this time the Prisoners' Aid Society is rescuing someone else!" (This was truly magnanimous of her; but she always tried to believe the best of people.) "After all, Mandrake *does* unlock the back door each day, if but for a moment — and should he pursue us, at a pinch I really believe I could arouse the populace," thought Miss Bianca, "to prevent the child's recapture!"

It must be confessed that Miss Bianca had quite a clear picture of herself doing this — from some convenient point of vantage, the populace cheering below, as in photographs of Royalty coming out on balconies. But she set vanity aside, and sensibly recognized that it would be easier, if possible, to make their escape with less *éclat* — that is, when Mandrake wasn't looking.

"Think, my dear child!" said Miss Bianca to Patience. "Surely there must be *some* occasions when the back door is unlocked for something that takes longer than garbage?"

Patience thought as hard as she could.

"Last month," she said at length, "the clockmaker came. To wind up the ladies-in-waiting . . ."

"Ah!" exclaimed Miss Bianca.

"And *then* the door was left unlocked quite a long time, because he had to go back for an oilcan — and Mr. Mandrake had the Duchess's dinner to carry up, so he just left the door on the latch. If I'd only been braver!" sighed Patience.

"Never mind that now," said Miss Bianca. "A man who forgets his oilcan once will no doubt forget it again."

"I'm sure he will," agreed Patience. "Mr. Mandrake says he always forgets *something*, he's so old and absent-minded!"

"Age takes its toll," said Miss Bianca kindly. Her

spirits were rising with every word! "No doubt this good old man comes regularly?"

"Oh, yes!" said Patience.

"And when does he come next?" asked Miss Bianca.

"Next year," said Patience. "That's why Mr. Mandrake says the ladies are so wonderful: they run for a whole year . . ."

Miss Bianca's spirits sank again. A whole year! It was beyond possibility to wait a whole year. After another year, Patience might well have turned into a little automaton herself! ("And *I*," added Miss Bianca mentally, "into a *shrew!*")

She racked her brains.

"But supposing," thought Miss Bianca, *"the ladies break down?"*

"If I'd only been braver!" repeated Patience sadly. "If I'd only been braver, I could have run away then!"

"Have no regrets, my dear child," said Miss Bianca briskly, "just prepare to run away tomorrow!"

4

The audacity and brilliance of Miss Bianca's plan must now of course be apparent.

Leaving Patience asleep in the attic, all through

that night Miss Bianca toiled — running from velvet skirt to velvet skirt, up by chatelaine and girdle to each velvet bodice, seeking within each steely rib-cage its center of mechanical energy. — Fortunately the Ambassador's son had a taste for clockwork; Miss Bianca, having spent more hours than she could count watching while he dismantled clockwork train or airplane or motorboat, at least knew how to *stop* clockwork. Be-

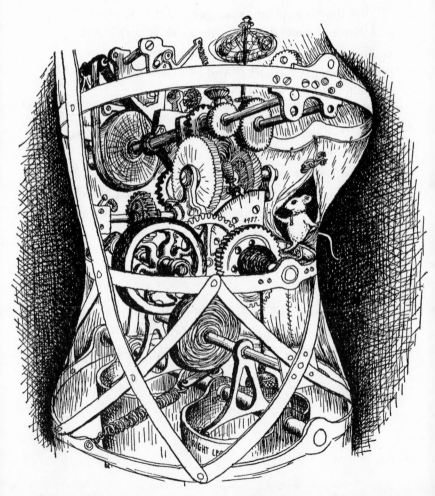

neath each velvet bodice, as she scurried down again, she left a spring loosed from its axis; as 4 A.M. struck, not a lady achieved so much as a carriage-bob, but were all collapsing where they stood!

The lady in carnation was the last to totter: as she only, in a last gasp, creaked out the inevitable formula.

"As your Grace pleases," creaked the carnation lady, *"as your Grace pleases, as your Grace pleases . . ."*

Then she too ran down!

Miss Bianca stole up onto Patience's pillow, careful not to disturb the child, and composed herself for sleep. It is always wise to get a good night's rest before any important event. — Even picnics, or clambakes, or Hallowe'en parties rate an afternoon nap: how much more necessary, therefore, that Miss Bianca and Patience should sleep soundly, before a dash for freedom from a Diamond Palace.

5

Meanwhile Bernard too had been coming to a resolution.

The track on his stamp-paper carpet was by now worn quite threadbare. Half convinced as he had been by the games mistress's clever insinuations, as more and more time passed — without a word from Miss Bianca — Bernard's anxiety grew and grew. Though it might be like Miss Bianca to enjoy luxury, surely it wasn't like her to leave a whole Prisoners' Aid Society — let alone himself, thought Bernard, with rare egoism — in such suspense!

Everyone else seemed quite happy; but not Bernard. So, just like Miss Bianca, he determined to act alone, and disguised himself as a knife-grinder.

This was because (acting alone) he felt he needed to be armed to the teeth. But when he *was* — with two swords, two hatchets, three daggers and a part of a lawnmower, he couldn't move. By loading all these deadly weapons onto a little handcart, and adding a grinding wheel, he could not only get about, but would also be less conspicuous, especially since it was his humble design to approach the Diamond Palace by the back door.

He took a few lessons in knife-grinding, just in case.

Bernard said nothing of all this to the Prisoners' Aid Society. He was too much afraid of telling the members what he thought of their complacency. A flaming row, however relieving to individual feelings, does a Society nothing but harm: for instance, if any number of resignations follow, a whole useful or-

ganization may split into factions and so be rendered sterile. On the other hand, the sudden and unexplained disappearance of a Secretary can be almost equally disturbing, so before he set out conscientious Bernard mailed brief mimeographed notices all round, as follows:

> *Dear Member,*
>> *I have set out.*
>>> *Signed,*
>>>> BERNARD (*Sec.*)

9

False Hopes

IS IT REALLY to be today?" asked Patience, as soon as she woke next morning. "Is it really today that we're going to escape together?"

"To be sure it is," said Miss Bianca confidently. "Have you anything you wish to take with you?"

"Only my handkerchief," said Patience.

"The very thing," said Miss Bianca, "for you must carry me in your pocket, and I will sit on it. Meanwhile, attend the Duchess's toilet just as usual, and then we shall see what occurs at the Morning Levée — which I really think will be something quite out of the way!" said Miss Bianca.

2

Indeed it was. As the Grand Duchess emerged to receive her ladies' morning salutation, nothing met her eye but a row of collapsed velvet gowns!

"What's this?" demanded the Duchess angrily —

stirring first one, then the next, with an infuriated toe. "What's wrong with 'em, Mandrake? What's wrong with my ladies-in-waiting — ordered upon your special recommendation?"

Mandrake in turn peered at each inarticulate heap; and raised an ashen face.

"As your Grace pleases," he muttered, "they seem to need a little attention . . ."

"A little attention!" stormed the Grand Duchess, bringing her cane down across his back. "And the clockwork-maker here only last month!"

"As your Grace pleases," muttered Mandrake, "perhaps I should summon him again . . ."

"Summon him this very instant!" screamed the Duchess.

How the hearts of Patience and Miss Bianca lifted! — Patience's hand, in her apron pocket, almost squeezed the breath out of Miss Bianca's body, in delighted congratulations. For of course she realized at once that this was somehow all Miss Bianca's doing. Bending her head down to whisper —

"We'll run away as soon as the door's open, won't we, Miss Bianca?" whispered Patience eagerly.

"Indeed we will!" Miss Bianca whispered back. "Poor Mandrake! I could almost feel it in my heart to pity him!"

But they reckoned without the Duchess's imperious nature.

"Only first call my coach!" screamed the Duchess.

"Your — your Grace's coach?" repeated Mandrake, stammering with astonishment.

"To carry me to my hunting lodge!" screamed the Duchess. "If I can't be properly waited on in my Diamond Palace, you and the child shall wait upon me in my hunting lodge!"

Even as she spoke her gaunt right hand, weighted with diamond rings, descended on Patience's shoulder. The big knuckles ground cruelly against Patience's collarbone, the long fingers, strong as an eagle's talons, almost met in the child's emaciated, shrinking flesh; Patience stood as helpless as if she'd been turned to stone.

And never once did that terrible grip loosen, all the time Mandrake, in the stables, roused the astonished ostlers, and bade them harness the no less astonished horses, and then set them with hammer and wedge to force open the great gates in the rock-crystal wall. — Not only the back door, but the great gates were to be opened! Even up in the State Saloon, Patience and Miss Bianca could hear quite plainly first the thumping, then the clanging, then the grinding over gravel, interspersed with wicked language whenever

an ostler hit his thumb. But they were powerless to take advantage. The Duchess held Patience as in a vise; and sounds which should have been music to their ears but deepened their despair!

"Ask if you should not prepare her baggage!" whispered Miss Bianca desperately.

"Please, your Grace, don't you want me to prepare your baggage?" gasped Patience.

"My Grace will find everything needful where she's going!" snapped the Duchess. "Stand still, child!"

"Her jewels, then!" prompted Miss Bianca — in whose experience no great lady ever traveled without her jewel box. "Ask if you may not fetch her jewel box!"

"Mayn't I even fetch your Grace's jewel box?" gasped Patience.

"I shall find jewels too!" snarled the Duchess. "And canes too, and whips too! Stand as I bid you!"

She never let go Patience's shoulder until she had pushed the child before her into the great, dirty, dilapidated coach. All the stuffing was coming out of the seats, cats had littered on the floor; for a moment, as the Duchess climbed in, it seemed as though the very springs would give, under her wicked weight. But though the whole vehicle sagged lopsidedly, it somehow held together. — Then Mandrake bolted

98

them in, and mounted the box, and whipped up the horses . . .

It was at this moment that Bernard, with his knife-grinder's cart, appeared making for the back door.

It stood wide open. Mandrake, so harried and hustled, had dispatched to the clockwork-maker not only a message, but a key. The message included strict injunctions not to leave the door unlocked, still less ajar even, for a single instant; but this time the clockwork-maker had forgotten his screwdriver, and really he was too old to bother.

So Bernard, his handcart with him, entered the Diamond Palace without the least difficulty or delay.

Only of course he didn't find Miss Bianca. He was just five minutes too late.

10

A Coach Ride

Miss Bianca hadn't seen him; but Patience had.

"Did you see that mouse with the little cart?" asked Patience cautiously. (Some few miles later, when the Duchess's great dirty wig began to nod.)

"I was in your pocket, child," said Miss Bianca. "I saw nothing."

"Well, there *was* one," said Patience. "Do you think it could have been Bernard?"

Miss Bianca shook her head hopelessly. She was in dreadfully low spirits. And no wonder: so nearly had her plan succeeded, and it was such a clever plan, bitter it was indeed to be cheated of the fruits! Moreover, there was no telling but that their future situation might be even worse than that they left behind: at least in the Diamond Palace there had been twelve ladies for the Duchess to abuse, whereas at the hunting lodge the full brunt of her temper would have to be borne by Patience and Mandrake — the child no doubt bearing the worst of it!

"Don't you think," persisted Patience, "we should throw out some sort of *clue,* just in case? Shall I throw out my handkerchief? Or suppose you threw out your silver chain?"

Miss Bianca flinched. At that moment of utter despondency her silver chain seemed her one remaining link with the happy past. It was a gift from the Boy's mother, fully an inch long and of the most exquisite workmanship, and it had never been off Miss Bianca's neck since she received it. She had worn it even in the Black Castle; each time she fingered it, what beautiful memories came flooding back! — of her Porcelain Pagoda, with its swansdown cushions; of Ambassadorial dinner parties, when it was so much admired; best of all, of the Boy himself, her kind protector and playmate . . . "I should never have let them make me Madam Chairwoman at all," thought Miss Bianca sadly, "if I am to be reft perpetually from his side! And am I now to sacrifice my precious silver chain — my last memento of him — just *in case?*"

She sighed again. So did Patience.

"It's the only one I've got," sighed Patience, as she

gently took her handkerchief out from underneath Miss Bianca and screwed it into a ball.

Miss Bianca looked at the grimy, crumpled scrap of cotton. If crumpled and grimy, it was because Patience had so often cried into it: the little blood spots showed where Patience had pricked her fingers on the diamond stars of the Duchess's wig . . .

"I'm afraid you won't be so comfortable, in my pocket, without it," apologized Patience.

"I should be ashamed of myself!" thought Miss Bianca — and with one swift gesture unclasped the clasp and threw her precious chain out of the coach window.

As soon as she had done so, she felt much better. It was the fact that nothing made Miss Bianca feel so low — not even hopes disappointed, nor fears for the future — as being selfish. Children know this feeling too, which was probably why Patience, prepared to give up her one-and-only handkerchief, had been able to encourage and support Miss Bianca instead of the other way round.

And in fact the idea of throwing out a clue, just in case, proved to be a very sensible and valuable one. Bernard *found* it!

2

Bernard wasn't a particularly clever mouse, but any involvement with Miss Bianca preternaturally sharpened his wits. Thus, discovering the Diamond Palace deserted, he immediately concluded that its occupants must have *gone* somewhere; also, probably by some means of transport. This notion led him back to the great gates to examine the gravel for hoof or wheel tracks. Discovering both —

"A coach!" thought Bernard.

Examining the tracks a bit further on —

"Bound outwards from the city!" he thought.

And then, with a really splendid feat of memory —

"Also a certain hunting lodge," recalled Bernard, from the speech he had made about the Grand Duchess at the General Meeting, *"situated in the forest"* — this was the bit he had been going to say when the Professor of Mathematics interrupted him — *"above the Happy Valley . . ."*

So at least he knew which direction to follow, even when the wheel tracks were obliterated by the marks of bicycle or motor tires. Sometimes pushing his handcart before him, sometimes pulling it behind, off in pursuit hurried Bernard as fast as he could.

All the same, the Duchess's coach was already some

miles ahead, and fast as Bernard hurried he was no
match for two coach-horses, however aged. He grew
hotter and hotter, and tireder and tireder, and the
hatchets rattled about in his handcart, and the part of
a lawnmower kept falling off, so that the finding of
Miss Bianca's silver chain was just what was needed
to put fresh heart into him.

What a mercy it hadn't been found first by gipsies!

It would have made a gipsy-daughter's wedding-dowry. But there it lay still inviolate, glittering like frost upon the bramblebush that had received it.

Bernard pressed it to his whiskers. He wouldn't have done so if there was anyone looking. Mice, for all their interracial connections, remain less Latin than Anglo-Saxon when it comes to any display of emotion. But since no one *was* looking, Bernard pressed it to his whiskers . . .

And now, just as though the chain possessed some white magic of its own, a lorry first overhauled him (having nearly over*run* him), then halted while the driver and his mate ate lunch. In large letters over the cab, FOREST AND HAPPY VALLEY PIT-PROP CO. read Bernard. He instantly made fast his cart to a trailing rope, and himself scrambled up over a rear wheel.

Once in motion again, they actually *overtook* the Duchess's coach. The lorry was well into the forest before Mandrake whipped his horses along the first broad ride between the first tall trees.

Then it broke down.

3

"Did you see that lorry?" asked Patience of Miss Bianca.

"No, child," said Miss Bianca — speaking now more cheerfully, but without any particular interest. "Remember that I am in your pocket."

"I might have called out," sighed Patience, "but we passed by before I thought of it . . ."

If only she *had* called out! — If only *Miss Bianca* had called out! The sound of that beloved voice would have spurred Bernard to nip driver and mate from their tea-making (they always made tea when the lorry broke down) and make them stop the coach (as probably containing some important person) to complain of the awful hazards their Union rules subjected them to, such as being mouse-nipped on the road. If this had happened Patience and Miss Bianca would have been rescued at once, lorry-drivers having in general very good hearts.

But Patience didn't call out; and on the coach rolled; and not until half-an-hour later did Bernard, fidgeting about while the kettle boiled for a second brew, recognize its wheel tracks; when in a desperation of impatience, as the driver and his mate began to make French toast, he unhitched his handcart and followed after — once more alone.

11

The Hunting Lodge

AT LAST THE coach halted. The last few miles of forest had been so dense, branches rattled on its roof: the clearing in which stood the Duchess's hunting lodge was no bigger than a tennis court: the building itself so closely hemmed by trees, they must have doubly darkened windows already half-blind with unclipped ivy. The Duchess's hunting lodge was as dark as her Diamond Palace had been bright . . .

Patience shivered; and Miss Bianca with her.

For welcome, out bounded two huge bloodhounds, fawning about the Duchess's feet.

"Down, Tyrant! Down, Torment!" she cried. — Yet their very names seemed to give her pleasure. She repeated them almost lovingly. "Brave Torment, brave Tyrant!" she cried. "Have you been too long without proper duties, that you slaver so? I put you upon duty again! — Where's your master?" she added. "Where's my Chief Ranger?"

Up behind the bloodhounds loomed a figure almost grimmer than Mandrake's — bearded like a pard, strong long legs booted to the knee, enormous hands gauntleted to the elbows, and one of them clutching an iron cudgel!

"I put *you* upon duty too!" cried the Grand Duchess.

2

Much as she had hated the Diamond Palace, Miss Bianca instantly hated the hunting lodge far more. If the Palace's diamond-studded vulgarity had often made her feel positive nausea, the hunting lodge, in all its plainness, Miss Bianca immediately knew was going to make her feel something even worse. She didn't give this emotion an exact name; but it was fear.

Patience wasn't to have an attic, in the hunting lodge, but a little cellar; or cell. Mandrake directed her to it at once, with instructions to stay there until sent for to undress the Duchess. "As you will stay there accordingly," ordered Mandrake, "whenever off duty!"

Between its narrow, damp, dark walls Patience and Miss Bianca looked at each other — each striving to conceal from the other that unnamed emotion.

"I suppose I shall spend *some* time upstairs?" said Patience bravely.

"To be sure you will!" replied Miss Bianca.

She gently rubbed Patience's shoulder where the Duchess's grip had bruised it.

"I wonder what the Duchess meant," said Patience presently, "about putting those dreadful great dogs *on duty?*"

Miss Bianca wondered too.

"Are they police-dogs, do you think?" asked Patience. "To prevent anyone trying to escape?"

Hitherto, such was the child's true affection for her only friend, the idea of escaping had never been mentioned since they were forced from the Diamond Palace into the Duchess's coach. Far from reproaching Miss Bianca with fruitlessly raising her hopes, Patience so suffered for Miss Bianca's disappointment, she immediately attempted a sort of apology for even using the word.

"I meant, to prevent anyone just going for a walk in the forest," explained Patience.

Just then, both Mandrake and the Grand Duchess shouted for her at once. Off poor Patience ran — leaving Miss Bianca, touched almost to tears, to rack her brains again as she had racked them in the Diamond Palace . . .

3

"It is evidently Tyrant and Torment we have to fear most," thought Miss Bianca. (She knew quite well that by *going for a walk in the forest* Patience meant *running away through the forest*.) "Without *them* on the scent, even the Chief Ranger, big and grim as he is, might well be at a loss. If only we could but win them to take our part!" thought Miss Bianca.

"Appearances may deceive," mused Miss Bianca. "We cannot all be born beautiful; beneath many a rugged exterior beats a kind heart; perhaps Tyrant and Torment are less bloodthirsty than they naturally (being bloodhounds) are forced to look. Who knows but what our predicament, put to them in a few simple words, may not even touch their hearts? I think I'll pay them a little visit."

If Bernard had been there (in fact he was still plunging about the forest), he would have of course tried to stop her, on the grounds that she would instantly be eaten up. But Bernard wasn't there, and actually Miss Bianca's confidence proved fully justified. There was ever the air about her, however modestly she bore herself, of a V.I.P. (or Very Important Person) such as police forces, far from consuming, turn out guards of honor for. As Miss Bianca entered Tyrant's and Torment's quarters, both blood-hounds rose smartly to their feet and saluted!

"Pray forgive me if I intrude," said Miss Bianca, bowing back with easy grace, "but I just happened to be passing; and dropped in for a little chat."

"Always honored to see a lady in Mess," replied Sergeant Tyrant readily. "Corporal Torment, find her a seat!"

While Corporal Torment looked about for something Miss Bianca's size, Miss Bianca too looked about, despite all her anxieties, with unaffected interest. She had never been in police quarters before. Even among military men she knew only Lancers and Hussars — with whom, after they'd jingled alongside the Ambassador's carriage, she and the Boy occasionally lunched. Here was certainly no glittering Regimental plate — no shelf of cups won at polo or cricket; but a well-scrubbed decency reigned, and she had no hesitation in sitting down when at last Corporal Torment produced what appeared to be a particularly well-scrubbed ivory bench. — "Whatever else I do," thought Miss Bianca, "I must *not* look like the Colonel's wife visiting Married Quarters!" — and so didn't examine her seat too closely, but instead launched out into light chat.

"What an agreeable *dépôt* this must seem to you,"

began Miss Bianca, "if you, like myself, are lovers of our famous forests? Such beauty of trees, and undergrowth! What very happy bloodhounds you must be, stationed in such exquisite, afforested surroundings!"

It will be seen that she wasn't using particularly simple words just yet, but most troops like being talked to a bit over their heads, and Tyrant and Torment were no exception. Their big ears wagged appreciatively as they listened, receptive to whatever the lady had to say. Only they neither of them said anything back, and as Miss Bianca wasn't there merely to give them pleasure, or even to teach them appreciation of natural beauty, after a few more well-turned phrases she *did* simplify.

"The dawn glimpsed through birch trees," exclaimed Miss Bianca, "what rare delights! What chiaroscuro! — I'm sure you both write to your mothers about it frequently."

Though they still didn't speak, she thought they certainly looked touched!

"Or if either of you has a little sister," continued Miss Bianca, much encouraged, "perhaps you write to *her?* — Possibly you have observed," she added lightly, "*someone's* little sister just come into residence here at this moment?"

At last Tyrant spoke again.

"Blue eyes, fair hair, height about four foot, weight about sixty pounds: description already circulated," agreed Sergeant Tyrant.

4

Miss Bianca was so shocked, it took even her a few moments to recover poise, as she suddenly realized that some appearances evidently did *not* deceive! Those few heartlessly professional words revealed Tyrant a police officer to the marrow, immune to every softer feeling. It was his mournful, touched gaze that had deceived — probably just due to the way his eyelids drooped — not the cruel set of his jaw! Probably he never wrote to his mother at all.

"Why, you make the poor child sound like a criminal!" cried Miss Bianca indignantly.

"Juvenile delinquent," corrected Tyrant.

"Such as is our duty to pursue," put in Torment, "with the full rigor of the Law."

"But *Patience* isn't a delinquent!" cried Miss Bianca. "She has never done anything wrong in her life!"

"But she *might*," pointed out Tyrant.

"Such as running away," added Torment. "They *do,* don't they, Sarge?"

Miss Bianca shuddered. But with a great effort she managed to conceal her true emotions.

"Naturally it is your function to pursue," she agreed. "And when giving chase to escaping murderers, for instance, your selfless devotion must be the admiration of all. I'm sure *I* admire the police-force quite enormously. But such a mite as Patience — only sixty pounds, remember! — is surely beneath your notice? Really, you'd look quite ridiculous — two such great bloodhounds as you are! If *Patience* went running through the forest, surely you wouldn't pursue *her?*" pressed Miss Bianca.

Sergeant Tyrant and Corporal Torment wrinkled their brows. — All bloodhounds' brows are perpetually wrinkled, because they are such slow thinkers. They never think a single thought their fathers and grandfathers haven't thought before them; and even so have to remember, and ruminate, and check up. But when they have done all this, they are as stubborn as only the stupid can be.

"If so ordered, we would," said Tyrant.

"By her Grace," added Torment.

"Seeing as it's her Grace's orders we're under," explained Tyrant.

It was just at this moment that Miss Bianca, as she lowered her eyes to conceal the contempt and repugnance in them, perceived precisely what it was she was sitting on. Her artistic studies had of course included Anatomy: what she was sitting on was a very small shinbone — gnawed.

"But she'll be too tired to run tonight — eh, Sarge?" grinned Corporal Torment.

5

"My dear child," exclaimed Miss Bianca, as soon as Patience returned from putting the Duchess's wig away, "we must flee this very evening! It is our only hope — if Tyrant and Torment are not to pursue us and probably tear us into pieces!"

"Oh, dear," sighed Patience, "I'm so tired already — and my shoulder still aches so!"

" 'Tis our only hope!" repeated Miss Bianca vigorously. "Also I have looked at the map in the hall —" (she had found it on her way back from Tyrant's and Torment's quarters) "— and discovered that we are no more than a league north from the Happy Valley! Once there, I promise you will never have to run anywhere again! Pluck up your courage, my dear child, put me in your pocket, and let us both make a last bid, however bold, for freedom and happiness!"

Tired as she was — her shoulder still aching — at

these words of Miss Bianca's Patience *did* pluck up courage!

6

At least the Duchess's hunting lodge wasn't nearly so well bolted and barred as her Diamond Palace. Or perhaps Mandrake was too exhausted after the journey to go round properly. In any case, there was a little window left half open on the ground floor. Patience needed only a very small space to squeeze through! — and lost only her handkerchief in the process.

Once outside they paused a moment, listening. All was still. They looked back at the high gloomy bulk of the lodge: not a light showed.

"Hold me up, child," said Miss Bianca, "so that I can see the stars!"

Patience held Miss Bianca up on her palm. Miss Bianca scrutinized the heavens. She recognized the Great Bear at once — his tail pointing to the north. "The Happy Valley lying to the south, we leave your honorable tail behind us, do we not, honored Ursus Major?" cried Miss Bianca. — She was so well-educated, she knew all the proper forms of address; and indeed the Great Bear, pleased at being given his classic name, seemed to shine all the brighter. "Quite right, you little atomy!" growled the Great Bear kindly. (In a charcoal-burner's hut in the forest it sounded like a clap of thunder.) "Off, away with you, and leave *me* to my duty of holding true the North Star!"

"So we must leave the North Star behind us," said Miss Bianca to Patience. "Can you remember?"

"I'll try to!" said Patience bravely — even though she shivered a little in the cold night air.

There was a wide opening in the very direction they needed to follow. Tucking Miss Bianca back into her pocket, Patience stole softly into its shade. Underfoot she felt moss and beechmast — so easy to run on, soon, as her eyes grew accustomed to the darkness, she was running quite fast, yet so smoothly that Miss Bianca felt the motion almost agreeable. "This is better than one could have dared anticipate!" thought Miss Bianca. "How right we were, to seize our opportunity!"

Though the air was cold, it was also sweet — with the breath of freedom!

7

But by what mischance, in the hunting lodge behind them, did the Duchess suddenly wake?

As a rule she slept heavily all through the night. She didn't even dream, for she had nothing to dream about. All she desired — wealth, and power, and especially the power to give pain — was hers to enjoy by day. Possibly it was the unaccustomed bed; but for whatever reason, the Grand Duchess suddenly woke — and when Mandrake came running at the furious peal of her bell, demanded the child Patience!

"Send me the child Patience," ordered the Duchess, "to come and rub my feet!"

Off shambled Mandrake in his dressing-gown and slippers — losing first the right-foot slipper, then the left, in his haste to do his mistress's bidding. After a thorough search of the hunting lodge, however, he returned at a slower pace . . .

"As your Grace pleases," mumbled Mandrake nervously, "the child doesn't seem to be about . . ."

"Not *about?*" shouted the Duchess. "If she's asleep, wake her up! What d'you mean, *not about?*"

"As your Grace pleases — not here," mumbled the Major-domo. "That is, nowhere to be found . . ."

Perhaps the worst thing of all was that the Duchess had faced the same situation before. As the little shin-bone bore witness.

"What, run off already?" screamed the Duchess. "Rouse my Chief Ranger!" she screamed. "Loose Tyrant and Torment! Bring her back, if not alive, then dead!"

Instantly all was bustle and confusion. — Bustle not unpurposeful, however, nor confusion undirected! Out to the Chief Ranger's quarters stumbled Mandrake, back they both hastened to unleash the bloodhounds. Patience's handkerchief (found caught on the window sash) was presented to their noses. Tyrant and Torment recognized upon it also a trace of mouse-scent. "Easy meat, Sarge!" bayed Corporal Torment. — It was so long since they had been let loose, they bounded forth absolutely slavering with anticipation. The Chief Ranger seized his cudgel and followed, as they galloped into the forest while the Duchess shrieked a view-halloo from her bedroom-window. "View-halloo!" shrieked the Duchess. "View-halloo, good Tyrant and Torment! Bring back your meat alive or dead!"

8

"Do you know," said Miss Bianca to Patience, as they paused for a brief moment, "though I wouldn't wish to alarm you, it does seem as though I just heard something that sounded *rather* like the voice of Torment."

They were in the very thick of the forest. Beneath

the close-growing trees an undergrowth of brambles sprawled their thorny trails across a path no longer mossy but strewn with biggish stones. Patience had once or twice been tripped up by them.

"I thought *I* heard it too," said Patience nervously.

"Then do you think you could run a little faster?" suggested Miss Bianca.

"I'll *try*," said Patience.

Of course Bernard was in the forest with them; but his handcart having bogged down against a giant mushroom, he was completely occupied in extricating it . . .

12

Bloodhounds in the Forest

IT WAS A long, dreadful night indeed, to Patience and Miss Bianca — running and running, pausing just for a moment when Patience had a stitch, then running and running again! — In the thick of the forest as they now were, they had certain advantages: so many rabbit and ferret runs, so many fox and badger paths, confused their scent. But it *was* Torment Miss Bianca had heard: fleeter of foot than his sergeant (as corporals often are), Torment had at once taken the lead, and well it was for Patience and Miss Bianca that his nose now and then betrayed him!

On and on they ran. Their only respite was in the hut of a charcoal-burner. The great forests above the Happy Valley were full of such; fortunately the fugitives happened upon one not only hospitable but honest. Its lighted window might have lured them both but to disaster — many of the charcoal-burners doubling their humble profession with that of jackals to the Chief Ranger, whom they helped to lay not a few poor poachers by the heels. And even here, after Patience had been given a cup of milk, and Miss Bianca a morsel of cheese, and both had been let sit an hour by the fire, it was plain that they weren't exactly welcome . . .

"I ask no questions," said the honest charcoal-burner, "nor no questions will I answer neither — to whomsoever be pursuing of ye! All the same — hearing her Grace's Chief Ranger's whistle — let alone the baying of her Grace's bloodhounds — also seeing as I'm a man wi' wife and childer —"

Patience looked wistfully at the warm hearth. But already contact with Miss Bianca had taught her true courtesy.

"Then I'll just run on again," said Patience politely, "and thank you very much for the milk."

2

"I'd almost rather they brought her back alive," mused the Duchess to Mandrake, as he obsequiously served her a horrible snack of warmed-up jugged hare.

"Your Grace's tender heart is well known," said Mandrake.

But even he, cruel as he was, shuddered to think of

the fate of the child Patience if the Chief Ranger *did* bring her back alive . . .

3

Every bramble-trail of the undergrowth tore at Patience's skirt and clawed her ankles, the lower branches of young saplings lashed her eyes, big roots tripped her up. If her fingers had bled from the diamond stars in the Duchess's wig, her poor legs now bled even worse, from thorn and bramble. Painful as was the sting of the Duchess's cane, much more so the whip of a hazel-wand! Yet on and on Patience ran — Miss Bianca in her pocket — as brave a little girl as ever lived.

Whenever she had to stop, Miss Bianca encouraged her in the coolest way.

"I was particularly pleased by your nice manners, dear child," panted Miss Bianca (actually feeling quite faint herself from so much bumping about). "You spoke very nicely indeed to that poor but honest charcoal-burner."

"Did I?" gasped Patience. "I wanted so much to stay!"

"Which makes it all the more creditable," said Miss Bianca. "Anyone can be polite in a drawing room, but to be polite while fleeing from bloodhounds shows a truly educated heart. — Now, can that be Tyrant's voice I hear as well? Perhaps you'd better run on."

On Patience ran again. After Miss Bianca's praise the trees seemed less thick, and the brambles less prickly, and she didn't stumble quite so often. Soon she was running downhill. With surprising suddenness the forest thinned and dwindled — first to mere scrub, then to a mere hedgerow bordering a sunken road. They were reaching the Valley at last! — and there, just where the road bent, stood one enormous oak . . .

Miss Bianca recognized it instantly.

"Just as far as the next turning," she cried, "and up the path beyond! Run, my dear Patience, run — for it really *is* Tyrant's voice!"

With a last effort Patience ran so fast that Miss Bianca was almost thrown out. She had to hold on to the inside of the pocket with both hands.

"We've come to a house!" gasped Patience.

"And safety!" panted Miss Bianca. "Ring the bell!"

"I can't reach it!" sobbed Patience.

"Then knock!" panted Miss Bianca. "Both Tyrant *and* Torment I hear! Knock louder!"

"I'm knocking as hard as I can!" sobbed Patience.

At that moment, the bloodhounds rounded the

corner by the oak tree — heads down, jaws drooling, eyes aflame. Why, oh *why* didn't the door open!

4

Inside, in the big comfortable kitchen, the farmer stood up and yawned.

"Time for bed, wife," said he.

"Aye, time for bed," said she.

She put out the two big lamps while her husband kicked apart the fire. A last flicker of light chased the shadows across the ceiling; the scarlet geraniums showed velvety-black against the warm, comfortable curtains.

"Seeing as I'll be up at five," said the farmer, "and the boys no later, for all they're still out dancing, the gay gallivants!"

"Gay gallivants, gay workers," said his wife. "There'll be hot porridge ready for ye. — But listen, husband, to the dogs' cry!"

"After a poacher," said the farmer, "that's all."

" 'Send he gets back safe to his littl'uns!" said the farmer's wife.

They neither of them heard Patience beating at the door. The big iron knocker was so heavy, and her hands were so small, and she was so exhausted, she wasn't making very much noise, and what she did the baying of the bloodhounds drowned.

"God bless this house," said the farmwife, "and all poor homeless ones abroad!" Then she and her husband went to bed.

5

"I don't think they're *going* to open!" sobbed Patience.

Miss Bianca glanced hastily back. For an instant the bloodhounds' pace was slower — they were alongside the pigsties; it was a moment's respite — but only a moment's. The thought of what might happen in *another* moment, absolutely there on the doorstep, so near to sanctuary yet so hopeless to achieve it, froze Miss Bianca's blood.

"At least we can't stay *here*," she gasped, "to be pulled in pieces! Run on again, child!"

"I can't!" sobbed Patience. "I'm too tired!"

It was a time for desperate measures. Miss Bianca did a thing she'd never done in her life. Baring her small white teeth, customarily employed on nothing tougher than cream cheese, right through apron and frock and petticoat she gave Patience a sharp nip.

"*Now* will you run!" ordered Miss Bianca. "If we

may but reach the dovecote — across that vegetable
patch to the right — there is yet hope!"

Patience ran.

6

Fortunate that Miss Bianca's preliminary investiga-
tion of the farm had been so thorough! — otherwise

she wouldn't have known about the dovecote at all. As it was, she remembered not only its situation, but also that there was a ladder inside leading up to a broad ledge below the first tier of nesting boxes. That bloodhounds cannot climb ladders is of course common knowledge, but it was Miss Bianca's conscientiousness in the first place that enabled her to profit by it.

"Now up the ladder!" ordered Miss Bianca — regretfully but sensibly nipping Patience again; and as they at last reached precarious, temporary safety, drew her first full breath for what seemed like years . . .

7

All around them the doves woke up and began to coo.

"Who's here, who, who?" cooed the doves. "Do *you* know who, my doo?" "Two, two!" cooed the doves nesting nearest. "But we don't know *who!*"

Since Patience obviously couldn't tell them, also it was obviously necessary that they should be reassured, how fortunate, again, that Miss Bianca was a perfect mistress of their language! — which she had studied in the course of singing-lessons.

"Pray forgive the intrusion," called up Miss Bianca

— pitching her voice with all the accuracy of a prima donna, and with a much better accent than most prima donnas have, in a foreign tongue — "and allow myself and my young friend to beg your hospitality! We are neither rogues and vagabonds nor fugitives from justice: there just happen to be a couple of bloodhounds following us."

"Who, who did you say?" cooed the doves interestedly.

But Miss Bianca felt it quite beyond her to explain the nature of bloodhounds to sleepy doves — who are stupid enough even when wide awake!

"Large birds," said Miss Bianca. "But they will not enter here, being afraid of enclosed spaces." ("True, true!" cooed the doves, not wishing to seem ignorant.) "Therefore, with your permission," continued Miss Bianca, "we will occupy this very commodious ledge until morning, and then be on our way — leaving you to the happy knowledge of a charitable act gracefully performed."

Miss Bianca's eloquence rarely failed of effect, nor did it now. Even though the doves understood few of the big words, they felt reassured and flattered, and after a few consenting coos all went back to sleep.

"Are these the doves you sang to me about?" asked

Patience, as she and Miss Bianca settled themselves on the ledge.

"No, indeed!" said Miss Bianca, rather sharply. "*They* had sense! — Now we have but to hold out till morning," she added cheerfully, "and help will surely come. Oh my dear child, what loving arms will then receive you!"

"I'm sure I'll try to hold out," said Patience. "I'm only afraid of falling off this ledge. — Will loving arms *really* receive me," she asked wistfully, "if the bloodhounds don't first?"

"You may take my word for it," said Miss Bianca bravely.

But morning was still many hours off; and the Duchess's Chief Ranger, who *could* climb ladders, was certainly following behind his hounds . . .

Miss Bianca hoped Patience had forgotten the Chief Ranger. She almost wished she could forget him herself!

"Where, oh *where*," thought Miss Bianca desperately, "is Bernard?"

13

The Last Stand

ONLY HIS FAITHFUL handcart kept him on his legs. Wearily poor Bernard struggled on, leaning on its shafts: when he came to a dip, and the cart could roll downhill, he even snatched a brief ride on them, otherwise he might have collapsed altogether. By this time he had lost all sense of direction, he was just keeping *on;* and it was by the merest chance that he stumbled into a little track beaten through the undergrowth where the going was easier.

At the end of the track stood a charcoal-burner's hut.

Bernard stopped outside simply because he *had* to stop somewhere. He didn't knock at the door. Only because the charcoal-burner was just setting out to do a little poaching on his own account, and saw him, did Bernard speak up — to show he wasn't a burglar.

"Any knives to grind?" asked Bernard hopelessly.

"Nary a one," said the charcoal-burner.

"No scissors of your wife's?" suggested Bernard automatically.

"No scissors neither," said the charcoal-burner, "to the best of my belief." — He looked at Bernard shrewdly: even the disguise of a knife-grinder, and after all his dusty travels, couldn't conceal Bernard's inherent respectability. "But since you're such a decent-looking sort of mouse, I'll ask."

"Don't bother," said Bernard.

But the charcoal-burner was already calling over his shoulder.

"Martha!" he shouted. "Any scissors to grind?"

"What, at this time of night?" called back his wife inside the hut. "Whatever makes you ask?"

"Just because here's a decent-looking mouse willing to grind 'em!" called the charcoal-burner.

At that, his wife came out to see. She too gave Bernard a good look, and shook her head regretfully.

"Neither scissors nor skewers," said she. "But I must say mice seem to be mending their ways! For let alone here's one earning an honest livelihood, that little white lady in the child's pocket had the prettiest manners ever seen!"

Bernard was up in a flash. All his weariness was cast aside like a mackintosh when the sun comes out.

"When were they here?" he asked eagerly.

"Why, this same night as ever is!" said the charcoal-burner's wife. "They left not an hour ago!"

"Which way?" gasped Bernard.

"Since there be only one track through the forest at all passable," said the charcoal-burner, "you'll have no difficulty in following 'em!"

With but the briefest word of thanks — barely re-membering the civility of a pull at his whiskers — Bernard seized his handcart and rushed off in the direction indicated.

He was but a mile behind Patience and Miss Bianca in the dovecote — but Torment and Tyrant, to say nothing of the Chief Ranger, were still *between* them!

2

The reason the Chief Ranger wasn't already up with his bloodhounds was that, like every other wicked person, he feared the brave farmers of the Happy Valley. They turned angry, contemptuous faces upon him even when he was hunting poachers; if they had guessed he was hunting a child — and a girl-child! — they'd have ducked him at least, if not tarred and feathered him. With his long booted legs he should have over-taken Patience in the forest itself — and indeed only the accident of her finding refuge in the charcoal-burner's hut had saved her. But when he perceived, upon examining her fresh tracks, that she had actually gained the Happy Valley, he held back, waiting till dead of night (when all the brave farmers would be asleep), and trusting to his bloodhounds to find and hold the quarry. He knew that at his whistle and call of "Come, Tyrant! Stay, Torment!" the one would rush bounding to fetch him while the other remained on guard.

So exactly it happened, when he at last reached the sunken road. — Shrill blew his whistle, carryingly echoed his voice; within a matter of seconds Tyrant slavered beside him under the oak tree. "What, no blood on thy jaws?" joked the Chief Ranger grimly. "Has one small maid been too much for 'ee? Ah, well, so maybe her Grace'll like it better to have her back alive!"

Then he followed Tyrant along the path to the dovecote.

One hardly knows whether it is a point in his favor or not that he'd have preferred to find the *remains*. The Chief Ranger himself thought it a great point, as showing he was such a kindly-natured sort of chap he'd much rather all was over before he got there. The pleas of poachers, regarding their wives and children, he used to say often quite upset him, as he broke their wrists with his cudgel and set his dogs a-tearing of their raiment. He was nonetheless prepared — duty being duty, especially with a pension in sight — to fling Patience over his shoulder and carry her back into servitude with the Grand Duchess.

Outside the dovecote lay Torment on guard.

"What, no blood on *thy* jaws either?" joked the Chief Ranger. "All work left to yours truly? Well, well! Why didn't ye go in after?"

"Ladder, ladder, ladder!" bayed Torment.

"Oh, so she's up a ladder, is she?" said the Chief Ranger — and pushed his big bearded face, grinningly, through the dovecote door . . .

3

Miss Bianca and Patience were still not quite so defenseless as they seemed — or at least Miss Bianca wasn't. Every word of this colloquy had been overheard by her, and as her ears were sharp, so were her wits keen. However exhausted, first by natural fatigue, then by watching (fearful lest Patience, who *was* asleep, should fall off the ledge), Miss Bianca still kept her wits, and perceived one last useful stratagem.

"Wake the doves again!" cried Miss Bianca. "Fire! Rats! Hawks!" she shrieked — conjuring up every peril most feared by their hosts. "Oh wake the doves," cried Miss Bianca, "till they wake the house! Call and scream, child, as loud as you can!"

As the big bearded face pushed through the door — "Fire! Rats! Hawks!" cried Patience.

"Hawks! Rats! Fire!" shrilled Miss Bianca.

"Rats! Fire! Hawks!" cried both together.

All the doves woke up at once, and without knowing precisely what was going on, took up the cry.

4

"Listen, husband! Seems as though there be something disturbable to my dovecote," said the farmer's wife. "I trust no rat's found entry!"

"Doves be so foolish, they'll wake and create at a shadow," said the farmer sleepily. "I'll still take a look in the morning, just to please 'ee . . ."

"What if morning's too late?" asked his wife.

"Five o'clock's early enough for any man," grumbled the farmer, sinking his big heavy head back into the big feather-pillow.

His wife was too good a wife to argue. She just sat

139

up a moment longer, hoping there was nothing really amiss in her dovecote, and then pulled her nightcap back over her ears and went to sleep too.

5

A flurry of blue-gray wings swirled down about the Chief Ranger's head; for a moment he was almost blinded by them, as the hubbub almost deafened him. The doves — at least a hundred of them — could have pecked his eyes out! But unfortunately they had no imagination: the Chief Ranger didn't look like any large bird, such as Miss Bianca had told them of; no hawk was in sight, and the cry of "Rats!" or "Fire!" being a favorite practical joke with their own teen-agers, within a matter of seconds each foolish dove had returned to its perch.

Reassured by the sudden calm, the Chief Ranger set his foot upon the ladder.

How easy, now, before dawn broke, before the brave farmers of the Happy Valley were awake, to throw a child over his shoulder and carry her off!

The ladder creaked beneath his weight as he began to climb . . .

"Oh *where*," thought Miss Bianca again, desperately — *it might be for the last time* — "is Bernard?"

140

6

He was at the dovecote door! — Having followed the right direction at a speed perfectly incredible!

The rumor of the frightened doves reached him just as he entered the farmyard; leaning on the shafts of his handcart he covered the intervening ground like a racing motorist. Crash went the handcart against the door sill — he dragged it across! "Bernard!" shrieked Miss Bianca — one upward glance, and he took in the whole appalling situation!

"Cut down the ladder!" shrieked Miss Bianca.

Bernard seized a hatchet off the handcart. How he wished he had four arms instead of two, to hew with both his hatchets at once! Even that would have taken too long, for the wood was hickory, the hardest wood there is. — Bernard snatched up a sword, and put himself in a posture to attack. But though he had taken lessons in knife-grinding, he had inexplicably omitted to take lessons in swordsmanship: the first flourish of the unaccustomed weapon nearly lopped his own ears off. Bernard flung it aside with a groan — hatchets and swords had betrayed him, and what use was a part of a lawnmower? — There remained only his daggers, compared with the bulk of the Chief Ranger no more than bee stings. But in sheer despera-

tion Bernard seized the one nearest to hand and flung it hard and true at the Chief Ranger's throat.

No more than a bee sting as it was, it made the Chief Ranger bellow. Like most people fond of inflicting pain on others, he himself couldn't bear even a prick without bellowing! — His unmanly roar was his undoing — for who now came running, at the uncouth sound, but the farmer's two big sons!

7

They had been out all night dancing. From the buttonholes of their velvet jackets the big nosegays given them by their best girls hung droopy but still sweet. Their hair was on end, but still glossy with traces of goose-grease. They were so young and strong and jolly — the gay gallivants! — that even after polkas thrice encored, and mazurkas innumerable, they were still ready to tackle any intruder in their mother's dovecote!

"Why, 'tis the Duchess's Chief Ranger!" cried the bigger boy fearlessly. "What be 'ee doing here, Chief Ranger, alarming of our mother's doves?"

"Arresting an escaping criminal," snarled the Chief Ranger, "upon her Grace's orders!"

Both boys stared interestedly up at the ledge. It

was beginning to be light: they could just make out Patience's fair head and slight childish shape.

"Escaping criminal?" repeated the younger incredulously. "Why, her looks just like our little sister!"

14

The End

OF COURSE THEY jolted him off the ladder without the least difficulty: it was from sheer *joie de vivre* that they ducked him in the mill pond. (Bernard added his mite by hurling his last weapon, the part of a lawnmower, in after, and scored a hit on the Chief Ranger's left ear.) As for Tyrant and Torment, the boys just dealt them a good wallop apiece, and left their master to finish the beating when he managed to haul himself out.

How lovely it was for Patience to be given breakfast sitting up in bed (two brown eggs, and four thick slices of brown bread-and-butter) before she sank into sleep under a buttercup-patterned quilt! And how lovelier still, just before she dozed off, to feel her thin little hand clasped in the farmwife's big warm one, and to hear a kindly voice promising she should never have to run anywhere again!

"Truly?" murmured Patience, half-asleep. "Can I truly stay here always?"

"For always and ever," promised the farmwife. "Seeing 'tis just such a little maid as 'ee us have lacked too long . . ."

Exhausted and sleepy as she was, Patience managed to keep awake a moment longer.

"And can Miss Bianca please stay too?"

"If she's that pretty white mouse on your pillow, and if she's been a comfort to 'ee, certainly, my dear," said the farmwife. "We'll fix her up wi' a nice shoe-box, and feed her bacon-rinds every day."

Miss Bianca felt it time to clarify the situation. But she was careful not to hurt the good woman's feelings.

"Personally," she said sweetly, "the idea of a bungalow appeals to me quite enormously. Pray do not imagine me for a moment untouched by so generous and thoughtful an offer! It just so happens —" here she hesitated a moment; and decided not to mention her Porcelain Pagoda — "that I possess a little nook in town already — quite probably spring-cleaned during my absence! Under the escort of the Secretary of the Prisoners' Aid Society (temporarily disguised as a knife-grinder), I shall have no difficulty in regaining it; and you do know how one wants to see nothing's been broken!"

"Indeed I do," agreed the farmwife warmly. "There's no trusting a servant-wench wi' so much as a bran kettle! — But what about the little maid here?" she added. "Will not she grieve for 'ee?"

Miss Bianca sighed.

"No," she said, almost sadly. "Not with two big brothers to play with; not with such kind foster-parents! She may remember me for a little, perhaps, in her dreams — but only in dreams. I would not wish it otherwise," said Miss Bianca gravely, "after all the perils she has undergone. So let me just sing her a last lullaby . . ."

Thus while the farmwife wiped away a sympathetic tear Miss Bianca for the last time sang Patience to sleep. She didn't sing the lullaby about the doves, but a variation composed on the spur of the moment.

Two big brothers and cowslip-balls and violets,

sang Miss Bianca sweetly,

Two big brothers and lambkins in the spring.
One big apron to lay a weary head upon,
A pair of big slippers for a little girl to bring.
Oh cowslip-balls and lullaby, oh lullaby and violets,
Oh lullaby and violets and lambkins in the spring!

As she finished, Patience stirred in her sleep; and put out a hand not towards Miss Bianca, but to the farmwife . . .

"You see?" said Miss Bianca, stepping lightly from the pillow.

"I see you're the cleverest little lady, and the best-hearted, 'twas ever my lot to meet," said the farmwife, "and that lullaby shall ever remain in our family, to be sung God willing to our grandchildren, as a most precious heritage."

2

Bernard and Miss Bianca actually traveled back to the city in the farm gig. It is pleasant to relate that this was chiefly in tribute to Bernard, generally so overlooked; the farmer's sons were so struck by the way he hurled the part of a lawnmower at the Chief Ranger's ear, they insisted on loading his knife-grinder's cart in behind when they drove to market. Bernard felt proud indeed, as he was able to hand Miss Bianca into so swift and commodious a vehicle. They sat together on a nice clean egg.

"Yet even on foot," said Miss Bianca, "and through the forest, at *your* side, my dear Bernard, I should have known no fear! What heroism you have displayed! Your attack upon the Chief Ranger I can compare only with the Charge of the Light Brigade as immortalized by Alfred Lord Tennyson."

Bernard glowed all over. His ears glowed particularly — where he'd almost lopped them off.

"Yet how did you know whither to follow?" asked Miss Bianca. "Did you by any chance — it was a notion of the child's — find my silver chain?"

"It's in my pocket now," said Bernard. "And once I *had* found it, d'you suppose mere bloodhounds would have held me back? — May I keep it, Miss Bianca?" he asked daringly.

She moved a little way down the egg. With every mile that spun behind their wheels she was nearing her Porcelain Pagoda; and the dear familiar company of the Ambassador's son; and all the social duties that so fully occupied her time . . . Fond as she was of Bernard, and much as she admired him, their backgrounds were too different for them ever to be more to each other than they were now. It wasn't that she grudged Bernard the bauble, it was just that to let him keep it would be raising false hopes!

"Dear Bernard, forgive me," said Miss Bianca. "As always, you are my most trusted friend. How many times have I not offered to be a sister to you —"

"Seventeen," said Bernard.

"— and ever with the truest sincerity! But since my chain was a gift from the Boy's mother — and since I'm almost sure there's a dinner party tonight, when of course I shall be expected to wear it — I really must ask you to give it back."

Slowly, reluctantly, Bernard drew Miss Bianca's chain from his pocket. With a peculiarly graceful gesture she bent her neck; as Bernard clasped the clasp, their whiskers, very lightly, brushed.

Then the gig stopped with a jerk. Rough but kindly fingers set down Bernard's cart; scooped up Bernard and Miss Bianca, and set them down too.

"Farewell, farewell!" called the farmer's sons. "And never fear for our new little sister, for her'll be the happiest little maid alive!"

3

The medal struck to commemorate this wonderful adventure caused a good deal of argument. The mice wanted to get the Grand Duchess onto it, and the two bloodhounds, besides the Chief Ranger; this was manifestly impossible, however, and in the end they compromised with the neater if less exciting design of a Ducal coronet shattered, surrounded by mouse-tails intertwiny. Miss Bianca was of course awarded the first, and Bernard the second, and these were in silver. The games mistress (representing the Ladies' Guild) got one in bronze.

The child Patience grew up to be as good and beautiful as she was happy, and married the elder of her foster-parents' sons. They still live all together in the farmhouse in the Happy Valley, and put bacon-rinds out for the mice every night.

THE END

THE TURRET

Contents

1   Miss Bianca at Home   **3**

2   The Lily Moat Picnic   14

3   At the Moot-hall   27

4   A Daring Adventure   37

5   Consequences   50

6   The Scouts   60

7   Good and Bad   71

8   The Plan   80

9   Sir Hector   93

10   To the Rescue!   104

11   In the Turret   118

12   The End   130

The Turret

1

Miss Bianca at Home

MISS BIANCA sat at her desk in her Porcelain Pagoda writing a letter of resignation to the Mouse Prisoners' Aid Society.

Everything in the boudoir was beautifully light, simple and elegant. The furniture was of cedarwood, so that it smelled as well as looked nice, and the few cushions on the chaise longue, silk stuffed with swansdown, were all of the same pale pink. — How different from the rough surroundings of the Moot-hall, from whose platform Miss Bianca, in her capacity as Madam Chairwoman, had directed, and if necessary quelled, so many a stormy meeting! How different too her own discreet private stationery — bearing just the address, the Porcelain Pagoda, in blue on pure white rice paper — from the thick official sheets headed M.P.A.S., or M.P.A.S.L.G. (Mouse Prisoners' Aid Society Ladies' Guild), with things like "Office of Madam Chairwoman" or "Sewers and Drainage Committee" typed below! The pen in Miss Bianca's hand felt light as a feather — which indeed it was: a wren's quill.

Nonetheless, before signing her name, Miss Bianca paused. She was as conscientious as she was beautiful; and though she had examined her motives with extreme strictness, like many another very conscientious person felt uneasily that anything she very much *wanted* to do was perhaps something she *shouldn't*. It was against every inclination that she had been drawn into public life at all: her Porcelain Pagoda stood in the schoolroom of an Embassy, she moved with enjoyment in the highest diplomatic circles, and in hours of leisure found even keener delight in the cultivation of a gift for verse. Nor was it an existence without duties; the Boy, the Ambassador's son, never learnt his lessons half so well without Miss Bianca sitting on his shoulder to help him concentrate on some hard sum of arithmetic, or to revive, by some appreciative exclamation, his flagging interest in a page of history; even the Boy's tutor admitted her good influence — just as the Boy's mother did, who always allowed him to take Miss Bianca with him in his pocket to such things as Military Reviews, or Charity Matinées, that go on for hours and hours . . .

Only these were such *pleasant* duties! — Miss Bianca's conscience pricked her again.

Then she recalled the many occasions of late when

4

public and private duty had actually conflicted. While she was away helping to rescue a prisoner from the Black Castle, the Boy pined until he couldn't get even a simple addition right. The rescue of a child captive from the clutches of the Diamond Duchess had made her nearly miss a big dinner for the French Ambassador. (*"Je n'ai jamais rien vu de plus joli!"* exclaimed the French Ambassador, as Miss Bianca stepped delicately between the wineglasses to make her bow to him — he little guessed that she'd just escaped the jaws of bloodhounds.) Such memories as these quietened her conscience at last: when Miss Bianca recalled her experiences at the Duchess's hunting lodge (peril of

bloodhounds) and in the Black Castle (peril of cats and jailers), she really felt she'd done enough.

"My constitution will stand no more!" thought Miss Bianca. "I should become a nervous wreck!"

Also she had a slim volume of verse to prepare for publication.

"One has a duty to one's readers too!" thought Miss Bianca.

She dipped her quill into the ink again, and signed.

At that moment, a bell tinkled at the gate of the pagoda's little surrounding pleasure ground. Miss Bianca smiled as she rose to answer it. She knew very well who would be there — the Secretary of the Mouse Prisoners' Aid Society in person: otherwise her dear old friend Bernard.

2

"I hope I don't disturb you?" said Bernard anxiously. — It was shortly after midnight, a very proper calling hour for mice; but he was always terribly afraid of seeming to intrude, at least upon Miss Bianca. (Upon members of the M.P.A.S. who hadn't paid their dues Bernard intruded as ruthlessly as a bailiff. It was partly what made him such a good Secretary. The other parts were his extreme reliability, and coolness of judgment, and lack of self-seeking.)

6

"Not at all," replied Miss Bianca. "I had just finished writing a letter . . ."

"*The* letter?" asked Bernard eagerly.

"I'm afraid so," said Miss Bianca. Of course she had let him know her intentions in advance; and indeed he had influenced the decision.

"I'm very glad to hear it!" exclaimed Bernard.

Unreasonably enough, Miss Bianca felt a trifle nettled.

"I'm told — possibly by flatterers — that I made rather a good Madam Chairwoman," said she.

"Of course you did," said Bernard warmly. "You made the best Madam Chairwoman our Society ever had — or any Society ever had anywhere." (There are branches of the Mouse Prisoners' Aid all over the world, because there are unfortunately prisons all over the world.) "But I can't help being glad you're giving it up, because it'll mean the end of your risking your life amongst cats and jailers and so forth. As you know, I was against it from the beginning: you're too beautiful," said Bernard simply, "to be *allowed* into deadly peril."

Very beautiful indeed looked Miss Bianca, as she smiled affectionately back at him. Through the school-room window the rays of a full moon frosted her ermine fur to argent; the fine silver chain about her neck gleamed like diamonds — but not less brightly

7

than her eyes. Or rather, the light in Miss Bianca's eyes was softer; they were brown (very unusual in a white mouse) and fringed by long dark lashes which lent them a most wonderful, tender depth. Bernard swallowed.

"Of course the Society'll want to give you a Dinner," he said huskily.

Miss Bianca sighed. Mice are very fond of giving Dinners, there is nothing they like better than to see six matchboxes end-to-end spread with shrimp tails in aspic and deviled sardine bones; all they need is an excuse. Bernard knew this as well as Miss Bianca, so that her sigh didn't offend him.

"Oh, dear!" said Miss Bianca. "With speeches?"

"Naturally with speeches," said Bernard. "First me, then the President of the Ladies' Guild, then you. If we can keep any of the others off their feet, it'll be a miracle."

Miss Bianca sighed again. Moving in diplomatic circles as she did she was used to a rather high standard of after-dinner speaking: the prospect of having to sit through perhaps half-a-dozen predictable and pedestrian orations thoroughly dismayed her. Also it was August, a month in which the best after-dinner speech always seems much longer than usual . . .

"Couldn't they give me something a little *cooler?*"

suggested Miss Bianca. "A picnic, for instance? —
However, do not let us meet boredom halfway, but
rather enjoy this pleasant evening by taking a little
stroll."

Bernard was only too willing; arm-in-arm they began to promenade the small but charming pleasure
ground. It was where they had first met, beside the
Venetian glass fountain: Bernard then but a shy young
pantry mouse, almost too awkward to speak, to the
famous Miss Bianca! Now he was stout and important,
but it seemed to him as but yesterday. Miss Bianca
hadn't changed at all. Her elegant little figure moved
with the same easy grace, her weight on Bernard's arm
was no more than a snowflake's; only as she looked at
the pretty swings and seesaws upon which she had
been used to disport herself, she smiled. She hadn't
swung on a swing for months.

"Time passes, my dear Bernard!" said Miss Bianca
softly. "I am ready indeed, to retire to private life! — I
didn't so much mind the perils," she added, "it was the
society one was forced into!"

"That Head Jailer in the Black Castle was the
worst," recalled Bernard.

"No," said Miss Bianca thoughtfully, "I believe
Mandrake was the worst." (Mandrake was the Diamond Duchess's steward.) "The Head Jailer's habits

were of course deplorable — indeed, the memory quite nauseates me now, of all those cigar butts left strewn about! — but *he* was being cruel, or so he believed, to desperate criminals; *Mandrake* was cruel to a defenseless child, whom but one kindly look or word might have saved from despair . . ."

"It was you who saved her from despair," said Bernard soberly.

"I must admit that to know her now safe and happy is one of my greatest comforts," said Miss Bianca, "but *Mandrake* I shall ever hold in abhorrence."

"Can't we talk of something more pleasant?" suggested Bernard.

— He really meant, more romantic. But Miss Bianca, though by her smile she seemed to acquiesce, just asked him to turn the fountain on.

"In this moonlight, it should look quite beautiful," said she, "and you know I'm not strong enough myself!"

Actually even Bernard had to sit down, on the spring that controlled the water supply, to make it work. He did so now almost too energetically: the resultant jet of water drenched Miss Bianca to the skin. But she took the mishap with her usual debonair good breeding, and in fact it gave her a splendid new idea. As Bernard, red in the face, respectfully wiped her down with his handkerchief —

"Bernard!" exclaimed Miss Bianca. "Could not the Society give me a *water* picnic? How long must it be, since we had a water picnic?"

3

The reason why the mice hadn't had a water picnic for so long was because it was so difficult to arrange. Everyone knew where a proper water picnic took place — on the lily moat beneath a ruined turret standing in neglected parkland some miles outside the city boundaries. Very old grandparent-mice remembered going there in celebration of the tercentenary of Jean Fromage — the heroic French mouse who'd once rescued a French sailor boy from slavery in Constantinople: since when the trouble of arranging transport, and hiring boats, and finding babysitters, had left the lily moat unvisited. But upon such an occasion as the resignation of Miss Bianca, and under Bernard's enthusiastic leadership, all obstacles were surmounted.

A mouse domiciled in the files at the General Post Office reported an outgoing mail van (room for any number) leaving at ten A.M. and halting in its circuit to empty a letterbox at the parkland's very gate: a second, returning, emptied the letterbox again at six; really quite an ideal schedule. Bernard personally made the whole trip in advance, in case the timetables had been altered, and while on site concluded a deal for boats with a colony of water rats established on the lily moat's brink. As for babysitting, when the great fatigue entailed by such an excursion had been pointed out to them, also after Miss Bianca had signed a few photographs for distribution amongst absentees, a more than sufficient panel of grandmothers was mustered ready to stay at home and babysit.

2

The Lily Moat Picnic

IT WAS THE most successful picnic imaginable.

Punctual to the minute set forth the Post Office mail
van: punctually, even early, while it still waited in the
Post Office yard, had the Mouse Prisoners' Aid Society
boarded it — hauling on hamper after hamper. All the
elder ladies wore best hats, and the younger ones floral
topknots; Miss Bianca's own elegant ears were protected by a most becoming light lace handkerchief tied
under the chin. Bernard brought his mackintosh.

Off the van rolled, tooting its horn. — As it approached each mailbox it gave an extra toot, to show
people their letters were really being collected, and
this the mice enjoyed extremely. Indeed, such an *esprit
de mail van* rapidly rose among them, they joined in
with hip-hurrahs. A special three-times-three saluted
the box at the park gate, before all scrambled down
and made for the lily moat, where (thanks to Bernard)
a score of handy vessels — skiffs, canoes and cata-

marans — were moored in readiness. As for the weather, it was quite perfect: not a ripple discommoded as upon waters azure as the sky one and all embarked.

The novel aquatic experience proved so delightful, hither and yon from lily leaf to lily leaf paddled or sailed the happy party all morning, ere landing on the largest leaf of all to unpack lunch. The Ladies' Guild, who provided it, had excelled themselves: there was everything mice like best — that is, cold; they couldn't have deviled sardine bones or toasted cheese, but no other delicacy lacked, while for centerpiece stood a splendid entire meringue with MISS BIANCA in pink icing. The Prisoners' Aid Society brass band played Handel's *Water Music*.

It was the most beautiful picnic imaginable — especially because as so rarely happens at picnics everyone got a good sleep after lunch. What with all the exercise, and all the fresh air, and all the food, even the youngsters curled up practically with their mouths full. One particularly happy result was that no one made speeches.

Then the refreshed brass band struck up anew, now launching into the livelier strains of jigs and schottisches. Sets were formed and partners taken — and how the lily leaf rocked at last! — not to any watery ripple, but to the stamp and patter of dancing feet!

They danced The Dashing Brown Mouse, and Roll Out the Walnuts, and Jenny's Whiskers; then they danced Hickory-Dickory, and Mousetown Races, and that oldest favorite of all, Belling the Cat!

Bernard and Miss Bianca sat a little apart under the shade of an unfolding bud. Miss Bianca had of course opened the ball with him, but though lily pads make the most wonderful dance floors, being so exceptionally well sprung, she was rather easily tired. (Her own choice, in preference to The Dashing Brown Mouse, would have been that charming minuet Le Camembert; but she was too thoughtful to ask for it, lest no one else knew the steps.) In any case, she altogether preferred to sit and admire the view.

"What an exquisite scene!" murmured Miss Bianca. "Do observe, Bernard, the reflection of the turret in the moat! It's quite like Canaletto!"

"It's a bit in need of repair," said Bernard.

"Which makes it but the more picturesque!" pointed out Miss Bianca.

They were both right. Though its top part was now no more than a wig of ivy tods, the turret commanding the moat even in dilapidation still rose slender and colorful. It was built of yellow marble, which where unconcealed by ivy gleamed softly in the now declining sun. The ivy grew thicker as it climbed: until about three-fourths of the way up but empaneled, between

twin stems thick as the trunk of an old vine, a long honey-colored shaft; in which, near the top, a single window still solidly barred provided the necessary dark accent . . .

"Exquisite indeed!" repeated Miss Bianca. — "But what, I wonder," she added, "can be that bit of white up there?"

Bernard followed her glance. There was indeed something white fluttering just above the windowsill.

"Probably a piece of paper," said Bernard, "or a paper napkin. I dare say some people who picnic here leave their litter to blow about."

"How shocking!" exclaimed Miss Bianca. Amongst the several other offices she was discarding was that of President of the Mouse Anti-Litter League; but old habit remained strong, and indeed Miss Bianca was anti-litter by nature. "Especially in such picturesque surroundings as these!" exclaimed Miss Bianca indignantly. "Bernard, do send someone to fetch it down!"

A Boy Scout paddling by on a twig seemed only too glad of the errand. So indeed seemed several more Boy Scouts: before you could say Baden-Powell half-a-dozen were scrambling up the ivy, and after some slight endeavor they returned to lay their trophy in Miss Bianca's lap. — It proved to be not paper after all, but linen, a long shred like a hem. *"Really!"* cried Miss Bianca. "To throw away paper napkins is bad enough, but to discard *linen* ones argues complete ir-responsibility! — Now, don't throw it back in the moat, Bernard; keep it till you see a bin."

At that moment the brass band struck up the mouse National Anthem.* All stood to attention, especially Bernard. It was time for Miss Bianca to return thanks; she rose, supported on Bernard's arm, and gracefully bowed. — She was additionally supported, of course, by the knowledge that she was looking her best: thanks to the lacy handkerchief not a hair was out of place. It also gave her rather the air of a court lady of the time of Louis the Fifteenth; and if half the mice present couldn't have told one Louis from the next, all instinctively applauded her aristocratic charm.

"Dear friends," began Miss Bianca, as soon as she could make herself heard, "pray believe that I do not exaggerate when I tell you this has been the happiest day of my life. I only hope it has been enjoyable to you too — "

"You bet it has!" cried one of the young dancers — who had actually got engaged to the mouse of his dreams halfway through Hickory-Dickory.

"So I see," smiled Miss Bianca, "by the set of your whiskers! You must invite me to the wedding! — But

* "Mice of the World, Unite." This is the solemn andante part. The chorus, allegretto, goes: "Cheese, cheese, beautiful cheese."

I hope we older, soberer folk have enjoyed this delightful excursion almost as much."

"Hear, hear!" cried all the mice.

"So that this picnic you have been good enough to arrange for me," continued Miss Bianca, "may ever remain as happy a memory to you all as it will to your grateful ex–Madam Chairwoman. Regretfully indeed I retire to private life — but warmed to the heart by your kindness!"

"Hear, hear!" cried all the mice again. Actually, some of the more conservative were rather glad Miss Bianca was retiring to private life. The Mouse Prisoners' Aid Society as a body were all for cheering prisoners in their cells — mouse-duty from time immemorial: Miss Bianca's revolutionary ideas of getting prisoners *out* was something else, and the adventures she'd led the Ladies' Guild into, for example, with this aim, many husbands still reprobated. Thus male voices in particular swelled the cheering, as Miss Bianca made her final bow and once more on Bernard's arm stepped lightly into a canoe to regain land and the returning mail van.

"It really has been a happy day!" sighed Miss Bianca gratefully. "Dear Bernard, I hope you have enjoyed it too?"

"Every minute," said Bernard sincerely. "Especially

as it means the end of your risking your life amongst jailers and bloodhounds."

"Of course you are quite right," agreed Miss Bianca. "I know myself that my nerves have become over-strained . . . What a happy day indeed!"

She cast a last backward glance, as the mail van moved off, towards the now deserted scene of revelry. Darkling lay the lily moat, yet still as beautiful as at noon; tall and slender rose the turret against the sun-set —

With, above its windowsill, *a second scrap of white replacing the first!*

2

All the way home Miss Bianca sat rather silent and preoccupied; but since most of the other mice were rather silent too, after their day's pleasuring, it wasn't remarked. Only Bernard glanced anxiously at her from time to time, and escorted her back to the Porcelain Pagoda with even more than his usual solicitude.

"Tomorrow I hope you'll take things very easily," said Bernard, as Miss Bianca untied the lace handker-chief from about her head and sank gratefully upon the chaise longue. "Let me get you a glass of milk."

"Thank you, no," said Miss Bianca, still in a preoccupied sort of way. "Bernard: that turret above the moat —"

"If you didn't like my calling it dilapidated, I'm sorry," said Bernard. "It's more like a Canaletto than any turret I've ever seen."

"Is that *all* you saw?" asked Miss Bianca.

"Well, yes," apologized Bernard. "You know I'm not very strong on Art . . ."

"This is not a question of Art, but of fact," said Miss Bianca gravely. "Bernard: I tell you that that turret above the moat *has a prisoner in it!*"

3

Bernard jumped. Then he smiled an indulgent smile.

"So that's what's been bothering you," he said. "Well, at least you haven't caught cold! Though why you should imagine any such thing —"

"I didn't imagine," interrupted Miss Bianca, "I *observed*. *I* observed, if you did not, a second signal fluttering at the window! — For so I am now convinced the first to have been; also no doubt *tied* to the bars (rather than blown against them) by some imprisoned hand within. Let me look!"

Reluctantly, with growing uneasiness, Bernard pulled the linen shred from his mackintosh pocket.

Before handing it over he took a quick look himself: quite plainly (and how unfortunately!) one end indeed showed the creases of a knot.

"I dare say some other picnic party tied it there, just for sport," he suggested. "Remember how our Scouts enjoyed the climb?"

But Miss Bianca was too busy examining the trophy even to consider this reasonable hypothesis.

"I was wrong," she murmured. "It isn't the hem of a napkin, it is the hem of a handkerchief. And with a name on it . . ."

" 'J. Fromage,' perhaps?" suggested Bernard, with a desperate attempt at facetiousness. But never was facetiousness iller-timed.

"No; not J. Fromage," said Miss Bianca quietly, "*Mandrake.*"

4

Bernard seized the scrap from her shaking hands; there, sure enough, the hateful name was still faintly visible.

"So he's got his deserts at last!" said Bernard grimly.

Miss Bianca nodded.

"One can see how it happened. The Grand Duchess would be angered to the last degree by his allowing the child to escape . . ."

23

"I dare say the turret belongs to her," agreed Bernard. "She owns all sorts of places she's let go to rack and ruin. — To think of Mandrake up there under the leads," said Bernard, with relish, "boiling in summer and freezing in winter, and probably starving all the year round! Well, at least no one's going to rescue *him!*"

To his astonishment Miss Bianca, whom he had naturally expected to share in his rejoicing, turned pale. — No doubt from shock, thought Bernard, or from the painful memories aroused; and added encouragingly that Mandrake was probably in leg-irons as well.

"I only fear so," said Miss Bianca gravely.

"You only *fear* — ?" began Bernard, astonished again; and paused, as an incredible suspicion dawned. "You don't — you can't — mean you think *Mandrake* ought to be rescued?"

"Indeed I do," said Miss Bianca.

5

"Of course he was completely odious," admitted Miss Bianca, some minutes later. (Bernard now pacing up and down as he always paced when thoroughly upset; as he'd paced until he wore a track in his postage-stamp carpet, Miss Bianca captive in the Duchess's palace.) "In fact, Mandrake was the most odious person it has ever been my lot to encounter —"

"Crueler than the Head Jailer," Bernard reminded her.

"There is nothing bad one can't say against him," admitted Miss Bianca. "He was the Grand Duchess's jackal —"

"Without a single kindly word for a poor defenseless orphan," reminded Bernard, tramping on.

"Exactly," said Miss Bianca. "You must know I hold no brief for him —"

"You held him in abhorrence," reminded Bernard.

"I still do," said Miss Bianca. "But confined as he is, what chance has he of reform?"

Bernard suspended his tramping to look at her. She appeared certainly rather fatigued, but in no way feverish . . .

"Let's get this straight," said Bernard, speaking very carefully. "You mean that *Mandrake* should be *rescued* in order to give him a chance to *reform?*"

"Well, he can hardly reform in a turret," pointed out Miss Bianca. "Who could?"

"What makes you," persisted Bernard, still very carefully, "think that he *would* reform? Have you any *grounds* for thinking he would?"

"No," said Miss Bianca simply. "I only hope."

For once Bernard lost all patience with her.

"Tell that to the Prisoners' Aid Society!" he exploded.

"Which is precisely," said Miss Bianca, "what I propose to do."

3

At the Moot-hall

THE NEXT MEETING in the Moot-hall took place
some three days later. Miss Bianca had meant to attend in any case, since not to do so, at the inauguration
of a new Madam Chairwoman, would have seemed
discourteous; and the very fact that she didn't much
care for her successor (a very tough games-mistress
mouse, in Miss Bianca's opinion far too fond of giving
orders) made her all the more punctilious. She had intended to sit as unobtrusively as possible, and certainly without speaking!

"But in such circumstances as these," thought Miss
Bianca, "I shall really *have* to speak; for Bernard won't,
and how else is Mandrake's case to be put forward?
For once, any refinement of good manners must go by
the board."

She still tried to *enter* the Moot-hall unobtrusively
— arriving, indeed, so early, it was only a quarter full.
An usher who attempted to lead her to a front match-

box she politely but firmly ignored, and sat down about the middle. To have sat down absolutely at the *back*, amongst the scuffling hobbledehoys eating popcorn, would have been conspicuous: Miss Bianca with her usual tact chose a place in just the right row (say about M), next to a short-sighted chemist. — He wasn't eating popcorn, but sucking lozenges, and politely offered one without recognizing her. Miss Bianca of course accepted it, though with but a smile; only the stone-deaf could have failed to recognize her *voice!* The flavor was perfectly innocuous, also there was a wrapping of silver paper, out of which she made a cocked hat while the Hall filled up. When upon her other side sat down a timid housewife who just said "Oh, my!" and relapsed into awestruck silence, Miss Bianca began to feel quite comfortable.

It still cost her a slight pang to see Bernard lead the new Madam Chairwoman out upon the platform. Miss Bianca had resigned of her own free will and didn't regret it; but there must ever be a sadness in seeing oneself supplanted. She stood up and applauded with the rest, however, and actually led a supplementary round, after Bernard's brief speech of introduction.

Then the new Madam Chairwoman made a speech. Her style was very different from Miss Bianca's: in curt, gruff tones she almost snapped out her thanks to the Society and Secretary for their confidence in her;

and was almost shouting, as she went on to adjure more general attention to physical fitness. (All incoming Chairwomen choose a special theme for their inaugural address. Miss Bianca's had been The Quality of Mercy.) As for *appearance*, Miss Bianca with the best will in the world couldn't help being critical: a pride in one's calling is entirely proper — but was it really necessary, wasn't it rather derogatory to the dignity of the Society, to appear on the platform in a *gym slip?*

However, all the mice seemed quite satisfied. ("The charm of novelty!" thought Miss Bianca wryly.) Some even sat up straighter on their matchboxes, under the games-mistress's harangue. It nonetheless went on far too long, and as the hobbledehoys at the back began to shuffle their feet about, Bernard seized the opportunity of a pause between two breaths to make a conclusion.

"Three cheers and thank you very much," interposed Bernard, stumping forward again. "I'm sure our new Madam Chairwoman's words will be taken to heart by one and all; now, since there is nothing on the Agenda save our welcome to her I propose the Meeting adjourns to supper. Any seconder?"

Half the front row shot up their hands. In another moment the meeting would have been over — which was exactly what Bernard intended. *He* had seen Miss

Bianca in row M, and hoped by this means to prevent her from courting a rebuff. But even as he reached for the Minute Book, Miss Bianca rose.

2

To do so required a considerable effort. Courtesy alone enjoined silence; also after having been given such a splendid picnic, any immediate further claim on the Society's notice smacked of a prima donna's post-farewell, positively-last-until-the-next reappearance. It was a true sacrifice Miss Bianca made, of elegance to altruism, as she rose and spoke.

"On a point of order," called Miss Bianca clearly, "may one raise from the floor a subject *not* on the Agenda?"

At once, at the sound of that famous silvery voice, every neck craned. Murmurings of "Look who!" and "She's here!" were heard on all sides.

"Well, I'm not sure —" began Bernard.

"Jolly well *out* of order, *I* should say," snapped the games-mistress.

But the mice applauded Miss Bianca so vigorously, there was no doubt of their wish to hear her, and even Bernard was so nettled by the games-mistress's tone, he made no attempt to overrule them but resigned himself to the inevitable.

"Thank you," said Miss Bianca. "Further to praise

31

our new Madam Chairwoman," she continued, "is obviously superfluous; but would it not be a happy thought to mark her inauguration, as it were with a white stone, by some distinctively heroic enterprise on the part of the Society as a whole?"

"Yes, yes!" "Go on!" "Tell how!" cried all the mice. Miss Bianca let them wait a moment.

"How little did we think," she began again, "dancing on the lily pads — on the occasion of that memorable picnic you were so kind as to offer me — that within the very turret that overlooked our revels, a prisoner still languished! How our gaiety must have mocked his ears! But such is the case; and what a glorious issue if, as a result, freedom should once more blossom for him like a splendid water lily!"

It must be admitted that half the members of the Society always listened to Miss Bianca simply spellbound by her beautiful delivery and exquisite choice of words. It was a sort of mass hypnotism, from which they awoke finding themselves committed to all sorts of surprising projects. But in this instance the magic had barely begun to work before the games-mistress, from the platform, broke in.

"Suggestion noted," barked the games-mistress. "Secretary, put it in the Minutes! — Can the speaker give any *particulars* of this prisoner? — such as his *name*, for instance?"

Far too soon, Miss Bianca had to.

"Mandrake," said Miss Bianca bravely. "His name is Mandrake . . ."

3

There fell a deathly silence. Every mouse in the Hall knew of Mandrake and how wicked he was. Ironically enough, it was Miss Bianca's own heroism, in rescuing an orphan from his and the Grand Duchess's clutches, that had made him so widely ill-famed! — Until now mothers scared bad children to obedience by the threat that Mandrake was coming for them . . .

Out of the silence rose a hiss.

Miss Bianca had never in her life been hissed before. For once she had to pause for words; her whiskers quivered. If only she'd been on the platform! How much easier, *from the platform*, Miss Bianca now realized, to sway the emotions of a Meeting! Quite a number of members couldn't even see her. But she had a place on the platform no longer, and in the moment while she paused to gather her resources the new Madam Chairwoman (having literally the upper hand) spoke again.

"The speaker's enthusiasm," she said loudly, "is I'm sure jolly creditable to her soft heart. I dare say a lot of *us* have soft hearts ourselves; but it needn't mean

33

having soft heads! — Anyway, I'll put it to the vote: all those in favor of rescuing the notorious criminal Mandrake, hands up!"

Not a hand was raised.

"Motion put," snapped the games-mistress, "no seconder, rejected nem. con.!"

4

"I knew how it would be," said Bernard sympathetically, as he walked back with Miss Bianca to the Porcelain Pagoda. (He should already have been heading the supper table, but he saw she wanted to get home, and couldn't bear to let her leave the Moot-hall alone.) "I knew you'd get no help from the Society."

"Nor from you either?" sighed Miss Bianca. "Not even from you, Bernard?"

"Nor from me neither," returned Bernard, reluctantly but doggedly. "Though our new Madam Chairwoman might have been more tactful, I'm bound to say I agree with her: to set Mandrake at liberty would be to loose a monster on the world. You have made a most gallant, if in my opinion misguided, attempt to interest the Society on his behalf; it has failed; so do, please, Miss Bianca, just forget him and give all your attention to your nerves, also to that slim volume of verse so eagerly awaited."

Miss Bianca sighed again. Then, very delicately, she shrugged her ermine shoulders.

"Thank you, dear Bernard," she said, "for your excellent advice. — Now surely they're waiting for you to serve the soup?"

With an unhappy look, off Bernard stumped; Miss Bianca entered the Pagoda. It was the first time they had ever parted so coolly.

POEM BY MISS BIANCA,
WRITTEN THAT SAME NIGHT

Alone in gloom the wretched prisoner writhes,
 Paying at last for all of evil done!
Yet is not Mercy still the strongest power
 To bring him back, repentant, to the sun?
                                    M. B.

She wrote another:

Alone the criminal? Lone too the hand
 Outstretched to rehabilitate and free!
No friend to aid — the heavy task unshared
 By e'en the Prisoners' Aid Society!
                                    M. B.

This was the first time Miss Bianca had ever been able to work the Prisoners' Aid Society into a poem, so she was naturally rather pleased. Even so, it was with a heavy heart and troubled mind that she at last sought repose between her pink silk sheets.

4

A Daring Adventure

BUT THOUGH Miss Bianca no longer had the backing of the Society, though even Bernard refused his aid, anyone who thinks she was going to abandon her project of rescuing Mandrake will be mistaken. However fragile her nerves, beneath Miss Bianca's ermine coat beat a heart of truest steel — compared with which combination an iron hand in a velvet glove is but peanuts.

Bernard, if not the new Madam Chairwoman, had nonetheless succeeded in raising several doubts in her mind. How *could* she be sure Mandrake would reform? Had she *grounds* even for hope? What if the ex-steward emerged from captivity wickeder than ever — a monster loosed upon the world indeed? The longer Miss Bianca considered these awkward questions, the more clearly she perceived it her duty to obtain reliable (and satisfactory) answers to them, before taking independent action.

Obviously the only person competent to supply such answers was Mandrake himself.

"We must have a good long talk together!" thought Miss Bianca next morning.

But how to reach him?

"The Scouts climbed the ivy," thought Miss Bianca daringly, "why should not I ?"

She enjoyed at this time unusual freedom of movement, because the Boy was having his tonsils out. Naturally Miss Bianca had accompanied him to the nursing home — and would gladly have remained with him; only the Matron, as absolute in goodness as the Duchess in badness, refused to let her. "Poor Miss Bianca!" said the Boy's mother kindly, as they drove home together. "I'm afraid you're going to be dreadfully lonely, all by yourself in your Porcelain Pagoda!"

Of course Miss Bianca *was* lonely. On the other hand, without the Boy's lessons to superintend, and his playtime to share, she had unusual freedom of movement. Moreover, the Boy's tutor had been given a holiday, and his mother, now that the Boy wasn't there, no longer paid her regular suppertime visit to the schoolroom. Thus nobody noticed when that evening Miss Bianca wasn't there either!

She had actually caught the last outgoing mail van at seven. (She knew from experience that it was always easier to contact a prisoner at night; and coming home from the picnic, while seemingly so preoccupied, had in fact committed to memory the whole of the timetable pinned up in the driver's cab.) Since the journey back would be at about midnight, she took with her a light wrap and a morsel of cream cheese.

It was rather a pleasant trip, through the darkling fields beyond the city; although now less tootful than silent, the driver being a trifle weary and disinclined for exuberance. He was also disinclined to make unnecessary speed; long before the turret above the lily moat came into view Miss Bianca had shared her provision with a homing field mouse — the simplicity of whose manners quite excused his appetite. "Come any time convenient, ma'am, and sup your fill with me and my missus!" urged the field mouse, gratefully licking his whiskers. "Just don't tell she what I lost amongst the thimble-riggers at the fair!" Miss Bianca smilingly accepted the invitation for some future date; dropped off at last at the letterbox by the park gate, made her way to the moat, and there blandished the first water rat she encountered into sculling her across to the turret's foot. "I shan't be very long!" promised Miss Bianca. "Why, didn't I see 'ee but last week, dancing the prettiest of all?" coughed the water rat. (All water rats are by occupation subject to bronchitis.) "Rely on I waiting so long as you care, ma'am!"

Pleased by this humble tribute, and with no jailerish sounds to dismay, Miss Bianca attacked the ivy quite gaily. It proved a less difficult ascent than she had feared, the main stems were so thick and the leaves so steady. To slip between the window bars presented no difficulty at all: within ten minutes from landing there stood Miss Bianca at the prisoner's side!

2

Mandrake it was indeed; though Miss Bianca hardly recognized him.

In the Diamond Palace, Mandrake, for all his wickedness, had always been clean and well shaven; dressed indeed rather richly — his close black tunic diamond-buttoned, his steward's chain diamond-studded, even a cast-off pair of the Duchess's diamond buckles ornamenting his shoes. What an alteration was now! Naturally the Grand Duchess, casting him into disfavor, had stripped him of every jewel: the lack of the buttons was the most obvious; without them Mandrake had been forced to hold his tunic together with lacings of ivy pushed through the holes on one side and on the other through the very cloth. His unbuckled shoes were similarly secured; while as though in pathetic remembrance of his old high office, a garland of withered ivy drooped about his neck . . .

But even these changes were as nothing compared

with the change wrought by the mat of long gray hair tangling first with his bushy eyebrows, then with a long gray beard. His face was scarcely visible; only the jutting beak of his nose identified him. Altogether, as he crouched upon an untidy pallet-bed, he looked far less like Mandrake the Duchess's cruel steward, than like some poor old hermit of the woods; or like a broken old tree hung with Spanish moss.

Mandrake for his part didn't recognize Miss Bianca at all. How should he? The child in the Diamond Palace had always kept her safe out of his way in an apron pocket.

"Let me introduce myself," said Miss Bianca gently. "I am Miss Bianca."

To her horror, Mandrake cringed. — There had been a time when she would have rejoiced to see him cringe; but not now. Now, before such a poor old man of the woods, Miss Bianca felt nothing but compassion.

"Sent by Her Grace?" whimpered Mandrake. "Of course, obviously sent by Her Grace! — otherwise how would you come to be here? Present Her Grace my humble duty," whimpered Mandrake, "even if she has but sent you, as I suspect, to eat up any little bit of food I was saving for my supper!"

His clawlike hands absolutely clasped to his breast — tried to conceal beneath his beard — a rough bowl half-emptied of some sort of disgusting porridge. Miss

Bianca was forced to close her eyes a moment; but as soon as she had recovered from the slight attack of nausea, mounted lightly beside him on the pallet.

"My good Mandrake," she said soothingly, "pray credit me when I assure you that I have come neither upon the bidding of the Grand Duchess, nor to share your interestingly frugal meal. Have you by any chance heard of the Mouse Prisoners' Aid Society?"

The reason Miss Bianca brought in the Society, which of course wished no part of Mandrake at all, was because she felt a diffidence about seeming to take too much on her own shoulders, as unbecoming to feminine modesty. In fact the reference proved a lucky one; Mandrake's expression, very slightly, brightened.

"The Mouse Prisoners' Aid?" he repeated wonderingly. "Long ago, when I was out in the world, I indeed heard such a Society spoken of, amongst ticket-of-leave men." (What circles he must have frequented, thought Miss Bianca!) "Aye, and a good work it did," continued Mandrake, "cheering and befriending the unfortunate! Can it really be that you are come to cheer and befriend poor Mandrake?"

Touched to pity as she was, Miss Bianca remembered the object of her visit.

"That depends," said she, rather sternly. "Also pray do not refer to yourself in the third person, as though you were Julius Caesar. 'Unfortunate' is a description

43

most wrongdoers apply to themselves: you, Mandrake, I fear have been *bad*. Your long service with the Grand Duchess is in itself a certificate of badness."

"I had no option!" pleaded Mandrake, beginning to whimper again.

"Quite so," said Miss Bianca. "Some crime committed in early youth — the details of which, believe me, I would rather not know — put you in her power. Had you but paid the penalty at the time, you would not now — at least I hope not — find yourself confined and starving within a ruined turret."

"From which I may never, never regain liberty!" groaned Mandrake.

"That depends again," said Miss Bianca. "How would you employ yourself, if you regained liberty?"

She gazed earnestly into his face — or what she could see of it, through the tangle of gray hair. Very much hung upon his answer: upon whether it spoke a mind truly repentant, or still corrupt!

There was a long silence.

"Would you return, for instance, if it were possible, to Her Grace's service?" asked Miss Bianca.

"Never!" groaned Mandrake.

"Then what *would* you do?" pressed Miss Bianca.

"Well, if I could, I'd go as gardener to an orphanage," said Mandrake.

3

Miss Bianca was so surprised, as well as pleased, by this unexpected yet promising reply, it was with but an eloquent glance of approbation that she encouraged him to proceed.

"You are right," continued Mandrake, "in saying that I have been bad; I've been bad all my life, but never badder than while in Her Grace's service I allowed how many a defenseless orphan to pine away, without a word, which I might so easily have spoken, of kindness! Though the last actually achieved escape — not that you can know anything of *that* —"

(Miss Bianca forebore to enlighten him!)

"— and though it was that very escape that brought about my undoing, the tears of her predecessors haunt me still. If ever I had my liberty again," sighed Mandrake, "and if any orphanage would receive me (without pay, just my keep), I'd make its garden the prettiest, and the fruitfullest, and the best to be played in, any orphanage ever knew!"

Again there was a silence — but briefer, more poignant — while with his long gray beard he wiped away the tears now streaming down his face. Miss Bianca herself was not dry-eyed: a shake of her whiskers sent as it were one last diamond to jewel the ex-steward's ivy chain.

46

"Say no more, Mandrake!" cried Miss Bianca. "You shall be not only cheered, and befriended: you shall be *rescued!*"

Mandrake flinched.

4

There was no doubt about it; he flinched. Instead of meeting her enthusiastic gaze, he looked away. Miss Bianca hoped that he was but temporarily overcome by joy; in the circumstance, it would have been quite natural! But his next words, uttered, or rather mumbled, in a low, despairing tone, showed that such was not the case.

"It's very kind of you indeed," mumbled Mandrake. "Very kind I'm sure . . . but considering Her Grace's extraordinary powers, perhaps it would be best to leave me where I am."

"What!" exclaimed Miss Bianca.

"You can see for yourself," said Mandrake — in tones which really should have been *more* despairing — "there's no *way* of rescuing me. These walls of solid marble admit neither ingress nor exit; while even could the ivy bear my weight, which it cannot, the window's too small for me to get out of. There's no *hope* of rescuing me."

"Then why did you tie a signal to the bars?" demanded Miss Bianca.

"Well, it gave me something to do," explained Mandrake. "But I never thought anything would come of it . . ."

Miss Bianca perceived that though the dream of becoming a gardener in an orphanage was undoubtedly very precious to him — had possibly saved his reason, as he mentally set seedlings, pruned an orchard, rolled a tennis court — when it came to translating that dream into reality, with all the hazards necessary to be faced before it *could* be so translated, Mandrake to put it mildly was unprepared for heroism.

For a moment she felt nothing but indignant contempt. Then she looked at his porridge bowl.

"My poor Mandrake," said Miss Bianca, "I see you have allowed yourself to lapse into complete melancholia; which is indeed not to be wondered at; you are sadly undernourished. Of course there must be some means of *ingress* at least! — or how could you receive any food at all?"

"I don't know," sighed Mandrake. "It just comes."

"But that is nonsense," argued Miss Bianca. "Food cannot just come — unless in the form of a rabbit from a hat, or an apple falling from a tree: in either case uncooked. That porridge you hold *has* been cooked, however badly; someone must have *brought* it to you."

"Then I have never seen them," said Mandrake. "I fall asleep at night, my bowl empty; when I wake in the morning, it is filled. In my opinion, it's by the Duchess's black magic."

Miss Bianca was really annoyed. If there was one thing she didn't believe in, it was magic. She was too rational and well balanced. Certainly she didn't believe in porridge materializing out of thin air!

"Mandrake," said Miss Bianca firmly, "tonight you must keep awake!"

"I can't," groaned Mandrake. "In the beginning, I tried to; but I never could. I suppose that's another of Her Grace's spells."

"Nonsense," said Miss Bianca bracingly. "It is because, I repeat, you are undernourished. 'Qui dort, dîne,' as they say in France! You must make one more effort."

"I'll try if you insist," sighed Mandrake. "But it won't be any use."

With growing concern Miss Bianca perceived that it wouldn't. Mandrake was beginning to nod already. The porridge bowl dropped from his hand and rolled away as flatter and flatter every moment Mandrake's gaunt, listless frame subsided on the pallet. Deplorable Mandrake! — incapable even of hope, equally incapable of self-help! Yet Miss Bianca did not abandon the potential gardener.

"There is nothing else to be done," thought Miss Bianca, "but that I should stay, and keep awake, myself!"

5

Consequences

FORTUNATELY IT IS quite easy for mice to keep awake at night. Night is the time when they by nature feel most active and alert. Miss Bianca took no credit to herself for her watchfulness; and not much for staying at all. Below a faithful water rat awaited, and if she didn't get back on the mail van she could always catch an early-morning milk cart. But she did wish Mandrake wouldn't snore so!

As the wind rose without and whistled through the ivy, each separate shrilling note was echoed by a positive blast from the ex-steward's hairy nostrils. Miss Bianca clasped her hands over her ears; then hastily dropped them again, fearful of missing some slight important sound. To occupy and distract herself she made a careful examination of each encircling wall. "For there *must*," argued Miss Bianca, "be *some* mode of entry! If only I knew more of architecture!"

But architecture was not yet among the Boy's studies, and Miss Bianca had never thought to take it up independently. Indeed, with all her other social and cultural activities, she could hardly have found time.

So as the night wore on, she just wrote a poem.

POEM BY MISS BIANCA,
WRITTEN IN MANDRAKE'S TURRET

Mandrake! Thou name once dreaded, now more meet
*   For scornful pity, than for righteous rage!*
How shall I ever get thee on thy feet,
*   To lead to some receptive orphanage?*

M. B.

She had barely completed the last line when the justice of her earlier speculations was dramatically confirmed by the sudden sliding into two parts of what had seemed a solid wall . . .

2

They slid apart, the two great marble slabs, so silently, Miss Bianca perceived at once why Mandrake never woke. — She still didn't suspect magic; she just appreciated the work of some very clever architect. Both the Grand Duchess and her late father the Grand Duke Tiberius had been known to employ the cleverest architects available, before beheading them.

51

Nor as the dwarfish bowlegged figure, carrying an iron pan, crept through, did Miss Bianca quail as at anything unearthly. In fact she recognized immediately one of the Duchess's criminal grooms. (Everyone in the Grand Duchess's household had been a criminal of some sort.) As he approached Mandrake's fallen bowl, he grinned. Grinning — and without even wiping it out first — he tipped in a new supply of porridge; and as swiftly and silently withdrew.

But not too swiftly for Miss Bianca! In the instant before the slabs kissed again — her tail actually brushing between — Miss Bianca had followed. There was no time to observe what machinery, what clever contrivance of weight and counterweight, operated; she could only follow — down a narrow circular staircase built within the thickness of the turret wall — down and down until at last she and her unwitting guide emerged together in a small malodorous apartment at ground level.

Probably it had once been the guard-room, when the turret formed part of a legitimate defensive stronghold. Now it looked more like a doss-house. Dirty blankets cumbered a floor otherwhere littered with empty tins, despite the summer heat a charcoal-burning brazier threw off fuggy fumes; while upon an old horsehair sofa with the stuffing coming out lolled a figure of definitely trampish, non-military aspect.

52

Miss Bianca recognized this figure also, as the second of the Grand Duchess's grooms.

"Duty done, George?" he yawned.

"Aye, duty done," grinned his comrade. "Thy turn tomorrow, Jack!"

"Which I must say will be a pleasure," grunted Jack. "Her Grace never put me upon a duty I liked more! — Were the tea leaves in, George?"

"Aye, and our nail-parings!" grinned George.

Miss Bianca shuddered. Even though she knew how harshly Mandrake had been used to treat the Duchess's grooms, she shuddered!

" 'Tis a marvel how the old chap holds out so long," mused George.

"The longer the better!" growled Jack. "The longer he lingers in misery won't thee and I be longer paid in idleness? 'Tis not as if he'd any chance of escape, that we need lose our sleep!"

"So you think!" cried Miss Bianca to herself. *"So you think!"*

But there was obviously nothing to be done at the moment, and the dreadfully stuffy atmosphere was beginning to make her feel quite faint. Fortunately she hadn't to climb down the ivy again to get away, she just slipped under the doorsill — and directly outside discovered in fact a narrow causeway linking the turret to the nearest shore. "My poor water rat!" thought Miss

Bianca remorsefully. "How long have I kept you unnecessarily from your bed!" But she still felt so confident of his faithfulness, she ran swiftly round the turret's base, and there indeed he was. "Pray forgive me!" apologized Miss Bianca. "I was unexpectedly detained!"

The mail van had passed hours before, but she successfully caught an early-morning milk cart, and was back in the Porcelain Pagoda before a footman brought her breakfast — no one having noticed her absence.

Except Bernard.

3

Bernard arrived while she was still sipping coffee. His peal at the gate was so violent (before he discovered that the footman had carelessly left it open), Miss Bianca fully expected to see the bell-pull in his hand.

"My dear Bernard!" she exclaimed, smiling. "Is the Moot-hall on fire?"

"No, it isn't!" shouted Bernard.

"Then good morning," said Miss Bianca. "May I offer you a cup of coffee?"

"Good morning! No thank you!" cried Bernard. "Miss Bianca, where *were* you?"

"When?" asked Miss Bianca innocently.

56

"Last night," said Bernard more moderately, and mopping his brow with his handkerchief. "I called just about one o'clock: when you didn't answer the bell I thought perhaps there was some banquet going on, so I waited. I waited," accused Bernard, "until a quarter to three."

"You must surely know," objected Miss Bianca, "that diplomatic banquets always break up ere midnight? My dear Bernard, did you think I was at a *stag party?*"

— Before his obvious distress, however, she put badinage aside. Indeed his concern touched her particularly, after the coolness of their last parting; Miss Bianca truly valued Bernard, and was only too happy to be on good terms with him again. At the same time, her very regard impelled her to conceal from him an activity which she knew he would disapprove, and which would worry him as well. So she just said she was very sorry, she had been not at home.

This was rather disingenuous of Miss Bianca. — The phrase "not at home" is disingenuous in itself; it means one *is* at home but doesn't want to be bothered by callers. On the other hand, convention has made it perfectly acceptable. So Miss Bianca was really misleading Bernard into comfortableness when she let him think she actually *had* been at home, in the Porcelain Pagoda, when the facts were far otherwise.

57

"If you went to bed early, I only hope my ringing didn't disturb you," apologized Bernard, looking relieved.

"I never heard it," said Miss Bianca — again rather misleadingly. "Now do let me give you that cup of coffee!"

But Bernard, much as he wanted to stay, had to hurry off to keep an appointment, and Miss Bianca, much as she appreciated his concern, was glad to see him go, for she had a great deal to think about.

4

It is difficult enough to rescue a prisoner in any case; but far more difficult still when the prisoner doesn't want to be rescued.

"Alas, poor Mandrake!" thought Miss Bianca. "Alas, poor cowardly but still repentant Mandrake! What *is* to be done about him?"

She curled up upon the chaise longue and meditated.

"Obviously he has been undernourished for years," reflected Miss Bianca. "It is not to be wondered that his whole system, nervous as well as physical, has completely collapsed. Therefore the first step, equally obviously, must be to build him up again to robustness and courage by means of a balanced diet."

This was entirely sensible. But there were still difficulties — such as how to introduce a balanced diet into a ruined turret heavily guarded.

"Perhaps a course of vitamin pills would do?" thought Miss Bianca.

Pills were small enough to be sent through the post. But she very much doubted whether his jailers allowed Mandrake to receive mail. What if George and Jack *intercepted* the pills — even ate them up themselves — and so became stronger and wickeder than ever? Nor did there seem any possibility of bribery — Mandrake in captivity as good as a pension to them!

"Still, they do not keep particularly good watch," thought Miss Bianca. "Neither observed Mandrake's signal at the window: that they did not observe me either, climbing the ivy, is perhaps understandable, for it was dark, and I trod with great precaution; but no more did they observe, by broad daylight, a whole troop of Scouts climbing up!"

The reflection brought not only comfort, it brought an idea. Miss Bianca was too tired to examine it thoroughly at the moment, but at least it enabled her to sink into a long, deep, much-needed sleep.

6

The Scouts

DURING THE DAYS that followed any curious observer might have found Miss Bianca taking a rather unusual interest in the Prisoners' Aid Society Boy Scout troop. — Actually every mouse in town *was* a curious observer, Miss Bianca being such a public figure; however, most just considered it very nice of her that upon relinquishing the proud position of Madam Chairwoman, she allowed her benevolent attentions to be so humbly engaged.

Only their mothers thought much of the Prisoners' Aid Society Scouts. They were rather a ragtag outfit and numbered but six all told.

It was easy to see how this had come about: a first excellent Scoutmaster emigrated, a second, fatally, encountered a weasel; a third just resigned — but hadn't been replaced, because on every Agenda at the Moothall the item "Scouts" always came last, when there usually wasn't even a quorum to decide what should be done. Only a young half-Irish mouse named Shaun held the troop together at all.

Miss Bianca not only reviewed the Scouts before church on Sunday — the first Church Parade they'd put on for months; she not only visited their down-at-heel headquarters in an old oilcan, and gave prizes for table tennis; she actually invited Shaun to tea in her Porcelain Pagoda. It caused quite a sensation. Not that Shaun himself (half-Irish as he was) appeared abashed. His half-grown whiskers shone with brilliantine, he was curry-combed all over, his mother had spent half the morning replacing all the badges on his armlet by clean new ones — with the addition of two or three he wasn't strictly entitled to wear, if only because there was no one to examine him for Proficiency. Altogether Shaun felt himself a very handsome boy-o indeed, and an ornament even to the famous Miss Bianca's famous dwelling!

Miss Bianca, sensibly perceiving that the first thing necessary was to cut him down to size, at once pressed upon him a slice of toast so thickly spread with patum peperium as to bring tears to his eyes. After a couple more slices (which his pride forbade him to refuse), young Shaun sat looking much more respectful.

"What a great many badges you have!" observed Miss Bianca. "One for Trap Recognition, I see, and actually *two* for Cat Evasion!" (Shaun wished his mother had been more careful; but he really was proficient at Cat-Evading.) "And another for Cross-Country Running!" continued Miss Bianca, who had of course made herself mistress of the whole system. "Dear me, with such an accomplished leader, why is it, I wonder, that the Society's troop is so little in evidence?"

"The Society's not interested in us, ma'am," replied Shaun, "that's the reason. Why, 'twas only upon the occasion of your ladyship's grand picnic we've been let participate in anything at all."

"But how useful you were then," said Miss Bianca kindly, "tidying up the turret above the lily moat!"

"Ah, think nothing of it, ma'am," said Shaun. "The lads enjoyed it uncommonly, as an Exercise. Would we could get more such! — but now here's the entire summer holiday near gone by, without so much as a night under canvas."

"A week still remains," said Miss Bianca thoughtfully. "Though it does not involve actual camping out, would your troop care to make the climb again, do you suppose?"

"Would they not!" said Shaun.

"*Regularly?*" pressed Miss Bianca. "Say every day, for a week?"

"For a month!" declared Shaun.

"A month must be out of the question," said Miss

Bianca, "for you will all be back at school; but if for just a week your cooperation is available, the next thing to do is to swear you to secrecy."

2

There is nothing in all the world a Scout loves better — and particularly a half-Irish Scout — than to be sworn to secrecy. Shaun's eyes glowed with dedicated fire. His half-grown whiskers quivered with enthusiasm. He swore himself to secrecy three times over. — Miss Bianca could hardly *stop* him swearing himself to secrecy, in order to explain her project. Then in few but well-chosen words she laid the matter before him.

Her plan was that the entire troop, each member with a vitamin tablet in his knapsack, should daily ascend the turret to build Mandrake up. Miss Bianca didn't think six tablets a day at all too many, considering the ex-steward's sad condition; also the company and regular visiting (as showing her interest no mere flash in the pan) she trusted would raise his spirits as the vitamins toned his system. At the end of a week, with *forty-two* tablets inside him, and probably a Campfire song on his lips, Mandrake should be ready to make a bid for freedom!

Actually, she said nothing to Shaun about the bid-for-freedom part, for it would almost certainly involve risks which when she thought of their mothers Miss Bianca was determined no Scout should run. She presented the matter simply as a junior branch of welfare work.

Even this was enough to delight Shaun. Here was an Exercise at last! — and Miss Bianca's reiterated warning that the Society was to be kept in ignorance of it delighted him even more.

"For they'd never let us Scouts participate at all," gloated Shaun, "if they knew!"

"I assure you the only reason why they *shouldn't* know," said Miss Bianca hastily, "is because this *particular* case of welfare work would overburden an already full program, and so cause fruitless mental distress." (As ex-Chairwoman she had to be loyal to the Society — and from old friendship to Bernard its Secretary.) "Otherwise, your gallant services, I know, would be a source of extreme pride."

"Ah, tell that to your granny!" said Shaun easily. "Wasn't I there at the Meeting? All our new Madam Chairwoman's interested in is the old one-two-three!"

Miss Bianca's heart quite warmed to him. If she could have wished for more true altruism — for more true compassion as regarded Mandrake — at least she had found an enthusiasm to match her own. All that was necessary was to keep it within bounds.

"You must on no account be away from home all day," said Miss Bianca, "during the last week of vacation. Take the mail van that leaves at two (after dinner), then catch the four-forty back, and you may all be home in time for tea. Moreover there is no need to hire boats; on the further side of the turret you will find a causeway; pray keep off the water altogether!"

Shaun promised that her instructions should be followed to the dot, and went off whistling like a stormcock.

3

Miss Bianca supplied the vitamin tablets from the medicine chest in the Ambassador's bathroom: his wife, the Boy's mother, had so often complained that the Ambassador practically lived on them, Miss Bianca felt no scruple about half-emptying four or five small bottles. Some were for the nerves, others for the blood, others again for General Lassitude; all quite peculiarly apt, thought Miss Bianca, for the building up of Mandrake!

It was an interesting scene indeed, as she distributed the first issue to the Prisoners' Aid Society Boy Scout troop assembled in their dilapidated oilcan. Shaun, with his instinct for stage management, made a proper ceremony of it: each Scout in turn stepped up to Miss Bianca (standing on a cotton-reel), saluted, shook hands, received his tablet, and saluted again. Then all buckled their tablets into their knapsacks, and Shaun led Miss Bianca round to inspect them. The Scouts enjoyed every moment.

"Now three cheers for her ladyship!" cried Shaun.

"Hip, hip, hooray!" shouted all the troop — making a quite respectable volume of sound, considering that none of their voices had broken. — Their coats, too, were still half-woolly; Miss Bianca, surveying them, felt a momentary qualm. But it was only a run up the ivy she asked of them, which they had achieved once already without accident . . .

"Thank you," said Miss Bianca gracefully, "not only for your kindness to myself, but also for your generous

endeavors in a cause so near to every mouse's heart.
— Shaun," she added, in an undertone, "mind they
are all back for tea! You'd better come to the Pagoda
and report."

Then all the Scouts cheered again and marched off
in Indian file.

4

Miss Bianca herself did not spend the afternoon
idly. There is little point in rescuing a prisoner if when
at liberty he has nothing proper to do and nowhere
proper to go: Mandrake's ambition of turning orphanage gardener was on both counts quite ideal, but all
the more essential was it therefore to find some such
establishment willing to accept his services. There was
only one orphanage Miss Bianca could lay her hand
on — a large bleak building in the center of the city,
but with at least two acres of grounds. Thither she
made her way; and was soon in conversation with a respectable mole.

"What a very charming orchard!" exclaimed Miss
Bianca. (They met beneath a Granny Smith.) "But
are not the trees — forgive me if I show my ignorance!
— a little in need of *pruning?*"

"Aye," said the old mole. "In need of pruning they
be indeed!"

Miss Bianca strolled on towards a herbaceous border.

"And your perennials, what a blaze of color! — shouldn't some by now have been *cut down*," suggested Miss Bianca, "in preparation for the autumn?"

"So they should indeed!" said the old mole, trotting after her. He was greatly impressed by Miss Bianca's fur coat, which surpassed even his own.

"And a tennis court!" exclaimed Miss Bianca. "How delightfully situated, and what a pleasure, I'm sure, to all your little guests! — But shouldn't it be *rolled* more often?"

Here she was treading upon delicate ground indeed, since to moles as a race even the Center Court at Wimbledon would be improved by a few neat molehills. But this particular old mole had been so long connected with an orphanage, he saw things quite from an orphan's point of view.

"Aye, so it should," he agreed. "Poor young critters, sometimes the ball rises so unexpected-like, they give 'emselves black eyes wi' their own bats. Trouble is, ma'am, we're shorthanded."

"Ah!" said Miss Bianca.

"Matron tells she can't afford a gardener not nohow," grieved the mole, "wi' the price of e'en bare bread so high. What *I* say is, what of all the apple jam that could be got, were our trees but properly tended?"

"So that any conscientious gardener, *unpaid,* would find a welcome here," suggested Miss Bianca, "whatever his background?"

"Lady, only find we such a one," said the mole earnestly, "and I'll warrant Matron content wi' no foreground neither!"

"You encourage me extremely," said Miss Bianca. "Pray forgive me for intruding upon your valuable time."

7

Good and Bad

R EALLY, EVERYTHING'S going quite beautifully!"
thought Miss Bianca.

Evening by evening Shaun arrived punctually at the
Porcelain Pagoda to report all members of the troop
safe home and having tea. ("I hope their mothers don't
miss them too much," asked Miss Bianca anxiously,
"away as they are all afternoon?" But Shaun said everyone's mother was looking a month younger.) He himself showed a disposition to linger, especially after
Miss Bianca, on the first occasion, rewarded him with
a slice of toast and patum peperium. (She in fact
offered toast and shrimp paste, but Shaun, who seemed
to regard the patum as a personal challenge, asked for
it particularly.) He also reported the prisoner Mandrake in increasingly good shape, and knocking back
vitamin pills like billy-o.

Miss Bianca was specially glad to hear this — even
so slangily expressed — because it had occurred to her
that Mandrake, in his pathologically suspicious state,

might have regarded the pills as poison sent by the Grand Duchess; but it appeared that Shaun's reference to the Prisoners' Aid Society had at once reassured. "The first couple went down a bit queasily," admitted Shaun, "but now Himself can't hardly wait, for the next issue!"

"And they are really doing him good?" pressed Miss Bianca.

"He's not the same man," Shaun assured her. "Why, if your ladyship could see him this minute, you'd take him for a proper Hercules!"

Even allowing for Irish exaggeration, if even half what Shaun said was true Miss Bianca really wondered whether she shouldn't write the pill-makers a testimonial!

Actually Shaun didn't report quite *everything* that happened, on the Exercise. He omitted, for instance, the hair-raising moment when the youngest member of the troop lost his footing on the ivy and plopped head-first into the lily moat. All the other Scouts enjoyed this incident extremely, it offered such a wonderful opportunity to practice first Lifesaving, then Artificial Respiration; each looked forward to two new badges for his armlet (awarded on the spot by Shaun). The young mouse was none the worse, though the vitamin pill in his knapsack dissolved and had to be reconstituted with chewing gum.

No more did Shaun report the equally hair-raising
episode of the bat. It was he himself who encountered
this uncanny creature, hanging upside down and
sound asleep under the window ledge. Shaun had
never seen a bat before, and the disconcerting physical resemblance to one of his own race, but *with wings,*
so startled him, he almost followed his junior into the
moat. — He slipped, he slid; only a particularly thick
leaf cluster saved him — while the Scouts behind,
alarmed at their leader's sudden declension, began
to run back down the ivy in near panic. To avoid a

73

complete débâcle Shaun had absolutely to awake and ask the bat to move — who, equally startled at seeing one apparently of *his* own race *without* wings, flittered off shrieking into the unaccustomed daylight. The entire troop thought they'd seen a ghost (as it were poor Aunt Maggie turned into an angel), and in the ensuing discussion Shaun accidentally blacked someone's eye . . .

In fact, there were several exciting episodes Shaun didn't report to Miss Bianca. But after whatever adventures the Scouts always got home to tea; and Mandrake punctually received his six tablets per day; so that everything really *was* going quite beautifully.

Which was more than could be said of the parent Society!

2

Not that under its new Madam Chairwoman the Mouse Prisoners' Aid Society had ceased to function — on the contrary. It was functioning more vigorously than ever: only not on traditional lines.

The games-mistress was so energetic, she called a General Meeting every single night; but then took all Minutes as Read, and gave short talks on physical culture, followed by exercises for each age group. Younger members touched their toes and vaulted, the elders

performed easy rhythmic movements; it was all very well thought-out and useful, but a decided change. Miss Bianca personally welcomed an excuse not to attend (she was already so slender and agile, no one expected it of her), but she felt very sorry for Bernard, who had to.

"Do you perform easy rhythmic movements too, Bernard?" she inquired curiously.

"No, I don't," growled Bernard. "We settled *that* in Committee."

"And in Committee, how do you get on with our new Madam Chairwoman?" asked Miss Bianca.

"Horribly," said Bernard. "She bosses everyone about."

" 'Tis an *esprit*, one must admit, *un peu fort*," said Miss Bianca. "But then what energy, and dedication! Also you must remember that she was voted to the Chair quite unanimously, which naturally gives her confidence."

"Who else was there to vote for?" asked Bernard wearily. "When you wouldn't carry on (though don't for a moment think I wanted you to), who else was there? I can't remember when we've had such a poor lot of ladies — that is, in an executive sort of way. We wanted someone who could speak up and was used to running things — and by George we've got her!"

He directed a passing kick at a flowerpot. (This

76

particular conversation took place in the Pagoda grounds, the gate of which he happened to be strolling by when Miss Bianca came out to water her plants.)

"But what is worst of all," continued Bernard, "and setting aside all personal discomfort, is that she's diverting the Society from its true aims. We're not to cheer and befriend prisoners any more, let alone rescue 'em; we're just to take a millimeter off our waists!"

Miss Bianca listened with growing concern. Whatever her own criticisms of her successor (and though she couldn't help feeling a *little* pleased that Bernard now evidently shared them), the interests of the Society lay ever close to her heart. It had been amongst the most famous branches of the whole international organization — one of its decorations ranking above both the Jean Fromage Medal and the Tybalt Star for Gallantry in Face of Cats. The thought of its now declining to a mere gymnastic course was painful indeed.

"The promotion of physical fitness," said Miss Bianca, after a moment's pause, during which she tied up a daisy, "is of course entirely admirable; but surely there must be *some* captive on the Agenda?"

(She phrased the question as discreetly as possible, in case Bernard should think she was bringing up Mandrake again. But Bernard, originally reassured by her silence on the subject, and then what with all his other troubles, had in fact forgotten Mandrake's existence.)

77

"If you mean, isn't the Society keeping an eye on the Police files," said he, "I'm afraid the answer's no. I don't know whether you recall the name of our contact there — "

"Tubby Embonpoint," supplied Miss Bianca.

"Exactly," said Bernard. "Our new Madam Chairwoman can't stand the sight of him. Every report poor old Tubby brings in she simply won't let him stay to read — and then as soon as he's gone just tears up. I can see you think me pusillanimous," added Bernard unhappily, "for not making a flaming row about it; but with attendances falling off as they are, I feel that a united front on the platform must at all costs be preserved."

"There is that, certainly," said Miss Bianca.

"So I suppose I must just soldier on," said Bernard, with a sigh, "and hold things together as best I can until her term of office ends next year . . ."

3

"One, two, three and touch your toes!" shouted the games-mistress. "All in front swing right, swing left!"

The by now diminished assembly in the Moot-hall more or less obeyed. At the back there was a good deal of horseplay; in front several of the more elderly mice just sat down. Bernard, who on the platform had been sitting down all the time, continued sedentary. "Goodness me!" shouted the games-mistress. "What a slack lot you all are! Now let's try the one-two-three again!"

The response was so poor, however, even she saw it was time to break up. After their first enthusiasm the mice were already tired of being bullied; in the jostle at the exit more than one was heard to mutter something about this being *the last time,* while others muttered things like *"Never again unless there's nothing on the telly,"* or *"Not unless your sisters drop in . . ."*

So the Meeting broke up. Bernard only hoped and prayed that the whole Mouse Prisoners' Aid Society wasn't breaking up too!

8

The Plan

BY CONTRAST, as has been seen, everything in Miss Bianca's own private maverick branch was going quite beautifully; yet oddly enough it was for this very reason that she began to lose sleep again.

Looking ahead to the actual *rescue* of Mandrake, she perceived the time almost ripe. The ex-steward had indeed been built up far more swiftly than she anticipated; and she had found future employment for him so easily! Truth to tell, Miss Bianca was caught unprepared, and had as yet no proper plan of rescue at all; and her pink silk pillows fell to the floor, and her pink silk sheets crumpled, as she tossed and turned trying to think of one.

"He cannot be got out through the window," thought Miss Bianca, "for besides being barred, it is too small; nor if he could is the ivy capable of bearing

his weight. There is of course the stairway, only I don't
know how to work the machinery! Mandrake would
need to be swift indeed, to slip between those two great
blocks on the heels of George or Jack! — and even if
he should succeed, would not George, or Jack, observe
him, and immediately summon the aid of Jack, or
George?"

However much Mandrake might have been built up
on vitamins, neither George nor Jack had looked in

need of building up; and they had the advantage of numbers.

"Really, one scarcely knows where to *begin!*" thought Miss Bianca.

Yet after too long a delay — the Scouts having ceased their ministrations and gone back to school — might not the effect of the vitamins *wear off*, and Mandrake sink back into General Lassitude?

Or supposing the orphanage found another gardener?

These were troubling thoughts indeed, and more than once Miss Bianca longed for Bernard's sensible advice and masculine support. But she was resolved to make no further attempt on his sympathies — not from pride, but because she recognized that from his own point of view (believing Mandrake such a monster) Bernard was right; and though fully aware of her power over him not for worlds would she have *wheedled* him into doing anything against his conscience. Besides being a perfect lady, Miss Bianca was also a perfect gentleman.

When Bernard anxiously remarked on her distrait air, she told him she was correcting proofs — always a very trying occupation.

"Your slim volume of verse?" said Bernard respectfully. "Put me down for six copies."

Actually Miss Bianca *was* preparing her poems for the press, but so preoccupied was she with the ex-steward's fate, even though the printers waited she kept breaking off to write new ones. Such as —

POEM WRITTEN BY MISS BIANCA WHEN SHE
OUGHT TO HAVE BEEN CORRECTING PROOFS

O Mandrake, on thy feet at last,
    Shall I not call thee rather Hercules?
Employment waits, thy crimes are past,
        Come forth to prune th' expectant shrubs and
        trees,
Come forth to tend each sweet neglected flower!
— But how to free thee from thy horrid tower?

                                        M. B.

2

She was actually thus engaged when Shaun came to make his penultimate report. It was so identical with all those preceding — every Scout safe home, Mandrake in fine fettle — Miss Bianca really didn't pay much attention. Shaun's lingering rather irritated her. He'd wolfed down quite four slices of toast spread with patum, of which he could now swallow any amount without a choke, but even so he still lingered while Miss Bianca rustled her papers about with a pre-occupied air.

"Only another two days before school," observed Shaun conversationally.

"Time flies indeed," agreed Miss Bianca — but rising from her desk to give him a hint.

Shaun didn't take it. From his now-customary position on the foot of the chaise longue he regarded her brightly.

" 'Twasn't so much that I was thinking of," said he. "What *I* was thinking of was, isn't it about time we set about planning the rescue?"

Miss Bianca's whiskers quivered with surprise. — Also with dismay: she had been so particularly careful to give the Scouts no hint of what their Exercise was really leading up to! It was far too dangerous! (Of course she didn't know about the Lifesaving or the bat, or she would have thought even the welfare part too dangerous.)

"My dear boy," exclaimed Miss Bianca, as lightly as she could, "whoever put such an idea as *that* into your head?"

"Why, Himself, of course," said Shaun. "Ever since he's been feeling a bit more lively he talks of nothing else but your ladyship's promise to rescue him . . ."

"Oh, dear!" thought Miss Bianca. "O foolish, irresponsible Mandrake, to babble so!" But upon a moment's reflection she saw the injustice of the charge: she hadn't *warned* Mandrake to keep his mouth shut.

84

"It is I who have been irresponsible!" Miss Bianca chided herself. Still, she couldn't deny her promise, for that would have made Mandrake out a liar.

"Indeed, rescued he is to be," she admitted cautiously. "But *your* part in the undertaking has already — and how gallantly! — been played, by supplying him with vitamin pills, without which he could never have found strength to cooperate. The actual rescue itself must be left to older heads."

"Then your ladyship won't be taking part either?" suggested Shaun — O the Irish flatterer!

"Naturally I shall," corrected Miss Bianca (though concealing a smile). "But whatever plan is adopted, you, I repeat, will have no share in it, nor any other Scout; so please don't bother me now."

Shaun sighed.

"No doubt your ladyship has a grand scheme already prepared?" he said respectfully. " 'Twould be a treat to hear it."

"I think you had perhaps better remain in ignorance," said Miss Bianca severely.

"Ah, come on!" cajoled Shaun. "Didn't we climb the ivy? And amn't I sworn to secrecy? Tell just the first step."

Miss Bianca hesitated. But he really deserved *some* reward, and his gaze was so very respectful, she felt she could easily satisfy him with a few generalities.

85

"Well, of course the *first* step," said Miss Bianca, "is to lead Mandrake forth from his turret-chamber . . ."

"By the stairway," supplied Shaun intelligently.

3

Miss Bianca sat down again. If she had been surprised and dismayed before, she was now even more so! — and really needed something behind her back.

"How can *you* know of the stairway?" she cried. "Coming back as you do on the four-forty van?"

"Isn't there another out at seven?" said Shaun. "I've been returning on my own several nights past, to see just what goes on. And as the window's too small, let alone being barred, the stair hasn't it got to be?"

"Exactly so," said Miss Bianca. "It was what I had decided upon myself. — I'm afraid you have far exceeded your instructions."

"Mine's an inquiring disposition," explained Shaun. " 'Tis a pity George, or Jack, carries that porridge up so late."

"What, have you encountered them also?" cried Miss Bianca. "The Duchess's criminal grooms?"

"I thought they'd been grooms," agreed Shaun. "Can't you always tell a groom, by the cut of his legs? A pair of rough tough boy-os they are too!"

"Which is all the more reason," said Miss Bianca —

striving to regain command of a conversation so unexpectedly developing — "why neither you nor any of the Scouts should have business with them. Suppose Mandrake indeed enabled to make his escape down the stairway at dead of night —"

"I'd say, better by day," interrupted Shaun. "I'll tell why later."

"— he would still find George, or Jack, on guard below," pointed out Miss Bianca, "and what could even the whole troop do, against such ruffians?"

"A couple of kicks might well make a mash of the lot of us," agreed Shaun. (Miss Bianca shuddered.) "Therefore their attention must by no means be attracted, at the crucial moment, but rather diverted. As to which," said Shaun, without false modesty, "I've a very fine scheme myself — if your ladyship would care to hear it."

Again Miss Bianca hesitated; though this time more briefly. Shaun was looking more conceited every minute, and he was quite conceited enough already; but at whatever damage to his character Miss Bianca, having still no clear idea herself how to set about rescuing Mandrake, couldn't afford not to listen to even a Boy Scout who *had*. She even sketched an inviting gesture towards the patum-pot. Shaun took a spoonful neat.

"Pray proceed," said Miss Bianca. "The distracting of George's and Jack's attention I agree highly desirable; I myself could easily get them seats to a Symphony Concert, or even to the Opera; but since I doubt whether they are musical, any suggestion, or opinion, you may contribute, will interest me extremely."

"Well, in my opinion," said Shaun, "the answer's horses."

4

"Horses?" repeated Miss Bianca blankly.

"Aren't they grooms?" explained Shaun. "What groom could ever resist the sight of a fine horse? A string of racehorses exercising in the park, what groom could resist nipping out to take a look? For an hour at least I'd warrant neither George nor Jack on duty — especially were Sir Hector in the lead!"

Miss Bianca listened with increasing attention. Though no race-goer, even she had heard of Sir Hector. He was the great national favorite, beloved by all for the regularity with which he brought small odds-on dividends to many a humble pocket. Even citizens who sensibly didn't bet at all turned out just to admire his majestic stride past the winning post. No jockey had ever pulled him; the only one who ever tried to Sir Hector contemptuously threw at the first fence — and then, such was his magnanimous nature, stood protectively above while the rest of the field thundered by.

"I should quite like to see Sir Hector myself," confessed Miss Bianca. "Also I begin to perceive why any hour of darkness is unsuitable."

"Six A.M. it must be at the earliest," said Shaun. "Sir Hector's never out exercising sooner. Any move on Himself's part in the meantime would attract attention for sure! — In my opinion, those great sliding slabs must be jammed apart overnight."

To Miss Bianca's eager but prudent inquiry *how,* Shaun at first easily replied, by the bodies of the entire troop, after which all could be buried together in one heroes' grave. But upon her pointing out how much this would distress their mothers he thought again, and suggested employing Mandrake's porridge bowl instead. Especially with a fresh supply of porridge spilling forth Shaun promised it fatal to any delicate machinery whatever; and he himself undertook to roll it instantly into place on the heels of Jack, or George.

"Neither of whom ever look back," gloated Shaun, "to see does the wall close or no. They're too confident altogether! As they gape after Sir Hector on the morrow, old Mandrake may stroll down the stair at gentlemanly ease!"

Miss Bianca was beginning to feel almost confident herself. She was still more experienced in prisoner-rescuing than Shaun.

"I don't know that I'd advise *strolling,*" said Miss

Bianca. "There is ever the slip between cup and lip; Mandrake must make all speed possible towards the park gate, where halts a city-bound milk cart."

"Trust your ladyship to look so far ahead!" said Shaun admiringly. "Without your ladyship I'm sure we'd get nowhere at all!"

Miss Bianca smiled. She knew she was being flattered; all the same, half her cares seemed lifted by Shaun's resourcefulness, as a proper plan took shape at last!

A doubt occurred nonetheless.

"Surely Sir Hector," she suggested, "does not usually exercise in public? Has he not — of course I know nothing about racing; one merely picks up a phrase! — his own private Gallops to exercise upon?"

For the first time Shaun hesitated.

"True enough," said he, "and very fine and private Gallops they are. — Just for this once, he'd have to be persuaded to make a change . . ."

"And who is to persuade him?" asked Miss Bianca nervously.

"Why, your ladyship, of course!" said Shaun.

5

Thus it was upon Miss Bianca's shoulders that rested the first, cardinal preliminary to Mandrake's rescue: that of inducing Sir Hector (whom she didn't even know by sight) to change the venue of his morning exercise from his own private Gallops to the parkland about the turret. Upon this all else depended.

"Oh, dear!" thought Miss Bianca. "I suppose I'd better call on him tomorrow!"

9

Sir Hector

THE BOY WAS still in his nursing home: no one noticed Miss Bianca's absence next morning, from the Porcelain Pagoda, as in the back seat of an Attaché's sports car she drove towards Sir Hector's famous establishment. (A taste for racing, on the part of his Attachés, the Ambassador rather frowned upon. Miss Bianca, having herself made free with the Ambassador's vitamin pills, felt in no position to be censorious.) The Attaché in question was actually lunching at the stables — so she had plenty of time in which to operate.

There was thus no occasion for flurry; but in fact Miss Bianca did feel just a *little* flurried. For a single lady to pay an uninvited call upon a perfectly strange single gentleman was a complete breach of etiquette: behavior not only unconventional, but almost bold; and Miss Bianca habitually reserved her boldness for such situations as fleeing from bloodhounds. Nor did

the first sight of Sir Hector's domain do anything to pro-
mote female confidence. All good racing stables are
beautifully kept — posts and chains whitewashed,
each stall immaculate — and this one was so particularly; wherever the eye rested, not a flake of paint
scaled, not a single blade of grass (in the center patch)
fell below or rose above the general accurate level; but
more characteristic still was the air of peculiarly masculine peace that brooded over all. Miss Bianca felt as
though she had intruded upon a very good Club —
such as the Athenæum in London.

Cautiously she advanced through the silent, dinner-
time-empty yard. Not an equine head showed, above
the half-doors of the stalls; over each, however, was
written the name of its occupant — Nutmeg, Galga,
Coquette; Patches, Timotheus, Golden Boy — so that
at least she was in no danger of calling on the wrong
person, always a very awkward thing to do. Sir Hector's stall was the ultimate, superior in size to all the
rest, and if possible more immaculately kept. The other
names were painted in black on white, but Sir Hector's
in letters of gold.

"I wonder what is the correct procedure?" thought
Miss Bianca.

There was no bell, or knocker, with which to attract
attention. She had of course a visiting card with her,
but mouse-size visiting cards are so small, she feared

that if she just slipped it under the door Sir Hector might not notice it — or he might even tread upon it. "Really, a person of such consequence should have a butler!" thought Miss Bianca quite crossly. — In fact, it was rare indeed for Sir Hector to be left so unattended, but all the common grooms were at their meal, and his own special groom had slipped out to visit a sick aunt. (With Sir Hector's leave: it was a mystery in the stables how explicitly the two communicated, but they did.) Miss Bianca was not aware of all this, so her censure was perhaps justified. But however in favor of the conventions, she wasn't bigoted about them, and however much she would have preferred to be properly announced, she had small hesitation in slipping her person, rather than her card, under the sill.

— For a moment, it seemed as though she emerged beneath a great golden waterfall. Crinkly and bright, silken-shiny and rustling, the glorious wave poured down and almost blinded her. — Was it a waterfall, or was it fireworks? — It was neither. It was Sir Hector's tail.

2

Nor did the rest of his person prove less breathtaking in handsomeness. Sir Hector stood seventeen hands high; beneath a skin soft as a lady's glove his splendid muscles rippled with easy virile power. His mane, unlike his free-flowing tail intricately plaited, lent a touch of dandyism that but enhanced this masculinity — like the knot of ribbons at a Cavalier's shoulder. His ancestral Arab blood showed in a short, strong, superbly flexing neck — swanlike for grace, bull-like in strength; while his eyes for topaz brilliance matched Miss Bianca's own!

For a moment Miss Bianca was quite overcome. Then, carefully skirting the most majestic forelegs imaginable, she ran lightly up upon Sir Hector's manger, and halted but an inch from his equally majestic nose.

"Pray pardon the intrusion," said she, a trifle breathlessly. "Also be assured that only on business of extreme urgency would I venture to disturb you. Let me introduce myself: I am Miss Bianca."

However much surprised, Sir Hector was far too well-bred to show it. Considering that he had just waked up from a sound sleep, his answering words displayed in fact not only his breeding, but also uncommon presence of mind.

"A lady I have long desired to meet," said Sir Hector courteously. "Miss Bianca's distinguished services to humanity have made her famous indeed!"

Miss Bianca, who never lost poise for more than a

moment, accepted the compliment with a modest bow.
— Anything else would have been hypocritical; she
knew she was famous, just as Sir Hector knew *he* was
famous; but by an accompanying smile and little shake
of the head she managed to imply that *he* was *more*
famous. If this sounds complicated, it was quite easy
to Miss Bianca, with her long training in diplomatic
circles, where volumes can be spoken by a raised Ambassadorial eyebrow.

As for Sir Hector, he was immediately reassured that
Miss Bianca hadn't come to ask for racing tips (as even
the finest ladies had been known to do) and added that
he much regretted not being able to offer her a proper
seat. Miss Bianca with equal politeness replied that she
always preferred to stand. "As I believe you do yourself?" said Miss Bianca. "Also I shall not detain you
long!" "The longer the better!" said Sir Hector.

Actually Miss Bianca already felt that she would like
to stay a very long time indeed. She felt there were all
sorts of things she and Sir Hector could talk about —
such as the *burden* of fame, and what to do when
people wanted one's autograph. (She could never dis-
cuss such problems with Bernard, because Bernard's
autograph was never wanted save on receipts for Prisoners' Aid Society dues. This was dreadfully unfair
to Bernard, who had been quite wonderfully heroic in
the Black Castle, for instance; the trouble was that he

lacked personality. Both Miss Bianca and Sir Hector had outstanding personalities.) But however enjoyable such a conversation, it wouldn't have been to the point; and Miss Bianca fully realized that she *was* disturbing Sir Hector's noontime repose. If he had a race that afternoon, how many humble wagers might not be put in hazard, through its lack! On the other hand, the topic of Mandrake did need a little leading up to; and in the slight pause that followed Sir Hector spoke again.

"My own family tree boasts a famous lady also," said he, "though but collaterally. Her name was — Rosinante."

"The coadjutator of Don Quixote?" supplied Miss Bianca swiftly.

"Perhaps you have seen her portrait?" said Sir Hector, with a smile. "Dear me, she'd hardly have won a Selling Plate! But it is the spirit that counts, even more than the bone; and it seems she had great magnanimity."

Miss Bianca siezed the opening.

"Which I am sure has been transmitted to every branch of the connection!" cried she. "You encourage me to be frank!"

And as briefly as possible she laid before him her whole plan.

3

Sir Hector listened with grave attention. Miss Bianca's task was in one way made easier because he already knew who the Grand Duchess was — a person whose wicked designs deserved thwarting whenever possible; less fortunately, he also knew who *Mandrake* was. As soon as he realized the object of Miss Bianca's benevolence, Sir Hector's brow darkened. Just like Bernard, he seemed positively to *approve* the ex-steward's incarceration! — and for all Miss Bianca's eloquence remained unmoved.

"My dear little lady," he pronounced at last, "you do not know, and I am happy to think it, the depths of human depravity. There is no more chance of Mandrake's true repentance than of my being beaten by a rank outsider."

"But he *has* repented!" protested Miss Bianca. "His ambition now is to become a gardener! Does not *that* show true repentance? — Did not Lord Bacon, the great English jurist, aver gardening the purest, the most *innocent,* of all human pleasures — or occupations?"

"If I remember my history," said Sir Hector, "Lord Bacon was no innocent himself. Much as it grieves me to disappoint you —"

"You disappoint me indeed!" cried Miss Bianca,

quite passionately. "As I am sure you would disappoint the Lady Rosinante also! She, I am convinced, would have heard my appeal with more sympathy!"

A small globule, like a dewdrop, rolled along one whisker and fell sparkling upon her silvery fur. — Miss Bianca hadn't meant to cry; if there was one argument she disdained to employ it was the unfair female argument of tears. She simply couldn't help herself; and immediately wiped her eyes with her tail. This can be a very graceful gesture, when elegantly performed, which was of course how Miss Bianca performed it, though quite unconsciously.

"Pray pardon my emotion," she apologized, with dignity. "My nerves are somewhat overwrought; I should

tell you that I am also in the middle of correcting proofs. Pray forgive me, too, for disturbing your repose. Perhaps one day I shall have the pleasure of seeing you on the racecourse; in which case, I assure you, I shall wear my very best hat!"

It wasn't Miss Bianca's tears that moved Sir Hector; it was her gallantry.

"If my mere presence, in the parkland —" he began thoughtfully.

Miss Bianca, in the act of descending from the manger, paused. Again quite unconsciously, just because all her movements were so graceful, she paused in a peculiarly charming attitude — one tiny foot advanced, the rest of her person sweetly balanced for the first jump. The connoisseur's eye of Sir Hector rested on her appreciatively.

"If my mere presence," he repeated, "without any further obligation —"

"But that is all I ask!" cried Miss Bianca joyfully. "Of course I wouldn't expect you to *speak* to Mandrake! And it is, isn't it, just a matter of a hint to your groom?"

"He will no doubt think me whimsical," smiled Sir Hector, "but perhaps I am entitled to a whim. Until tomorrow, then, upon the parkland!"

4

No one ever quite knew, in the stables, how the idea originated. It was just generally accepted that whatever Sir Hector's groom said, went. Sir Hector's groom himself (their communications being always wordless) didn't know exactly how the idea had been put into *his* mind. But Sir Hector having given him leave, also wordlessly, to visit a sick aunt, he loyally promoted the favorite's whim to exercise for once upon the parkland, instead of upon his own private Gallops; and of course Sir Hector's jockey had to agree.

POEM COMPOSED BY MISS BIANCA ON HER WAY BACK
IN THE ATTACHÉ'S SPORTS CAR

My beautiful, my beautiful! that standest meekly by,
With thy proudly arched and glossy neck, and dark and
fiery eye!

She had got just so far when she realized that this poem had been written already, by the Hon. Mrs. Norton. So she had to start again, and in fact achieved one of her very best.

Wind's flashing speed, great Ocean's force,
 In one majestic frame combine!
But ah, the spirit is the Sun
 That animates with life divine!

                    M. B.

10

To the Rescue!

SIR HECTOR'S cooperation thus assured, Miss Bianca and Shaun sat down together to prepare in detail the full plan for Mandrake's liberation.

— Shaun was waiting at the Pagoda to hear *Miss Bianca's* report; and she had by this time recognized the hopelessness of trying to keep him uninvolved. All the other Scouts, however, she insisted should play no part; and Shaun, as always brimming with self-confidence — and, it must be admitted, rather a hog for glory — entirely agreed.

"Now take a piece of paper, Shaun," directed Miss Bianca, "and write down *One*."

Step One was to climb the ivy to Mandrake's chamber in plenty of time to prepare his mind for his release. Also Miss Bianca — Step One-A — would take a pair of scissors with which to cut his hair.

"What about a shave?" suggested Shaun.

"Quite impossible," said Miss Bianca firmly. "But at

least by extensive clipping he can be made presentable at the gates of an orphanage."

Step Two was to instruct him to feign sleep, concealing his newly shorn head under the blanket, at the moment when George or Jack came up with the porridge. Then immediately the groom withdrew — Step Three — Shaun would swiftly roll Mandrake's bowl between the sliding marble slabs and jam them apart.

"Leave me alone for that!" promised Shaun. "Amn't I the best dribbler on the football team?"

Step Four was perhaps the most difficult of all, as comprising the period of waiting. — Miss Bianca thought they should all go to sleep, to recruit their energies, and suggested taking an alarm clock. Of course she didn't possess such a vulgar mechanism herself, but Shaun said he could easily borrow one, to be set for five-thirty.

That left half an hour — Step Five — in which to tidy up and watch for Sir Hector from the turret window. Then as soon as the latter had rounded the moat, thus coming into view of George and Jack below, rescued and rescuers alike would descend by the stairway to find, if all went well, the guard-room unguarded.

"As I'll lay any odds 'twill be," cried Shaun, "and the door swinging open! A sight of Sir Hector'd draw Jack and George from their graves, let alone from their duty! Step Six is easy as pie — and as for Step Seven, 'tis but old Mandrake's skating off to catch the milk cart!"

"Which we ourselves I trust may take also," said Miss Bianca, "and so be back in time for lunch. Now go home, my dear boy, make a good supper, be sure to borrow the alarm clock, and meet me at the G.P.O. at seven."

2

Shaun left. Miss Bianca ate a little cream cheese herself, and put her feet up on the chaise longue.

Even the whole Prisoners' Aid Society, she thought, couldn't have conceived any *better* plan for rescuing Mandrake!

Of course the Prisoners' Aid Society had refused to consider rescuing Mandrake at all.

So had Bernard refused.

"Oh, dear!" thought Miss Bianca. "I do hope I'm not making a mistake!"

Such doubts necessarily cross the minds of even those most dedicated to good causes, when it comes to the actual point of doing something others equally dedicated thoroughly disapprove of. (The Society, under its new leadership, possibly wasn't quite so dedicated as it used to be; but Bernard certainly was.)

"Also I have involved Sir Hector," thought Miss Bianca, "and if in any unworthy cause, how shall I

106

ever forgive myself? O Mandrake, do *pray* show yourself worthy!"

None of these qualms, however, altered her resolution; having set her hand to the plow Miss Bianca was
not one to turn back; but it was perhaps fortunate that
she couldn't find her scissors. She was always losing
them — and this time she had to hunt through her
workbox and her bureau drawers, and look behind ornaments and feel down chairs — all she could find was
a pair from her manicure set, with which she would
really have to clip Mandrake one hair at a time! Miss
Bianca was looking for her *big* scissors, and like many
another lady couldn't remember where she'd put them.
They came to light at last between the leaves of an
illustrated volume on Byzantine Art. Miss Bianca was
quite distressed, she was as a rule so respectful of
books, and it just showed how worried she had been;
but the search most usefully distracted her mind from
further brooding, before she met Shaun at the G.P.O.

3

It was actually just as Shaun and Miss Bianca settled
themselves comfortably among the mailbags that Bernard, most *un*comfortably, though in his own home,
received a deputation from the Prisoners' Aid Society.

Bernard's home was a very nice bachelor flat in the

bottom drawer of an empty cigar cabinet. (Since the Ambassador gave up smoking, this was about the best address possible for a mouse; there were waiting lists inches long, and most of the other flats were occupied by doctors and bankers.) Bernard was rather proud of his cedarwood paneling and postage-stamp carpet, and as a rule welcomed visitors; but eight angry members crowding in at once promised less of social pleasure than of official embarrassment.

"Now, look here, Bernard — or rather, Mr. Secretary," began the spokesman (thus confirming Bernard's worst fears), "we've had about enough of it!"

Bernard, as he pulled up chairs, ran a hasty but experienced eye over the whole party. Four were old and stout, but four quite young; five were male, three female; altogether a very representative group . . .

"Of what?" he asked uneasily.

"Of being badgered about by our new Madam Chairwoman," said the spokesman. "That's what."

His seven companions uttered a low "Hear, hear." Bernard poured out bottled beer all round. Though every word, including the Hear-hears, found an echo in his own heart, he owed it to his office to uphold the dignity of the Chair.

"The lady to whom you refer," he said severely, "is undoubtedly a bit of a pill; but it was you yourselves who elected her, and as I remember, unanimously."

"In error," said the spokesman.

"Goodness me, you can't pretend you thought she was anyone different!" exclaimed Bernard.

"Maybe not; but we thought she'd *behave* differently," said the spokesman. "That is, differently from the way she's behaving now. — When have we ever before," demanded the spokesman, with rising indignation, "attended at the Moot-hall merely to receive *pep-talks? —* to be harangued into doing *exercises?* Quite apart from the fact that I like my wife's figure as it is —"

"Darling!" exclaimed the stouter of the ladies.

"— slimming is not the object, nor ever has been, nor ever should be, of our famous Society. What sort of example is being set the junior members? — one of whom I believe has a word to say on the subject himself? — Speak up, boy!"

Instantly one of the younger mice rose, consulted a piece of paper, closed his eyes and said all in one breath:

"On behalf of all junior members of the Prisoners' Aid Society I wish to state one and all distressed, disappointed and dislocated." Then he opened his eyes again and added, more colloquially, "Which means that if there's to be no more facing of jailers, or bearding of cats, or at least cheering of prisoners going on, us'll just switch to the Y.M.C.A."

He had scarcely sat down before up rose the spokes-man's wife in turn.

"As we members of the Ladies' Guild shall change our allegiance also," she stated, "to the Townswomen's Institute. What *we* have to say" (and here she too con-sulted a piece of paper) "is where is the point in pre-paring suppers if there can't be anything *nice?* Is Mr. Secretary aware that the new Madam Chairwoman has actually supplied us with a *calorie chart?*"

"And tape measures!" put in another lady.

"And dumbbells," added the spokesman grimly. "Well, Mr. Secretary, you see the situation. Voted into the Chair unanimously or not, unless her term of office is cut short I for one prophesy the complete disintegra-tion of our Society. What do you propose to do about it?"

Again poor Bernard agreed with every word. But he could only take refuge in the rules.

"A term of office can't be cut short," he pointed out. "A year's a year and there you are. Unless the incum-bent resigns or dies, she's in for a year."

"She won't resign," said the spokesman dourly. "She's too fond of giving orders."

"And she appears to enjoy uncommonly robust health," said Bernard. "Of course there *is* assassination, but I hardly suppose you'd recommend *that?*"

"In the interests of the Society I'm not sure that I

wouldn't," said the spokesman. "However, we leave it to you."

4

What a painful situation was Bernard's, left alone washing up the glasses! Of course he knew he wasn't really expected to assassinate the games-mistress; but undoubtedly *something* was expected of him, in the way of getting rid of her. Vain now were his hopes that he could hold the Society together by just soldiering on!

He had been prepared to. He had been prepared to stomach every rudeness of the new Madam Chairwoman in Committee, and then back her up on the platform, in the interests of the M.P.A.S. He was even prepared, if it came to the point, to swing a dumbbell himself. He knew he'd look pretty silly with a dumb-bell, but he was prepared.

The heroism of people like Bernard isn't the showy sort. Other people often don't recognize it as heroism at all. But it is.

Only now that it seemed that just soldiering on wouldn't be enough, what else could he do? As Bernard thought and thought he became so agitated and upset, he cracked his best engraved goblet against the tap; and answered a knock at the door with still shaking hands.

It was Mrs. Spokesman, come back for her umbrella. Or that was why she said she'd come back, and there indeed it was, in the hall. But as Bernard politely pointed it out to her —

"Bernard," said she, in a low, meaningful voice.

"Well?" said Bernard.

She hesitated. Then she looked over his shoulder into the kitchen and saw the broken glass, and in a busybody sort of way bustled in before he could stop her, and began picking up the fragments as though *that* was what she'd come for . . .

"It wasn't my best," lied Bernard — like all men jealous of his prowess as a washer-up.

"At least let's hope not one of a set," said Mrs. Spokesman. "But my poor dear Bernard, how you need a wife!"

5

Bernard froze on his feet. It was as though some dreadful lurking notion at the back of his own mind had suddenly leaped out red in tooth and claw.

"It isn't the first time I've thought of it," continued Mrs. Spokesman kindly. "Of course we all appreciate your devotion to Miss Bianca — as indeed who isn't devoted to Miss Bianca? I'm sure all we members of the Ladies' Guild are! — even while appreciating *her* resolve to remain single. Only Jean Fromage (were he alive) could be an acceptable match! What *you* need is I will not say an *ordinary* wife, but certainly a wife who besides taking a keen interest in public affairs would also wash up your glasses for you!"

Bernard backed against the sink.

"I see you take my meaning," said Mrs. Spokesman, with an arch smile. "And I'm sure Someone Else would agree with me! Someone Else having such a very particular regard for you!"

Of course Bernard knew at once who she meant. She meant the games-mistress.

"I don't believe a word!" he cried desperately.

"It's true as I stand," said Mrs. Spokesman. "Haven't you noticed how often she calls a Committee?"

"Because she likes taking the Chair!" implored Bernard.

"Not at all; to enjoy the pleasure of Mr. Secretary's company," corrected the spokesman's wife, with another horribly arch smile. "We women know one another! Beneath that gym slip, in the opinion of the entire Ladies' Guild, beats a heart so overflowing with unrequited affection, once it *was* requited immediate resignation from all public duties would inevitably follow, as that Someone Else dedicated herself completely to a husband's interests. — Just think about it, Bernard."

With her umbrella in one hand and the broken glass wrapped up in newspaper in the other, the spokesman's wife then left. Bernard staggered into the sitting room and collapsed on the sofa. He felt dreadful.

Had he really no option but to marry the games-mistress, to save the Society from disruption? It looked like it.

"I suppose I could spend a good deal of time abroad, visiting other Branches," thought Bernard. *"Here,* I suppose, there'll be nothing but dumbbells all over the place and a calorie chart in the kitchen . . ."

He uttered such a groan, the sofa springs twanged in sympathy.

"And I suppose I could still go and see Miss Bianca," thought Bernard.

Painful as it had been to hear her resolve to remain single spoken of as an accepted fact, he himself (the point put so plainly) humbly acknowledged only the fabled Jean Fromage indeed worthy of her hand, and this in a way was a consolation, because Jean Fromage was dead. So long as Miss Bianca didn't marry *anyone,* Bernard felt he could be almost content with her affectionate friendship and the privilege of visiting at the Porcelain Pagoda whenever he liked.

Immediately, however, his main consolation was that at least she was out of it all — out of all squabbles and disagreeableness, let alone deadly perils. And since it was partly by his own influence that she had been led to retire (thus putting the whole Society in jeopardy, owing to the unexpectedly horrible character of her successor), he recognized the obligation to pay any price to keep the Society on the rails, lest she should start worrying over the consequences of her defection, to the detriment of her nerves.

Brave Bernard was steeled to every sacrifice by the picture of Miss Bianca in the peaceful security of the Porcelain Pagoda, tranquilly correcting proofs of her forthcoming slim volume of verse . . .

Who was in fact at that very moment engaged in cutting Mandrake's hair in the turret above the lily moat!

11

In the Turret

BEND YOUR HEAD a little to the left," said Miss
Bianca. "What a pity it is you can't put your ears forward!"

Mandrake under her scissors sat passive — or rather
subduing an impatience she was delighted to observe.
Not a trace in him now appeared of General Lassitude;
instead of cringing, he had seemed ready rather to
chide her for delay; and instead of flinching before the
prospect of being rescued, he showed positive impatience! There had been no need to prepare his mind
at all; it was prepared already . . .

"I really must write those pill-makers a testimonial!"
thought Miss Bianca, clipping away.

At least a foot of hair, at least a yard of beard she
clipped off, while Shaun ran back and forth stuffing
the fallen Spanish-moss-like tangles under the bed.
Since she couldn't give Mandrake a shave she left him
a neat Imperial; then she clipped his eyebrows; and

118

when she had finished, Step One-A also was successfully achieved. Any orphanage in the world, thought
Miss Bianca, would have welcomed Mandrake as gardener, such was his respectable and even distinguished
appearance, especially unpaid!

Step Two equally succeeded. (One reason why Miss
Bianca was so good at rescuing prisoners was because
she never forgot the necessary order of Steps.) Mandrake, as instructed, lay down upon his pallet and was
soon emitting such truly convincing snores Miss Bianca
quite feared lest some of the pills had been for Insom-
nia. But by from time to time opening one eye he
showed he was just entering into the spirit of the thing,
and making the most of his temporarily passive part.

"Mind you set the alarm clock all the same!" said
Miss Bianca to Shaun. "I do hope it's reliable!" — It
had gone off three or four times in the mail van,
though according to Shaun only because he was training it. As soon as it was set Miss Bianca took it away
from him and into her own charge.

Step Three was the most exciting. As at about an
hour after midnight the marble slabs slid apart; as,
grim and grinning, one of the grooms (it happened to
be George) stumped through with the porridge pan,
and emptied it into Mandrake's bowl, and grinningly
withdrew —

"Now!" breathed Miss Bianca.

In a flash Shaun was on the ball. — The best dribbler on the team, he shot Mandrake's bowl accurately
between the closing stones. Though they shattered it,
shards of earthenware mingling with porridge still
jammed them apart. Nor did George look back. Too
confident altogether stumped George down the stair —
leaving the path to freedom open!

"Now for Step Four," said Miss Bianca coolly.

2

She had always known that Step Four would prove
the most testing, and so indeed it did. Shaun, after she
had taught him the first verse of Keats's Ode to Autumn (Miss Bianca never let slip a cultural opportunity), curled up and slept easily enough; Mandrake's
histrionic snores were soon genuine; but Miss Bianca
herself remained wakeful and a prey to nerves for
hours and hours.

She had no reason to be nervous — or at any rate,
not *quite* so nervous. Wasn't everything going really
beautifully? — and her faith in Sir Hector absolute?
As sure as the sun would rise, Sir Hector would keep
his appointment; and when had any project failed to
which he lent his countenance? Miss Bianca seemed to
recall more than one County Show saved from utter
disaster — rain falling in buckets, the ground a quag

— by his stately appearance, even under wraps. On the occasion when a race-course stand caught fire, his calm canter from the paddock to inspect the flames averted a panic and enabled him to win the National Cup with a full complement of spectators. In association with Sir Hector, how could any project fail?

Miss Bianca assured herself it couldn't.

— A sudden louder snore broke in upon her thoughts. She glanced towards the bed; and all at once the obscure source of her uneasiness became apparent.

The blanket now thrown aside, Mandrake's newly revealed profile jutted arrogantly forth — the nose like an eagle's beak, the thin cruel mouth that shut like a trap. Miss Bianca remembered it all too well, as that of the pitiless steward in the Diamond Palace. Asleep, Mandrake looked his old wicked self . . .

Miss Bianca trembled. "O Mandrake, do pray prove worthy!" she had implored — only a few hours ago, in her Porcelain Pagoda. With what earnestness did she now add the rider, "Or at least not thoroughly *un!*"

She was so agitated, she actually ran up upon the pallet and bent above his ear — intending to inject therein, for his subconscious to absorb while he slept, a few such phrases as "Meekness is all," "Pity the poor," and "Be not proud." But since she had felt a certain (very natural) repugnance about clipping the hair in Mandrake's ear-holes, she couldn't be sure her words penetrated; and upon descending, fell at last into a sleep almost as unrefreshing as wakefulness. She was glad indeed to hear the alarm go off at half-past five, to end such a restless, troubled night!

Luckier Shaun knew no such anxieties. He was up and spruced already, and out watching from the windowsill, as Miss Bianca first made her own hasty toilet, and then roused the now disturbing object of so much benevolent endeavor . . .

"Here they come," cried Shaun, "through the park gate — and Sir Hector leading!"

3

There is no prettier sight in the world than a string of racehorses out at exercise. The scrubbiest moorland or sandy track is adorned by their fleetness, and any natural beauty enhanced. The park about the ruined turret had long been considered by courting couples romantic; but not a butcher at odds with his wife could have failed to see it beautiful, as Sir Hector, followed by his five companions, paced forth upon its turf. The grass beneath their hooves took on a brighter green; trees about to shed their leaves saluted with a last flourish of rich foliage, as Sir Hector led in Galga, Coquette and Golden Boy, and Timotheus and Patches!

Miss Bianca, leaning over Shaun's shoulder, thought

of three poems at once. Shaun in his enthusiasm almost fell out and had to be pulled back by the tail. — Actually Miss Bianca leaned out nearly as far herself, in an attempt to catch Sir Hector's eye: the distance was too great, however, and racehorses rarely look up; but just a bird's-eye view of his glorious tail sufficed to raise her spirits. And that he had forgotten nothing of his promise was proved even as he rounded the moat and was lost to view: passing the ground-floor window of the guard-room, Sir Hector neighed so loudly, even had George and Jack been cooking breakfast, their attention must have been attracted.

Patches was the last to go by. (He always brought up the rear, being frankly too old for the work, and owing his place just to Sir Hector's kindly remembrance of past glories.) But though the excitement in the turret was by now intense, Miss Bianca restrained Shaun with one hand, and Mandrake with the other, until old Patches had vanished too, and only then gave proud Shaun the honor of first setting foot on the stair.

"Run down, Shaun, and see have George and Jack quitted the guard-room," she bade. "If not, stay until they do, then return and give word!"

But Shaun was down and up again in a trice.

"They're out both," he reported, "and the door just as didn't I tell you swinging open!"

"Then now for Step Six," said Miss Bianca (coolly).

4

Fortunately Mandrake was still so emaciated, even he could squeeze through the narrow gap. The stairway was steep and tortuous indeed, but with Shaun running before — and now, with the familiarity of an experienced guide, warning of a particularly high step or of one crumbled quite away — all gained the guardroom in safety. Empty it was indeed! — and the door swinging open! — so hastily had George and Jack run out!

Out ran Mandrake and Shaun and Miss Bianca too. Then they paused. It was still a moment for caution.

Sir Hector had by now cantered some quarter of a mile — in a direction opposite to the park gate where would halt the milk cart. Jack was panting after as fast as he could, every pant taking *him* farther from the park gate too; but George, the fatter and slower, waited still on the causeway's farther side to watch the rest of the string go by. Of course he wouldn't have noticed Shaun and Miss Bianca slipping behind him, but he would certainly have noticed Mandrake. "We must wait," breathed Miss Bianca, "until he too makes after!"

All three shrank back into the doorway. It seemed an age, while first Galga, then Coquette, then Timotheus and Golden Boy, cantered past; George seemed rooted to the spot. — Miss Bianca very much feared she heard Mandrake utter an unregenerate oath: the distressing thought that he might teach the orphans bad language for a moment, but unpleasantly, distracted her; she glanced up at him with a reproving, anxious look. Then she fixed her eyes again on George . . .

Would he *never* move? — or what if he moved in the wrong direction, *back,* to precipitate disaster?

But it was his own disaster George precipitated. Deceived by the long gap after Golden Boy, imagining the whole string gone by, with a whoop off he started in their wake — and straight into Patches's path!

On pounded old Patches, intent only upon following Sir Hector — contemptuous of his jockey's pull, too blind himself to see the need of swerving. George's back was turned; if Patches was half-blind, so did he seem half-deaf, as full in the path of those iron-shod hooves he lumbered forth! Another moment, and his criminal career would have been terminated for good in a mash of blood and bone —

Had he not been snatched to safety by whom but — Mandrake!

In a series of energetic leaps Mandrake bounded across the causeway and shouldered George to the ground, and rolled out of danger the last obstacle in his own path to freedom!

He had proved himself worthy indeed!

Shaun let out a cheer. As for Miss Bianca, she almost fainted with joyful emotion, to see her faith so justified. "O Mandrake, thou art even more reformed than I could hope!" she cried to herself. "O Mandrake, how could I ever doubt thee!"

— The next moment she almost fainted again. George, still upon the ground, as soon as he saw who his savior was, with the most appalling lack of gratitude seized Mandrake by the ankle, at the same time bawling out to Jack to come quick, their prisoner was escaping!

5

Mandrake wrenched himself free. "Oh, hurry!" cried Miss Bianca. "Hurry, towards the park gate!" "My ankle!" gasped Mandrake. It was sprained. He could but limp. Fortunately George, more severely incapacitated, couldn't rise from the ground at all. But Jack, in the distance, was already pounding towards them . . .

Shaun and Miss Bianca could run. (Shaun, it may be remembered, actually had a Badge for Cross-Country Running.) But how could they abandon the now crippled Mandrake to face even Jack alone? They couldn't. Yet what could they do when Jack caught up — as undoubtedly he would? Though the groom was

no greyhound, Mandrake could barely hobble. Nor could the mice support him; they were too short. One on either side they encouraged him to fresh efforts, they tried to encourage each other; but it was like a nightmare, to be forced to such slow progress in the face of such deadly peril!

"Look back, Shaun," whispered Miss Bianca. "Is Jack gaining on us very fast?"

"Fast enough," returned Shaun grimly.

"Then you at least must run," whispered Miss Bianca, "for your mother's sake!"

But Shaun suddenly said he was an orphan, and on they desperately, painfully labored.

Jack was no more than a hundred yards behind.

When he was but fifty yards behind, Mandrake stumbled; and all was lost.

12

The End

OR SO IT seemed.

At that very instant a glorious thunder of hooves shook the ground — Sir Hector was beside them! He had witnessed all — Mandrake's heroic act, George's base ingratitude, Jack's pursuit, and had covered half a mile in forty-nine seconds. His splendid eyes blazed with indignation, his saddle was empty; for the second time in his life, Sir Hector had spilled his jockey!

"Up on my back!" cried Sir Hector. "Up, all three!"

With a last astonishing effort Mandrake mounted. Shaun made a stirrup for Miss Bianca to reach Sir Hector's tail and himself swung up after. "Ready?" cried Sir Hector. "Aye!" responded Mandrake, in a loud, firm voice. — He was worth rescuing indeed! His ankle throbbed in agony, his hands on the reins were powerless, as Sir Hector began to canter it was all he could do to keep his seat, but not for a moment did his courage fail. "Carry me where you will," exclaimed Mandrake, through clenched teeth, "if need be to my death, but at least out of captivity!"

Miss Bianca quite palpitated with admiration — but nonetheless ran swiftly past the saddle to gain Sir Hector's ear.

"Not to his death, just to the Orphanage!" she begged.

"Sit close all the same," returned Sir Hector, breaking into a gallop. "For once, I'm going to show my paces!"

2

Like a whirlwind, like a sheet of flame over dry bracken, galloped Sir Hector through the parkland — a sight so glorious, the few early-morning pedestrians lucky enough to witness it never forgot it in all their lives. His tail streamed like a comet, the plaits of his mane like candle flames; from his nostrils (at least so one pedestrian asserted) flashed sparks of fire! Miss Bianca's silvery fur blew about like snowflakes; Shaun, even in the lee of the cantle, had to hold his whiskers on; Mandrake crouched ever lower and lower until he lay almost flat (thus accidentally offering the least wind resistance possible). Not only Jack was left far behind, but Sir Hector's stable-companions as well; though their dismayed jockeys took out the whip, Sir

Hector outdistanced them all with such contemptuous ease, when he at last entered the city it was at a walk.

"The Orphanage, I think you mentioned?" he inquired courteously of Miss Bianca. (He wasn't even out of breath.)

"If you would be so kind," said Miss Bianca. — She quite regretted that the ride was over. She adored speed, and clinging to Sir Hector's mane, had felt as safe as in the Ambassadorial car. But then one always *would* feel safe, thought Miss Bianca, with Sir Hector!

It seemed that their esteem was mutual. While Mandrake rang the Orphanage bell and waited for the door to open, the noble steed stooped his majestic head to Miss Bianca's level.

"By Pegasus, what an escapade you have led me into!" he said gently. "Mandrake's excellent conduct I admit fully justifies your faith in him; your feminine instinct was right; he *has* repented. But what *I* do not repent is having entered upon such an escapade solely for the sake of Miss Bianca!"

Miss Bianca blushed. Before she could reply — and indeed she would have found any reply difficult, such was her emotion — the Matron opened the Orphanage door. (The old mole had been quite right; they really were shorthanded.) Once again, how invaluable Sir Hector's aegis! The most respectable-looking gardener, without any references and asking no wages, might well have aroused suspicion; but seeing Mandrake as it were sponsored by the great national favorite, Matron engaged him at once.

"So now we part," said Sir Hector to Miss Bianca. "That is, unless I can drop you anywhere?"

Miss Bianca shook her head. After that wild and glorious ride, a mere *lift* would have been an anti-climax.

"Yet not, I trust, forever," said Sir Hector, smiling. "Perhaps one day you will visit me again; or even come to see me run, in your best hat? Though never, I suspect, better than you saw me run today!"

So low he stooped, his velvet nose brushed Miss Bianca's whiskers. But she braced herself for a final adieu. After all, Sir Hector stood seventeen hands high, and herself no more than two inches . . .

"Perhaps I shall prefer to keep a treasured memory," said Miss Bianca softly. "Today, was I not *up* with you?"

3

No medals were struck to commemorate this particular rescue, because it wasn't an official one — the Mouse Prisoners' Aid Society having played no part in it. Miss Bianca just invited all the Scouts to a splen-

did tea, and personally presented Shaun with an inscribed wristwatch. It had luminous hands.

Nonetheless, since everything concerning Sir Hector was news, the details somehow got about, and the more they heard the more all members of the M.P.A.S. regretted that they *hadn't* played any part, to share the glory. As has been seen, it was mostly their own fault, in allowing the games-mistress to bully them out of generous enthusiasm into mere self-regarding physical culture; they still so shouted her down at the next Meeting, while she was explaining *why* no medals, even she saw the necessity to retire as fast as she could.

So Bernard hadn't to marry her after all; and was so glad that when no one else would subscribe for the usual presentation silver tea-tray he paid for it out of his own pocket. The new Madam Chairwoman elected in her place was a nice fat member of the Ladies' Guild, who proved quite as executive as needful. She was also a great admirer of Miss Bianca's, upon whose advice and inspiration she so relied, the future of the Society was in safe hands.

Mandrake as gardener to the Orphanage turned out a great success. He truly labored there day by day to make the orchard fruitful, so that apple jam flowed free, and the flowerbeds brilliant, and the tennis court playable upon. One of the orphans who played on it actually became Junior Champion, and was subsequently tapped for the Wightman Cup.

Miss Bianca's slim volume of verse went into three editions, after unanimously favorable reviews.

Her testimonial to the vitamin-pill makers was quoted throughout the popular press, and helped to save many a reader from General Lassitude.

The jockey spilled in the parkland Sir Hector had carefully spilled into a bracken-patch, and so received no injuries.

The mouse who got engaged at the picnic married his dream-mouse next week. Miss Bianca not only attended the wedding, but stood godmother to their first six children.

If Bernard was surprised to find her taking in all racing editions of all evening papers, he was just surprised. Miss Bianca never hurt his feelings by revealing what admiration had been aroused in her breast by Sir Hector's splendid appearance and heroic conduct. Bernard, on the other hand, blurted out all about having been prepared to marry the games-mistress; but since the ghastly sacrifice (as he forthrightly described it) had been envisaged solely in the interest of Miss Bianca's nerves, she was less jealous than touched. She ever treated him with all her old affection, and he spent most evenings at the Porcelain Pagoda.

There was even a new bond between them, since together they had saved the Prisoners' Aid Society from disaster — Miss Bianca by reminding it of the glory to be won by its proper work, Bernard by his gallant soldiering-on over an extraordinarily difficult period. Miss Bianca's contribution was the more exciting, Bernard's the more solidly practical; but each merited equal praise, and their joint achievement must ever be accounted a notable triumph by every thoughtful mouse.

THE END